THE BRO CODE

THE BRO CODE

ELIZABETH A. SEIBERT

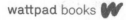

wattpad books

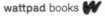

wattpad books

Published in Canada by Wattpad Books, a division of Wattpad Corp.

36 Wellington Street E., Toronto, ON M5E 1C7

www.wattpad.com

First Wattpad Books edition: September 2020

ISBN 978-1-98936-532-8 (Trade Paper original)
ISBN 978-1-98936-539-7 (eBook edition)

Library and Archives Canada Cataloguing in Publication information is available upon request.

Printed and bound in Canada

1 3 5 7 9 10 8 6 4 2

Cover design and illustration by Elliot Carrol
Typesetting by Sarah Salomon

This book is for the girls who aren't allowed to read this, for anyone reading past their bedtime, for giraffes, S&B, A&M, M&D, Mr. Dog, everyone who was/is/will be a total dork in high school, for me, and for you.

And for Kevin, who really didn't want to be mentioned.

Dear Nick,

What keeps sticking out is the first thing you said to me: *Tell me I'm wrong.*

I wasn't so special, though—you made everything about you.

It happened during the sultry summer right after Carter and I moved here, the kind where Olivia made us wear sneakers to play in the coarse sand by Bonfire Beach so our feet wouldn't peel off, and your bangs were perpetually plastered to your forehead.

Carter and I had it easier than most new kids because we had a trampoline *and* a pool. Still, when you came over, you always went straight for Carter's soccer ball. From after lunch until Olivia called for Carter to set the dinner table, you'd pretend the trampoline was a goal and Carter was to defend it like it was extra time in the

World Cup. You'd score, clap your hands to focus, and want to go again. I hope this rings a bell for you, Nick, because that's how you got to be Carter's best friend.

On the afternoon you first spoke to me, Carter transformed muggy July into a barbeque with ice-cold watermelon and corn on the cob. You invited the sixth graders to our yard without asking, which was the boldest move ever. One of them brought water balloons and you lined us up in the sticky grass for a toss-off: everyone would get a partner and throw a balloon back and forth until it broke.

There was an odd number of participants and you declared that I, the fifth-grade girl, should be the one to sit out. I wouldn't, according to you, be able to throw as far as everyone else.

"I'm telling," I'd said.

"Tell me I'm wrong."

You had a perfectly straight face, but the delight in your eyes still gave you away.

For whatever stupid reason, you starting a water balloon fight stirred up warm fuzzies in my ten-year-old heart (whatever). You had dirt in your unkempt hair, a chin that dripped with water, and a stupid grin that felt like it was just for me. I was toast.

It didn't matter. When school started, you'd hang out at any and every girl's locker except for mine. (I know this part sounds familiar.) You played with the girls' hair and they shrieked back, and you loved them for it. Though I get that's nothing compared to what Carter did.

Elizabeth A. Seibert

I'd really hoped, Nick, that six years later you'd be different.

That one's on me.

I'm writing this so you can remember. *You have a choice.* Things with Carter aren't as black and white as they may seem. Whatever you decide about the life or death of your *Bro Bible*, the holy script of *man*kind, the hallowed creed worshiped by geeks, athletes, and every guy in between—the ever-sacred Bro Code . . . this one's on you.

You've heard my thoughts on your situation. You know *I know* what you're about to do.

Tell me I'm wrong.

—Eliza

RULE NUMBER 1

BROS* BEFORE HOES.

*Any bro shalt be referred to only as "bro**," "dude," "man," "amigo," or "homie." A bro is never a "peeps," "pal," or "stand-up guy." A bro shalt be a bro forever until the end of time.

**"Brother" may be used in some circumstances. Never ironically.

Contrary to what you might have heard, I didn't sleep with Eliza O'Connor. Did I want to? *Have you seen her?* Could I have? *Have you seen me?* But I didn't, even though people will tell you that I did, because I attend high school with a bunch of world-class trolls. They'll regale you with other gossip about me too, some of which is true, like the prank I pulled on Mr. Hoover (the purple in his hair wouldn't come out for a week), and most of it is somewhat true, like I once picked up a girl by walking up to her by the concession stand at a football game and saying "No." (I *actually* said, "No, we haven't gone out before, and I vote we change that.") A few of the stories are definitely *not* true. And me sleeping with Eliza O'Connor is one of them.

Elizabeth A. Seibert

Some dudes will claim I'm the one who started the rumor. I wish I had—it'd have way better details than whatever version you heard. If you find out who did, hit me up, tell them to meet me out back where we can handle this like grown-ups. I do know *how* it started—not at Jeff Karvotsky's party, like everyone thinks. It really began a few months earlier, as most rumors do: with a bunch of stupidly hot people eating pizza.

It was a Wednesday afternoon and I played air hockey in Straight Cheese 'n' Pizza with half of the senior class, soaking up our last first day of school together. We'd ordered fifteen greasy pizzas and unlimited soda. Our haul was scattered across the countertop bar, pushed-together wooden tables, and a few booths lining the dining room, near the arcade games and infamous Chef Pizzeria. Chef happened to be a life-sized copper statue of a guy in a fancy hat tossing a pizza in the air. And yes, he was absolutely the crowning glory of a Cassidy High School senior prank every single spring. (Most recently, he'd been taken to our school's roof and dressed up in a mustache and wig to look like our principal.)

Cassidy High, of course, was the high school in North Cassidy, Massachusetts. It was the kind of school where the science team got more funding than football, and there were just enough kids for us to avoid being a regional high school. My classmates and I knew everything about each other, from who farted in music class back in third grade to who farted in biology class this morning. North Cassidy was where we'd all get married, stay forever, and then our kids would be friends too. Except me—I was holding out for a soccer scholarship, but that was a long shot anyway (pun intended).

"Yo, Nick! I want to hear that ghost story again," Robert Maxin, the only senior on the soccer team who had never kissed anyone, called to me.

"Promise not to pee your pants this time?" I said.

Robert sat on a bar stool at the counter and had spun around to face the rest of us. He held a slice of pepperoni that was so greasy it dripped onto his lap. He wiped it, staining the jeans his mom had *just* bought him. Robert was an obvious choice for this year's 'best dressed' yearbook superlative.

I winked at the girl on the bar stool beside him: Hannah Green, the brunette beauty, and one of the few cheerleaders at Cassidy High with straight As. Robert wanted me to tell the ghost story (about how our high school was haunted and one of the teachers turned into a vampire at night) as a last-ditch effort to keep her sitting next to him, but I was occupied with trying to keep my undefeated air hockey record.

Austin Banks, the man, the myth, the legend, and part of our bro trio, lasered the air puck at my goal like this was the most important game of his life. It wasn't, but Austin always played that way.

"Trying to hit a man when he's distracted . . ." I said. My shot glided back with expert spin. Before Austin could register what had happened, the puck clanged sweetly into his metal goal.

"Ten to nine. And the crowd goes wild! Ahhhh."

"Whatever." Austin adjusted his thick, black frames and pulled up the hood on his Cassidy soccer sweatshirt, despite the still summer weather outside. Austin was also famous for wearing basketball shorts after a snowstorm. We all have our things.

"Good game, Nick." Austin held out his fist to bump mine. We slid onto plush, red seats in the nearest booth, across from the third member of our bro triumvirate, the bleached-blond Carter O'Connor.

If Austin were LeBron James, Carter would be Michael Jordan—the OB (Original Baller). 'Course, you'd have to ban soccer everywhere but on Pluto for Austin or Carter to switch to basketball, but we're trying to make OB a thing so I use it whenever I can. Our mothers are very proud.

Carter had taken over his half of the six-person booth with a calculus textbook and a notebook's worth of scattered paper. He leaned over them, tapping his pen absentmindedly between his teeth. He'd colored them blue only the one time.

"Yo," I said, "You find your x yet? 'Cause I'm pretty sure she ain't coming back."

Austin snorted. "Hey, are we getting pizza soon—"

"Dude, this is no joke," interrupted Carter, "We're going to have to actually do homework this year. Guess I've got math." He scribbled an answer in a fat notebook. With his pen. Because Carter believes in himself.

"No fair, you got math last year," said Austin. "I ended up with fifteen essays for Ms. Peterson. Which was really forty because I had to do them times three so they'd all be different."

"I've *definitely* got math."

"Not it." I touched my nose. "*Quiero español.*"

"Dibs on AP bio," said Carter.

"AP psych," I added, "Which leaves you, Austin, with . . ." Carter, still head-down in his (our) homework, chuckled as I paused, "English and AP history. Sorry for your loss."

"Dicks."

We divided our homework load every year so one person would do it for the three of us per subject and it wouldn't take as long. It worked because we were legitimately always together: same sports, same classes, same irresistible personalities . . . we had a lot in common.

Austin slumped in his seat and surveyed the restaurant. Straight Cheese 'n' Pizza was awesome because not only did it have the best pizza, grilled cheese, and mozzarella sticks (the owners were the true geniuses of all things bread and cheese) that Massachusetts suburbia could supply but it also had free arcade games and a legit jukebox. Austin observed the different cliques of our classmates, who were segments of the popular kids wearing slightly different clothes, and laughed at Robert's wild hand gestures as he tried to retell that ghost story about our biology teacher. Hannah had tightly crossed her legs and smoothed her printed skirt as far down as it would go. Austin grinned like he was watching videos of people falling down on YouTube.

"How long you think it'll be before Hannah comes over?"

"Two minutes," I said, "Shorter if he tells her about when we went to Build-A-Bear."

"Poor guy. Does *not* know how to talk to girls."

"You two should give him lessons." Carter turned a page in his textbook.

"Jesus Christ," I replied so loudly that the guys closest to us looked over, "we said we're sorry about Sarah, okay? Get over it."

"I am over it," Carter said.

"You can't blame us for daring you to get with her and then get mad when it's actually easy."

"I said I'm over it."

"Bullshit."

The shift in the restaurant's atmosphere was palpable—most

people, especially those sitting in the booths nearest to us, now stared, letting their pizza get as cold as this conversation. Whispers replaced the whooping and hollering, and even the statue of Chef Pizzeria seemed to eavesdrop nervously.

"Woohoo, go Owls," said Austin.

That got a few laughs and soon people were back to minding their own damn business. Cassidy High's mascot worked every time.

Carter's phone vibrated on the table. Because all mobile forms of communication between bros occur in the sacred group chat, it had to be a girl.

"Who's that, then?" Austin asked.

Carter pushed Austin's arm off him. "My sister. My mom has an event again. Eliza's going to eat with us. Hope that's okay, dude."

"She's your sister," Austin said, as if someone had asked him if he wanted vanilla cake or vanilla cupcakes. (Trick question, chocolate or bust.)

The Bro Code clearly states that a bro will *never* date his friend's sister. Austin, however, is the absolute boss and Eliza does what she wants anyway, and Carter had little say when they dated two years ago. It ended badly, I hear—I don't know what happened because Austin can't say a word without Carter stepping in to defend his sister's honor.

"Maybe she forgot about it," I suggested. Whatever "it" was . . . Eliza had spent all last year in Australia as part of some foreign exchange for dorks. She'd gotten back last week and had (so far) been too busy with her friends to bother with us nerds.

"Whatever." Austin stomped on the carpet as he went to track down a pizza. He returned shortly with a fresh-out-of-the-oven pie, a basket of semi-warm mozzarella sticks, and none other than Hannah Green.

"Hey, guys. Robert told me about when you all went to the mall together." Instead of looking at me, her eyes were pinned on Carter. "I'd love to see the teddy bear you made some time."

Austin cleared his throat, half choking on pepperoni. That had been an amazing line on her end. But Carter was a bro. He stuck to the code. He'd never take another bro's girl.

At exactly that moment, a jingle signaled the door to the restaurant swinging open. Cue the fanfare, because in walked *the girl*.

She had the same bleached hair as Carter. She'd grown since the last time I saw her, and she had a perfect Australian tan. Because of course she did.

Carter scooched to make room for his sister.

"Hey, Hanns," Eliza said, dropping her book bag on the floor, "you eating with us?"

"Sorry," Hannah replied, actually sounding apologetic, "already have a ton of homework. Summer's def over." She waved good-bye to us. Mostly to Carter.

"Thanks for letting me come, broskis." Eliza reached for a pizza slice. "Olivia and her buttercream frosting have currently taken over our house. I barely got out before it became a true hostage situation."

We were getting even more stares from our classmates than when I'd made my outburst. Though Eliza, in her extremely normal white V-cut shirt and comfy leggings, pretended not to notice.

"Look at it this way, now you get to see me," I said.

"Same old Nick Maguire, huh?" Eliza asked.

Elizabeth A. Seibert

"The one you know and love."

"Dude, stop," said Carter. Eliza whacked his shoulder. She met my eye a moment later, catching me watching her for a second too long.

Austin drummed the table with his fingers and asked what we were all wondering: "Did you bring us any?"

"What?" She turned to Carter, who was back to his (our) math homework.

"Cupcakes," Carter answered, "same old Austin Banks too."

Ms. O'Connor, whom Eliza referred to as Olivia (and whom Carter merely called Mom), was the most popular mother at Cassidy High School, if not the entire town. After her cupcake start-up was featured in the *Boston Globe* as the area's cutest side hustle, Ms. O'Connor went all in. From the comforts of her next-level professional kitchen, she catered events all over the Northeast. Austin and I were big fans of her work.

"Ah." Eliza leaned back against the cracked leather cushion. "Yes, let me check my bag for the four dozen cupcakes Olivia donated from her fundraiser to these hooligans."

She gestured to our classmates, who now sat on the tables and played pizza crust football. (A game like paper football, but with delicious carbs.) Austin slowly ducked to glance under the table—just in case. Her blue bag rested against her neon running shoes with no cupcakes in sight.

The lights dimmed to signal the evening atmosphere.

"How was Australia?" I asked.

"Awesome. Good to be back, though. I never want to see another kangaroo again."

"In that case, Carter," I said, "you should probably leave."

"Burn." Austin coughed.

"Good one, Nick. Real wit right there," Carter replied.

After inhaling her slice, Eliza stood to go talk to her other friends. Apparently, she was too cool for us now. Good for her. "Thanks for the pizza, guys," she said, "Cool glasses, Austin."

Austin's glasses had been the talk of North Cassidy when he got them a few months ago. Scared of sticking contacts in his eyes and paranoid of becoming a classified dork, Austin went around without wearing them for a year after they'd been prescribed. After Carter and I refused to let him drive anywhere anymore, Austin picked out the most hipster frames he could find, which girls claimed perfectly matched his brown eyes. He should not have been worried. He'd gotten them a month before celebrities started wearing glasses exactly like his, and now they were popping up around the whole school. Austin's ego would never be at risk again.

Austin barely waited for her to be out of earshot. "Hardly recognized her, dude. Can't believe it's only been a year."

"I know." Carter shuddered. "Josh Daley asked her out yesterday. A month ago he didn't even know who she was."

Josh Daley? I wanted to scream. Josh Daley and I had been on thin ice ever since he tried to get me cut from soccer in sixth grade.

"That kid is such a tool," I said.

"She shot him down, thankfully. That's not going to be the end of it, though." Carter took the last bite of his pizza as a few families with super little kids entered the restaurant. Normal people's dinnertime meant our afternoon was ending.

"Sorry, man," Austin said.

"You're in a bunch of Josh's classes, right, Mags?" Carter asked.

"A couple electives, since we procrastinated taking them. Wish I could skip, but the lame school board calls that 'truancy.'"

"Same gym class?"

"You know it."

"Yeah, Eliza's in some of those too," Carter continued, "Do me a favor and make sure she's all right."

Austin reached for the last slice of pizza but withdrew when I made the same move—no questions asked. Generally, a bro is free to take the last slice of, well, anything. But while I'd been talking to Eliza, Austin finished the mozzarella sticks, so I had dibs on the pizza.

"Nick?" said Carter.

"She's going to be fine, dude," I said, "but sure."

I would have given away my last slice to keep Josh Daley away from her. *Be cool, Nick.*

Looked like I'd be attending class after all.

As if I had a choice.

RULE NUMBER 2

A BRO SHALT NOT GET "OUT" IN DODGEBALL.

Two mornings later, it was the third day of my fourth and final year of torture, otherwise known as high school. My Mustang gently clanked as it came to rest in our favorite parking spot: last row, last space in the student lot before the neighboring baseball field. Whoever had come up with the idea to end an outfield right at the parking lot was an evil genius—every time a player hit a home run, it could fly right into some kid's windshield—which turns out to be an extremely effective way to stop students from loitering after school.

Mr. Hoover, the morning hall monitor, was for sure going to give me a tardy slip. Even though the school day had started ten minutes ago, I still stopped to rest my head against the steering wheel, a soft buzzing making my thoughts fuzzy.

Last night's sleep had been a frenzy of *kind-of* worries and *almost* solutions. There were too many things to think about, from my stupid psychology homework to how super annoying my dad was to the possible extinction of bananas and how devastating that would be to pancake breakfasts everywhere.

The student parking spaces were in the back of the high school, and the faculty lot was in the front. Only upperclassmen had spots, since you needed a license to get a permit, but that didn't keep freshmen and sophomores from hanging around the rear entrance with their disgusting smoking and worse gossip.

Seeing them, I groaned and forced the sticky car door to creak open, wincing as the muggy August air welcomed me to hell. My backpack weighed on my shoulders as if trying to prevent me from taking another step.

"*It's my backpack's fault.*" Yeah, Mr. Hoover would give me two tardy slips if I'd tried that one.

The sun hid behind damp clouds, which made the school's "Go Owls!" graffitied brick walls and fractured sidewalks stick out even more. You'd never guess the entire building had been renovated three years ago—glistening hallways, no more fluorescent lighting, and alarms that'd go off if you tried to leave through emergency exits. A handful of students loitered around the back staircase, greeting me with fist bumps and "'Sup, Maguire?"

Their puffs of grassy weed hung in the muggy air like sad balloons. Holding my breath, I nodded back and hurried past them, careful not to get any whiff of it on my clothes, or Coach Dad would run me extra hard for a month. It had never occurred to the teachers that students would start smoking that early in the morning, though you'd get suspended on the spot if you tried it in this same exact location a few hours later.

As I reached the top of the dank, dirty staircase, the door clicked open and crashed into my shin. This would've hurt, except all my years of soccer had shot those shin nerves ages ago.

"Oops," came the voice of Madison Hayes. Her rosy perfume did not mix well with the smoke, making me cough when she stepped closer.

If someone were to say I was "in a relationship," it would be with Madison. We were the total opposite of official, though we'd been known to have some PDA that could rival any other couple, Instagram relationships included. Madison was cool about it, though, and didn't make "us" to be a whole big thing. The few times we did talk to each other, it was mostly complaining about our families.

Madison pushed her chest into mine and trapped me against the rusty railing. Her wavy black hair tossed itself onto my shoulder, sending shivers down my arms as she pulled back.

"Long time no see, handsome," she said.

I cleared my throat. "Yo."

"Nick Maguire, don't ignore me." She put her foot out, somehow filling an entire doorway with her crystal eyes and stick-thin stature.

Despite the heavy humidity, she wore an oversized sweatshirt and cut-off shorts. Other (probably jealous) girls often said that Madison tried too hard to look like she wasn't trying hard. I had it on good authority, however, that the sweatshirt was intended to cover up whatever, um, teeny tiny little hickeys might have, uh, appeared on her neck a few days before.

"Madison . . ." I said, "I have to get to class."

"Wow, ease up." Her cheeks flushed pastel pink, which was her favorite bait to hook me with. "Ummm, want to do something that'll make you feel better?"

Elizabeth A. Seibert

"And miss gym?" Her rosy scent had swirled out of reach, making me long for more. "You bet—" I stopped. "Wait no, can't. Gotta do a thing for Carter." My two new besties were in gym class, so I didn't really have options. She frowned and I patted her on the shoulder, swiftly sidestepping her before she had a chance to work any more voodoo.

Eerie emptiness, dirty-mop streaks, and the lingering odor of tuna sandwiches greeted me as I entered the government-funded underworld. Being late, I realized everyone else was already in class. It was me and . . . "Mr. Maguire!" Mr. Hoover, the middle-aged, balding hall monitor, called out.

I squeezed my eyes shut, trying to make him disappear. Had to be worth a shot—anything was. His loafers squeaked on the wet floor until he stopped in front of me. I opened my eyes to see a familiar yellow slip in his hands.

"Three slips in three days. And this is only the third day of the school year. Someone get this kid a medal."

"Genius observation." I jammed the slip into the back pocket of my jeans. "I can see why they made you the hall monitor."

Mr. Hoover sighed. "I thought we were past this, Nick. See?" He gestured around the vacant hallway. "There's no one out here to impress. It's no wonder you can't respect other people, you don't even respect yourself."

This is why he can't get a girlfriend. Although he was the man with the detention slips, I couldn't help myself. "Whoops, meant to say, genius observation, *sir.*"

Mr. Hoover ripped another slip with one smooth flick of the wrist. "And we have ourselves a winner. See you after school, Mr. Maguire."

"Looking forward to it." The paper's sharp edges stung when I crumpled it in my hand. Coach Dad was not going to be happy.

Luckily, the first fifteen minutes of gym class account for the time it takes to change, so I jogged onto the gleaming indoor basketball court having barely missed a thing.

"Move along next time, Maguire." Ms. Johnson, the gym teacher, swatted my shoulder blade and marked me "present" on her clipboard. Ms. Johnson is like thirty-five and used to play Olympic volleyball. She legitimately teaches us sports things, likes her job, loves kids, and doesn't really care about the rules. In conclusion, Ms. Johnson is a straight-up hero.

I went to stand with my boy Robert Maxin and, unfortunately, Josh Daley. He somehow managed to always be on the periphery of my friend group. Because of this, as per the rules of high school, he got to metaphorically "sit with us."

Where there are rock stars there are groupies. What can you do?

"Mags," said Josh, "you seen O'Connor's sister?" An irritating pain shot up my side as he nudged me and nodded to where Eliza and her friends sat on the bleachers. They were who Austin and I called "cool nerds." As in, nerds who weren't "hot" but had great personalities? He probably still wasn't her type.

Right?

"Don't let Carter hear you say that. Hey, how's it going with HG?" I changed the subject to Robert's favorite topic: Hannah Green.

"Too soon to tell." Robert put his hand over his heart. "Talking about it will probably put a curse on her and our firstborn child so . . . maybe don't?"

Douchebag Josh almost doubled over, laughing so hard Eliza and her friends looked our way. I shuffled my sneakers, wincing. *Chill, Nick.* What kind of universe did we live in where Douchebag Josh was getting to me?

Tweeeeeeeeet. Ms. Johnson blew her whistle to start class, gathering us under the bright stadium-style lights. "All right, gang. It's Friday, which means . . ."

Oh, heck yeah. Fridays were for dodgeball, and dodgeball meant absolutely dunking on freshmen at 8:00 in the morning.

"Maxin, Daley, y'all are captains," said Ms. Johnson. "Alternate choosing guys and girls. You know the drill."

"Mags," said Robert, high-fiving me.

No surprise there, since the Bro Code states that a bro must be a ride-or-die dodgeball fanatic. I embraced that rule to the fullest. Robert was able to choose Eliza before Josh could, and she waited next to me.

"How come you were late?" she asked. She wore an old cotton tank top that said, *I need my space*, with a picture of the NASA logo. Cute.

"Selena Gomez forgot to roll over and wake me up."

"How unfortunate."

"Truly."

She watched Josh line up his team. He gave her a tiny wave. The gym's stale air, suddenly, felt overwhelmingly stuffy.

"My dad went extra hard on my workout this morning," I admitted. "Didn't feel great after."

"Want to talk about it?"

Absolutely not. "Nah."

"Nick—" Eliza brushed my elbow. Thankfully, that's when Ms. Johnson blew her whistle and it was time to play. I followed Robert to the back of the court and ignored the goosebumps sprouting under my baggy T-shirt.

Honestly . . . yeah, I was *that* guy in dodgeball. Every time I picked up the ball and nailed someone square in the chest, a kind of weight lifted off my body, until all my stress and negative thoughts had transformed into endorphins and empowerment, like I *could* do something. Dodgeball can really cheer a bro up, am I right?

Don't hate us 'cause you ain't us.

My team won two games in a row. It wasn't until the third game that Josh personally targeted me, whipping fast ones right at the moneymaker. A true compliment. While I ducked to keep my nose from being broken, a sophomore on Josh's team arced a big, fat rubber ball right into my knee, in what should have been the biggest upset of the week, except they followed it up with a string of outs for my team. Robert got out, and then a few other kids, and then Eliza, until finally the only person still in was this five-foot freshman named Stephen Ross.

He was up against the entire other team.

"Here we go, Steve!" I shouted. I'd never really talked to Stephen before, and admittedly, I did not know much about him besides the fact I'd umpired his baseball team once.

I took my time on the bench as an opportunity to lie on the dirty floor and lift my legs. A smooth strain stretched my hamstrings. Ever since freshman year, my dad got me up way before any teenager should reasonably be conscious to run extra soccer drills before school. Still acclimating to being back in "school mode," the sessions left me extra slow-moving in the mornings and my muscles super stiff. I could practically feel the tiny tears in my calves begging me to rest, wanting to properly build themselves up again. Yeah . . . no way was *that* happening. You'd think my dad would prioritize stretching, since he's had his share of soccer career–ending injuries, but he didn't want to stand around and wait for me to stretch out my adorable butt.

My mom and dad were not the most open books, but they were particularly tight-lipped when it came to my dad's injury. Over time, I'd gathered that it happened between his junior and senior years of college, right before he was eligible for recruitment to the majors. It had to do with his knee, and although it led to him becoming a teacher, father, and coach . . . he'd probably still say it ruined his life.

Eliza was the closest person to me on the sub bench. She cheered for her friends on Josh's team, and I had to shake off a dizzying vertigo when I heard her voice—as if hearing a ghost.

I leaned against the metal bleachers. By this point, Stephen had gotten most of the other team out and a few of our team back in, which was a treat, since the cacophony of smacking rubber balls helped me relax.

"Nick, what's a good shoulder stretch?" asked Eliza. She flexed her arms in front of her. Like Carter, Eliza was tall and lanky, her upper body strong from playing volleyball. Ms. Johnson had recruited her for the school team while Eliza was still in middle school and would've excused Eliza from gym all month if she'd caught the tiniest whiff of a possible shoulder injury.

"That looks pretty effective."

She stuck out her tongue.

I laughed. "No really though, that's what I would do."

Eliza studied me, trying to discern if I was bullshitting her. Fair. "Thanks, pal," she said.

Literally anytime.

■

I left gym class with a productive energy. In fact, I'd almost completely forgotten how hard my dad had pushed me that morning and my half conversation with Eliza until I had to attend detention.

Before I could submit to Mr. Hoover's cruel and usual punishment, however, I had to find Carter and let him know I wouldn't make it to soccer practice, which brought me to Mr. Hoover's health and nutrition classroom exactly one minute late.

"Can't even make it to detention on time. Definitely a *great* look for your college applications," Mr. Hoover greeted me from his steel desk.

Like Mr. Hoover had any pull over my applications. Geez. He was the least important teacher in the school. *Which is definitely why he takes his sad, boring life out on me.*

Mr. Hoover proceeded to give me an hour-long lecture about the importance of being on time and how I was being disrespectful to him, my teachers, my classmates, and the rest of the school when I "arranged my priorities around my own sleeping schedule."

Then he made me clean his whiteboards. All six of them, multiple times, until they were pristine enough to perform surgery on. For his own sadistic sense of enjoyment.

■

After six hours of school and additional purgatorial suffering, my sorry ass finally made it back to home sweet home. It was only a ten-minute drive from school, but with the detention and then an extra workout afterwards, I arrived well after dinnertime. Hopefully my parents would have saved me some food.

My Mustang squealed into the gravel driveway and I winced. Could I have drawn any more attention to the fact that I was home two hours later than I was supposed to be? Only my mom's antique vehicle was parked, but impending doom still filled my stomach. My engine puttered off and I took a deep breath. It was time to channel my inner ninja.

With stealth-mode activated, the gravel cracked as I gingerly stepped to the tiny, unkempt back porch. I entered the back hall, where the leftover scent of spaghetti sauce sent a rumble up my stomach. When I thought it was safe for me to jog up the back stairs, the back door's latch made a shrill *click*.

"Look who decided to come home," a tired voice came half a second later. "Let's talk, Nick."

I couldn't treat my mom like I'd treated Mr. Hoover, no matter how many lectures she gave. No matter how many punishments I received. That was my resolve after she'd started working even more hours for my inevitably too-high college tuition: I wouldn't make things harder for her.

Instead, I tiptoed around her, trying to avoid conversations like the one we were about to have, and she found ways to have them anyway.

"What's happening?" I entered our messy kitchen—with several chocolate chips long lost under cabinets and a pot with spaghetti sauce drying on the sides—to see her already in her bathrobe, hot tea at the ready. My mom and hot tea were like peanut butter and banana, or like Oreos and Jell-O shots: next-level iconic. If I ever saw my mom without her soothing, peppermint herbal tea, I'd initiate DEFCON 1.

She motioned for me to take the hot seat on the other side of the magazine-covered table. "Where's Dad?"

"The Maxins."

Right. Robert's house. Our dads, just two bros, reclined in front of whatever game was on, with cold ones and mini-pizzas—this is what I pictured whenever someone mentioned the American Dream.

"Which is lucky for you," my mom continued, "because you get the lecture from me."

So lucky.

My parents had lived in the same house since before I was born. Essentially, they'd bought it as a starter house (apparently that's a thing), but then decided that having one kid (yours truly) was enough and stayed put. I didn't mind because I wasn't at home much. Our house being small was probably the main reason why I stayed out. The second reason? Carter's house had junk food.

Nonetheless, it meant that when I sat across from her, every line on her once beautiful skin was basically right in my face. Most of these lines existed because of me.

"Sorry, I know I said I wouldn't get detention this year. I was late and . . ."

"Buying doughnuts on the way to school can make you late, can't it?"

"I needed the coffee—"

My mom raised her eyebrow, stopping me in my completely screwed tracks. I didn't question how she knew about the doughnut. As frustrating as she could be, the lady was smart. Chief scientist/*X-Files* professor/Hermione Granger–level smart. Companies hired her to interview potential applicants and evaluate their employees. She'd conduct twenty-minute interviews and, based solely on that, determine whether people should be hired or promoted.

"And how was the coffee, Nick?" Having heard this lecture many times before, I said it in my head as she said it aloud: "*Was it worth it?*"

If Mr. Hoover had asked me that, I'd have mouthed off. I'd have said yes, of course it was worth getting disciplinary action on my permanent record and jeopardizing my chance of a soccer scholarship. Hot diggity dog. And I'd have frolicked off to whatever class I was probably blowing off. Probably biology.

"Mom, I'm sorry," I said, meaning it a little more than my last apology.

She lifted her *World's Best Wife* mug to her pale lips and drained the last of her tea. She didn't bother pushing back—we'd been down this road before. While my dad and I had both woken up at the crack of dawn, somehow *I* was late to school and he was able to get there *early* to tutor eighth graders about the Oxford comma. Besides, it was *my* soccer scholarship at risk. If I even got a scholarship. If I even made a college soccer team. If my mom didn't kill me first.

"I'm going up." Her chair legs scraped against the floor.

"Can I get you anything?"

"Lock the door if you go out." She rinsed her mug and examined it with her hand towel at the ready, sure to dry every last drop. With a satisfactory nod, she plodded up the stairs. I glanced at my iPhone, a hand-me-down from Carter: 6:50 p.m. New record.

A text message blinked in my palm. *You coming over?*

I leaned back and ran my fingers through my dark hair. Carter O'Connor was my best friend for three reasons: First, he knew what my phone password was (and I didn't even have to show him). Second, he liked *The Hangover* as much as I did (maybe even more). Third, he had a sixth sense for when I simply couldn't stand being home, and always welcomed me to crash at his place.

Thanks, man. I texted back.

That's what it was like when your parents simultaneously treated you like a kid and a grown-up, and their emotional unavailability was both suffocating and lonely. Carter always understood that. And from the way gym class went this morning, it looked like Eliza might too.

■

Boo hoo. Poor me.

Yeah, I know.

When I occasionally complained to Madison about my family, she'd mock me and say, "Wahhhh, your life is so hard. Check your white, male, upper-middle-class privilege. Sheesh."

And then I'd have to say, "I'm not denying that I'm another cog in the system of white male supremacy, Madison." Because I know that's exactly what she would want to hear, whether or not it was true, or if I even understood that. "Hashtag blessed."

Madison would roll her eyes and we'd fight about it some more, and eventually I'd ditch her to go hang out with Carter and Austin, my fave (white, middle-class) buddies.

Real talk: whenever Madison called me out on it, of course I became crazy-aware of the fact that my bros and I have it *made*. Though, it's not about the privilege we're born into, it's what we do with it that counts, right? Whatever that means.

I admit it, sure: the world definitely wouldn't feel great if the saying were *hoes before bros*.

But.

It's not.

RULE NUMBER 3

A BRO SHALT ALWAYS FINISH TELLING HIS JOKE. HE SHALT NEVER, UNDER ANY CIRCUMSTANCES, LET IT GO WITHOUT A PUNCHLINE.

Carter's house could put Tony Stark's personal playground to complete shame.

It had a swimming pool *and* a trampoline, a surround-sound IMAX theater in the basement, and more gaming systems than any kid could ever ask for. As if that weren't enough, the swimming pool converted into an ice rink in the winter, something Carter's dad had set up before he Irish-exited his own family.

To top it off, the walls were actual colors: none of that beige crap that my parents used. When I'd climbed to the top of the driveway, the valet even took my keys.

Got ya . . . the O'Connors don't have a valet.

"Look who it is!" Ms. O'Connor exclaimed as I let myself in

the back. The peaceful aroma of salted caramel welcomed me.

She stood at the blue marble kitchen island with a spatula in one hand and a velvety, brown cupcake in the other. I'd have offended her if I assumed it was a chocolate cupcake. *Not just any chocolate,* she often criticized me, *it's Oreo.* Or cinnamon spice. Or s'mores. Or peanut butter chocolate fudge.

Eliza perched on a bar stool at the island—a striking blond in the middle of a sea of cupcakes and mixing bowls filled to the brim with pale pink or blue icing. She wore Carter's sweatshirt with one arm out of a sleeve, resting a heavy-duty icepack on her exposed shoulder.

She dipped a finger in her mother's giant steel mixing bowl. "Got to make sure it tastes good," she said.

I nodded. "Can't go all the way to the event without realizing you used salt instead of sugar."

"Rookie mistake." Eliza licked pink frosting off her hand. I smirked. She pretended to throw a cupcake at me.

"Need an extra hand?" I asked. I didn't always suck up to Ms. O'Connor . . . wait, yes, I did. She let me come and go from her house as I pleased and fed me unlimited cupcakes. Those four words were a small price to pay.

Ms. O'Connor spread pale blue frosting onto her confections as if she were waving a magic wand. "I can always use another decorator. Liza has to rest and I'm down a player."

"Went a bit too hard in dodgeball this morning," Eliza said as she resituated her ice pack. Ms. O'Connor handed me a bowl of blue sugar crystals.

"Sprinkle these on the ones with the pink frosting."

Ms. O'Connor always gave me the easiest tasks, but I still found myself second-guessing my every move with them. Like sprinkle how? How many sprinkles per cupcake? What if the sprinkles end up in the wrapper and when someone eats the cupcake their hands turn blue and they don't realize it and give a big speech and embarrass themselves and become doomed for all eternity?

I turned back to Eliza. "Really, dodgeball? As I recall you spent most of gym on the bench . . ."

"Kidding, Maguire. Had a rough volleyball practice. Olivia is very concerned about me."

"Don't know why it had to be volleyball," said Ms. O'Connor. "Couldn't have been cross-country or swimming. Just one of the most concussion-heavy sports."

"The danger makes it more fun," said Eliza, "like riding a motorcycle."

The color drained from Ms. O'Connor's already pale face. "Where are you riding motorcycles?"

"Nowhere, Mother." Eliza relaxed into the bar stool. "It's too easy with you."

I kept my head down and flaked some of the sugar crystals onto the frosting as instructed. There must have been a hundred cupcakes on the counter. Half of them were brown, the other half white. I was about to ask Ms. O'Connor what the occasion was when we were interrupted.

"Dude."

Carter stood in the doorway wearing flannel pajama pants and a Clarkebridge College sweatshirt.

"Sometimes I feel like you only come over here to hang out with my mom," he said.

"Someone has to." Ms. O'Connor approached Carter and nudged him with her frosting-covered spatula. "Here, sweetie, try this."

"Ew. Stop."

"Can't blame me for trying." She shook the frosting in his face, but Carter wrinkled his nose.

Carter was the one person in their family, and perhaps the world, who didn't like Ms. O'Connor's cupcakes. He claimed it's because when she was starting out, Ms. O'Connor fed him four cupcakes a day trying to perfect her recipes.

"If you'd gone through that," he often said, "you wouldn't eat another one either."

"Have fun with your video games." His mom smiled at us, relieving me from my decorating duties. "If you need anything, let me know before nine. Have to be up early tomorrow to drop these off. They're for Stephanie Kaplan's gender-reveal party."

She picked up one of the brown cupcakes and broke it in half, exposing a deep blue center.

"It's weird that I know the gender of the baby before she does . . . She came over with a slip of paper from the doctor. Said she hadn't even read it yet."

"You should've made these bad boys green," said Eliza. "Tell her she's having alien babies."

Carter chuckled. "I'd go to *that* party."

"And," Eliza continued, "why does gender have to be binary? What if it doesn't know what it wants to be yet? Like, we are *literally* color-coding babies to let strangers know what type of private parts they have. Pretty freaking weird, if you ask me."

"Too bad no one did."

"Carter," his mom warned, shutting down a showdown between the O'Connor siblings real quick.

"Whatever. I gotta change." Eliza put her ice pack in the

freezer, between the gallons of frozen dough, and gave her mom a quick kiss on the cheek.

"Where are you—" I started, but Carter shook his head. *Don't ask.*

Carter led the way up to his room, though I could've gotten there from his kitchen blindfolded, spun around a hundred times, and in forty steps or fewer.

A spicy vanilla aroma followed us. When I was younger, I used to be jealous of Carter and what seemed like having the best, most fun family. As I got to know them better, I realized the baking and wafting smells were there to fill the extra emptiness in their house, left over from when Mr. O'Connor went out for cigarettes, found a new European family somewhere in the chip aisle, and never looked back. His dad was still around when they first moved to North Cassidy, though he'd left pretty soon after. I'd met him a few times, but I didn't really remember him. No great loss if you ask me. But it wasn't my dad. They kept his last name—apparently "Olivia O'Connor" was too quaint for her business to give up.

Despite the IMAX theater in his basement, Carter's room was where we hung out the most. Until late afternoon, sunlight flooded through several tall, bay windows making it impossible to sleep past 7:00 a.m., but also so you could never be unhappy. The walls that weren't taken up by the windows were covered with autographed posters of his favorite basketball players and shelves holding an endless supply of gummies and pineapple juice.

Carter's pineapple juice addiction had started before he moved to North Cassidy, so I never got the full story—but if a normal human's body is 60 percent water, Carter's was at least 50 percent pineapple juice cocktail. Maybe that was why the girls loved him so much after soccer practice—even his sweat made them want to be around him.

Carter's hamburger-shaped beanbag chair made a satisfying crunch as he melted into it, clicking feverishly on his video game controller. I took the Oreo beanbag chair beside him and waited for him to fire up the game.

Three rounds of *Fortnite* later, I assassinated his lameness and the screen went black.

"And that's how it's done," I said. "C'mon, man, you were practicing all afternoon and that's the best you can do?"

"I know how you get when you lose."

"Fine. I'll let you have *another* rematch." I thought Carter would have learned by now to not mess with my competitive side, though he was almost as competitive as I was. (But not quite.)

"Don't cry when I shoot you." Completely focused, Carter held his finger over the start button. "Ten . . . nine . . . eight . . ."

"Carter?"

He pressed pause. There were two things that we'd stop gaming for: an alien attack (awesome) and Eliza interrupting us (sometimes awesome), though it hadn't happened in a year.

Stop it, Nick. I commanded myself to be cool as I took in her appearance. *Anyone but her.* Eliza hung in the doorway, glittering like a firefly in dusky July twilight. The pale glow of the TV still revealed her tight leather pants and a flouncy top that could definitely be featured in some fashion magazine, and makeup that made her brown eyes flare. *Where is she going, and can I come?*

She pressed a light switch on Carter's wall, illuminating us since the sun had fully set while we played. "I'm leaving now.

Don't make Olivia freak out while I'm gone." Her gaze shifted from him to me. "You staying over?"

"Thought you'd never ask, babe," I said. "Where are you taking me?"

She tapped her silver flats on the hardwood floor and shifted her weight from one leg to the other.

"Eliza has a date," Carter said.

"Who's the lucky guy?" I crossed my fingers that she wouldn't say the name of a certain, rotten douchebag with a slimy—

"Josh Daley." Damn. She did anyway. "We're hitting up a parrrr-tay."

Somewhat in shock, I uttered the two saddest words in the English language: "What party?"

"Juniors only," she replied.

Were we seriously not going to crash this?

Carter shook his head. "It's at Sarah Rosen's house."

Ah. Sarah Rosen. The one girl Carter had "been intimate" with, without calling her his girlfriend.

Sarah Rosen, one of the most straight-as-an-arrow girls at our school, was a sore subject. Carter had hooked up with her at a party two years ago, and things were different for him after that.

Which meant, on principle, that he'd never enter her house without an invitation. I was totally free to attend, except that the Bro Code clearly states to never leave a bro behind. *Goddamn Bro Co*—I caught myself. *Close one.* I'd almost blasphemed bro-kind.

"I'm kind of nervous, though," said Eliza.

"I cannot be here for this, not again." The beanbag chair swished in protest as Carter jumped up, escaping to the bathroom. He slammed the door behind him.

"Let me guess," I said, "You guys've already had the pre-date boy talk?" (But for real, who wanted to sit around and talk about freaking Josh Daley?)

Eliza slid into Carter's seat, playing with the ends of her shirt.

"What if he thinks I'm boring?"

Not possible. "In those pants it won't matter," I said instead, though that probably wasn't better.

"Ha."

"Here, I'll help you." I stood up.

"Um . . ."

I took her long hands and she rose to meet me. "What're you doing, Nick?"

"If you're ever in a jam," I said, "tell this joke: what's the difference between a pregnant woman and a lightbulb?"

Eliza gave a little shake of her head.

"You can unscrew a—" I stopped. There was no way I'd make that kind of fool of myself in front of her . . . for the time being.

"Never mind."

Eliza blinked back at me. "Wow. I can't believe you tried to tell me that."

"Same." Unable to stop myself, I reached for her wrist and gave her a quick twirl.

"Oh my gosh," her voice cracked as she caught her balance, her hands on my shoulders. Just four inches away from me.

"Not bad," I whispered.

"Likewise."

We stayed like that for what felt like minutes but was probably a few seconds. Long enough for me to wonder what it would feel like to stand even closer. *Stop, Nick. Cool it.*

"Say hi to Josh for me," I said.

Eliza blushed, her wild eyes filled with bashfulness and a hint of something else. My shoulders felt empty as she removed her hands from them, our moment over.

"You'd be a good dance partner, Maguire. Any girl going out with you would have a lot of fun."

"Duh," I teased. "Remember, if your date with Josh is sub-par and you ever want a redo."

"You wish."

Great, now it's weird.

"I should go now, before this gets any more . . ." Eliza's shoes clicked as she walked like she couldn't get out of there fast enough.

"*Bye, Carter!*" She called. She nodded in my direction. The light seemed to follow her as she left the doorway.

"Is she gone yet?" Carter's voice was faint.

"Yeah, dude." I sank back into the Oreo beanbag. The refreshing hiss of a pineapple juice can opening came behind me. "Josh Daley. Gross."

"You had one job, Nick," Carter sighed. "One freaking . . . ugh. In any case." He paused for a sip. "What're we waiting for? This is the first time you've been here since Eliza came back from Australia. Remember all those ideas we had? My mom's probably in bed now so . . ."

"Oh, hell yeah." We'd had many pranks in store. "Did you get a new gun yet?" By gun I meant a Nerf 2000. He broke his old one a few months ago when we'd decided to test Austin's reflexes. We'd completely forgotten Austin spent two summers at karate camp (a fact he *likes* us to forget), but when we hid in the coat closet and fired at him, he'd jumped into a karate stance and chopped Carter's plastic toy in half.

The definition of tragedy.

Carter shot me the evil smirk he reserved for these moments. "Better than that. C'mon."

We tiptoed through the hallways until we reached an old, squeaky set of stairs that led to his attic. As fancy as Carter's house may have been, his attic always reminded me that it was not made in this century. Arguably, that tidbit made it even cooler.

"Did those bats leave yet?"

"Looks like." Carter lifted a piece of yellow newspaper in a cobwebby corner.

"Damn." Two weeks ago, we'd found a family of six baby bats flying around. It had been cool, kind of like a vampire family was living there.

"I know. They could've come in handy. It's okay, though. I saved the dung beetle from Austin's birthday party."

I high fived him and we set to work. Once the musty, rodent smell wears off, the attic's really not that bad.

"Dude." I opened one of the less dusty-looking cardboard boxes. "This it?" I held up the biggest Super Soaker I had ever seen in my life. It was easily a foot and a half long and the tank looked like it could hold about three liters of water. I had to carry it with two hands. "You know how much waterpower we can get with this thing?"

"I think we have to test it and see," Carter said.

And so it began.

■

Ten minutes later, we stood inside Eliza's bright orange room with our equipment. Eliza's room was decorated like an artist's studio, since she was the "creative type." Carter knew better than to go anywhere near her artwork. Tonight we'd rewired her computer monitor so every time she clicked her mouse the screen would change colors, and we'd filled her sock drawer with flyers for foot fungus cream.

But the *joya de la corona* was the alarm clock we'd stored under her bed: we'd set it to play the Beatles' "Help!" at 4:00 a.m. and we'd hooked it up to Carter's water gun so that if she tried to pull it out from underneath her bed, she'd get drenched.

"This isn't too mean, is it?" I asked.

"Nah," said Carter, "she's been having trouble with the jetlag. This is the perfect way to restart her system."

I considered this and decided to agree with him. There was no better cure for sleeping issues than a splash in the face. Joking, of course, but we had to justify this to ourselves somehow.

"This is going to be epic," I felt like an eight-year-old boy again. It was my second favorite feeling of the evening, second to earlier when . . . *stop, Nick.*

Carter kicked the water gun securely under his sister's bed. "You know, I bought two more Super Soakers . . . want to let them taste the fresh air?"

"Definitely. Those guns need us."

We raced to his attic, forgetting to be quiet for his mom. Carter pushed me against the thin railing and I almost tumbled down the stairs, but it was all worth it when we reached his grassy yard and turned loose the rusty spigot to fill neon orange tanks the size of my forearm.

The O'Connors' heated pool remained uncovered for probably the last weekend of the year. We kicked off our shoes and socks, since there was a good chance we'd end up in the water. Neither of us cared if our shirts or sweatpants got wet, but shoes take forever to dry. Plus, I had these fresh blue Nikes and if those got ruined my life would be over.

It was well past nightfall, but Carter and I knew every inch of his backyard. In good form, we waited for both our weapons to be filled with ammo before commencing in battle. The second I screwed the plastic cap onto my tank, Carter tore into the blackness where he'd wait to either hunt or be hunted.

I stepped suspiciously towards the pool—if he wanted to jump out at me, he'd have to reconcile with the water. A warm breeze rustled through the trees, stirring crickets and spooking squirrels, who scurried on the bark and gave away that Carter was not, in fact, hiding in a tree.

The concrete edge of the pool dug into my knees as I crouched and listened for movement. If Carter could've blasted me there, he would've, which meant he had to be somewhere out of reach . . . shadows squared against Ms. O'Connor's favorite hydrangeas, right before the white picket fence that separated their yard from the neighbor's. One of the bushes' shadows stretched longer than the others.

My brand-new, not-yet-broken-in trigger cut against my finger, and my ears strained as I closed on the bushes. Breathing so quietly that the squirrels wouldn't be able to hear, I sprinted to attack. I shot water in front of me, splashing as I ran to the yard's edge. As I narrowed in, I realized the long shadow hadn't been Carter, but a shovel resting against the flower buds.

"Any last words?"

Carter's gun scraped the back of my neck. I weighed my weapon—it felt light, probably about a quarter tank left. Digging

Elizabeth A. Seibert

my bare heels into the dirt, I spun to face him before he completely drenched me.

"Nice try," said Carter. As if I were caught in a rainstorm with a personal black cloud, Carter dumped his tank over my head. Cold dripped from my chin to my ankles, even as I shot a few revenge squirts.

Violent. Totally unnecessary. And great.

After two more rounds of that (best out of three and Carter won all of them), we ended up covered in the world's record for mosquito bites. We defrosted some frozen pizzas and sat pooling puddles in Carter's kitchen. Our water guns took a well-deserved rest on the kitchen table.

The slow treading of tires in the driveway interrupted our haphazard dinner. I checked my phone. It was 10:35. The same time that Carter and I would have even arrived at this so-called party.

"She's back early," Carter said.

Taking it way further than necessary, as was his specialty, Carter grabbed his Super Soaker and stomped down the driveway. Josh's pickup had barely rolled past the curb before he shut off its headlights. Carter scowled, squinting to no use as he tried to see inside.

"If she's not out in the next three seconds I'm going over there to slash his tires."

"Chill, bro," I said. "Be cool. On my lead."

Channeling our inner ninjas yet again, Carter and I slunk to Josh's truck. It blocked the streetlights so I couldn't see what I was doing, but I soon heard a "good-bye," and the closing of a door, and then the car slowly drove away.

"Go!" I shouted. Carter and I opened fire on the back of it, using all of the water left in our guns. Josh squealed down the street faster than I could call after him, "Night just got real, Daley!"

"*What are you doing*?!" A silhouette stormed over to us. "Are you kidding me right now? Oh my god, you guys. Grow the hell up!"

"We're sorry," I said, because I knew Carter would be at a loss for words. "It was an accident—"

"*Nick Maguire!*" Eliza cut me off. She came closer and my stomach sank—her white shirt clung to her, dripping and soaked. If she hadn't been mad at me, I'd have enjoyed the moment.

"Go away." She scooped up two fists of dirt and threw them at our faces.

She had great aim. Carter surrendered his water gun on the pavement. I did the same and we slunk into his house. I hadn't felt this bad since the time we accidentally-on-purpose destroyed the model of the solar system she'd been working on for two days. We thought it would be more realistic if the solar system had been ravaged by Darth Vader's Empire.

I now see why she was upset about taking that to school.

"Whoops," I said.

"I think my mom put fresh sheets in the guest room for you." Carter shuffled his feet. "Your stuff should still be there."

So, we weren't going to talk about Eliza. Perfect.

I puttered to the guest room, past the white wallpaper etched with silver sunflowers in the upstairs hallway. That wallpaper always made me think of the time Eliza had told Ms. O'Connor it was the ugliest thing she ever saw, and Ms. O'Connor had replied, "It's a good thing you never saw your father naked."

Carter denies that conversation ever took place.

The light was already on in the guest room, probably from Ms. O'Connor double checking that I hadn't left anything half-eaten in there after the last time I'd stayed over two weeks earlier. Right before the return of her favorite daughter. Even though they referred to it as the guest room, I was the sole person who ever used it—one of my old duffel bags with some extra shirts and a spare toothbrush sat permanently in the closet. We all pretty much considered it my home away from home.

In addition to a bed so big and comfy it made my bed at home seem like a cheap sheet of sandpaper, the room was decorated with posters of golden beaches that said things like, "Namast'ay at the beach" and "Keep palm and carry on." And it had book-shelves full of volumes with titles like *The Arabian Nights* and *The Adventures of Sherlock Holmes*.

Instagram-worthy for sure.

Stripping off my wet clothes, I tossed them into a pile by the door and wrapped one of the freshly laid-out towels around my waist. I reached under the bed, feeling around the pristine, cob-webless carpet. If Ms. O'Connor hadn't found it, there should be . . . *yes*. I pulled out a half-eaten chocolate bar. *Score.*

"Nick?" Eliza rapped softly on the door.

I jumped, tossing the chocolate onto the bed and quickly pull-ing on my Cassidy High soccer pants.

"What's up?"

The door scraped open. Eliza had changed into fresh, comfy clothes. Her hair dripped onto her sweatshirt.

"Whoa." She pointed to my lack-of-shirt.

"Sorry." I pulled the towel around my shoulders.

That was one of the good things about playing soccer for

Cassidy High: my dad put an extreme emphasis on his athletes' physical being. The core abdominal muscles did not go overlooked. I liked to flex that when I could. Who wouldn't?

"As long as I'm apologizing, I'm sorry about earlier," I said. "I obviously didn't think it through."

"Josh deserved it. I was mad about my shirt, but apparently it can get wet, so not a big deal."

She stood right in front of me and brushed some of the ground off my face. Her hands were freezing. I didn't dare flinch. "Sorry for throwing dirt at you. Hope I didn't get any in your eyes."

"This is making up for it pretty well."

"Great, I'm glad." She took her hand away, which left my cheek somehow colder. She flipped her long, wet hair over her shoulder, filling the room with the scent of her cinnamon shampoo. "By the way, you owe me."

"For the date? Can't say I'm not flattered—"

"No. I found the present you left under my bed. You really haven't changed at all."

"Which one?"

"Funny." She leaned against the door. "Need anything else for tonight?"

"Hey," I said, before she could leave. "Want to tell me why Daley's car deserved to be attacked?"

"Maybe when you're wearing a shirt. Maybe."

As the clock in the hallway rang eleven, Eliza slipped away, leaving me standing in her guest room with a wide, stupid grin on my face.

RULE NUMBER 4

THE DATING CLAUSE: IF A GIRL MATCHES ANY OF THE FOLLOWING CRITERIA, SHE SHALT BE OFF-LIMITS FOREVER UNTIL THE END OF TIME: A) WAS A BRO'S EX-GIRLFRIEND; B) YOUR BRO, OR YOUR BRO'S BRO*, SPECIFICALLY TOLD YOU HE WANTED HER; C) IS YOUR BRO'S SISTER.

*Does not apply to your bro's bro's bro, etc.

A couple hours later, even though I was lying on the most comfortable mattress in the world and my head rested against a pillow like a grass skirt in a tropical paradise, I still couldn't fall asleep. My phone said it was 1:22 a.m. I had two unread texts from Madison. One minute later than when I last checked it. Two texts that would remain unread.

For the last year or so, I'd had trouble sleeping. It usually wasn't as much of a problem when I was at the O'Connors' as it is when I'm in my own house, but tonight it seemed like the sleeplessness wasn't going to go away. It wasn't like there were a million things on my mind either. Okay, I guess there was my mom freaking out at me, and Mr. Hoover, and Josh, and soccer-slash-my-dad . . . whatever.

I rolled out from under the sweat-covered sheets and rubbed my hand against the back of my neck, trying to get some of the knots out.

Except for my moans and groans, the house slept quietly—too quietly, like it was holding its breath for an adventure. *Stop imagining things. Not every moment of your life has to be a goddamn action movie.*

I did what I always do whenever this happens: I pulled on a wrinkled hoodie and dug around for yesterday's socks, then I tiptoed across the creaky flooring to hit up the basement.

Second to Carter's room, the seriously legit, totally soundproof basement was my favorite spot in their house. It had everything a guy could ever ask for: an IMAX projector, surround sound, a pinball machine, a pool table, and it even had these little chocolate pudding cups lying around. No lie.

Being the absolute man that he is, Carter lets me come down in the middle of the night to play with his toys. Toys, in this case, being defined as his movie projector. One of the benefits of being friends with Carter, besides that his refrigerator holds an endless supply of ginger ale, is his movie selection. It was as if every streaming service in the universe teamed up with the Library of Congress and decided to camp out in some random town in Massachusetts.

That's better. Reclining on the leather couch, with the cool basement air weighing on my muscles and the remote, heavy in my hand, was way more my scene than a five-star guest room. *The Dark Knight* sat at the top of Carter's movie queue, half-watched from two weeks ago. I pressed Play and pushed back against the squishy pillows, my back relaxing into all of the right places.

The possibility of sleep spiraled closer with every scene change, but right in the middle of Heath Ledger explaining exactly how he got those scars, my cushions shuffled under a new weight.

"Aren't you living the dream?" Eliza whispered. In her old-school One Direction T-shirt and Cassidy High volleyball sweatpants, she couldn't have looked cuter. I mean, more chill.

"Wouldn't you like to know." I lowered the movie's volume so I wouldn't have to yell. "Why are you up?"

"Heard the movie from upstairs and had to come down." She relaxed against the end of the couch, bending her knees to keep her feet from touching me.

"Haven't seen *The Dark Knight* in forever," she added.

"It's your lucky night." It made sense that Eliza would love Batman. All the cool kids do.

Eliza shifted from lying on her back to viewing the movie on her side. As much as I tried to turn my attention back to Christian Bale, not even Batman could compete with how close her mismatched socks (one pink, one yellow) were to my legs.

For the millionth time, stop, Nick. Anyone but her. She's Carter's smart-ass little sister.

Luckily, the nighttime basement masked the constant movement of my own feet, fidgeting as they tried to scratch the nagging itch inside my brain—which was difficult without magical powers. In case it wasn't obvious by now, I'm not, in fact, Professor

Albus Percival Wulfric Brian Dumbledore. No matter how much I resented my parents for being Muggles, it wouldn't change the fact that if I ever went to Hogwarts, I'd probably be expelled for exclusively playing Quidditch and not studying. Ever.

Maybe I was magical after all, because ten minutes later, the riddle staring at me like a middle school crush cracked open. Sensing she had an audience, Eliza glanced over her knees, as if her sleepy dreams of calorie-free grilled cheese and no-limit credit cards were shattered by being pulled back into reality.

"What?"

The basement air felt warmer as I debated how to respond, when the truth was, she'd lied. Her room was on the second floor, and Carter's told me their fabulous movie theater/game room/woman cave (since two-thirds of his household is female) is soundproof like seven or eight billion times. There was no way she'd heard the movie from upstairs.

"Never mind."

If I asked her what she was doing awake, she would ask me what *I* was doing awake. Carter had mentioned earlier that she had a problem with jetlag. We'd go with that. Not that I was Sherlock Holmes or anything, but I was good at math; when it comes to putting two and two together, I can usually come up with a solid answer.

The credits soon rolled, and Commissioner Gordon's final lines simmered around us. Familiar goosebumps sprouted on the back of my neck as I realized she was taking in every inch of my silhouette. A whirr came from the projector shutting itself off, encasing us completely in silent darkness. As eerie as the basement could have been, something about being there with her kept it from seeming like the start of a *Twilight Zone* episode.

Of course, there was still time.

"Thanks," she said.

"For what?"

"Not asking."

"Anytime." My fingers tap-danced against my legs and the stillness around us grew louder. I could pretend my heightened senses were due to the darkness and it being well after 2:30 a.m., but I'd know I was kidding myself.

"You tired yet?" She asked.

I shook my head. "You?"

She sat up, pulling her pink and yellow socks away. "I'll put the game in."

"I'll get the guitars," I said, "And break."

While Carter's room was the main video-game arena, some games could be played only on the big screen. After I'd dug around for our equipment and Eliza forwarded through the credits, we stood ready with white plastic guitars slung over our shoulders. *Guitar Hero* has always been one of my favorite games, and Eliza and I played it together all the time—or at least we used to. Carter never really got into the whole "musical notes = points" thing, so when Eliza needed someone to show her how it was done, I taught her everything I knew.

Well, not *everything*. It's not like Obi-Wan straight-up handed Luke a copy of *How to Be a Better Jedi than I Am 101*. Some things Eliza would have to figure out for herself.

The game characters we'd created when we were twelve still existed in the system. Eliza played as a pink-haired rocker chick and I selected a cool guy with a mohawk. Previews of the songs blasted as Eliza scrolled through our choices.

"You want a practice round?" I asked.

"Only if you do."

I let her think she had the last word. She pressed Start for "I Love Rock 'n' Roll," the easiest song in the game. Guess we were doing a practice round. Maybe it was because it was late/early in the morning, but Eliza played her guitar like a zombie trudges for brains. Jumping onto my knees and strumming like a total idiot to cheer her up, Eliza gave me a tiny laugh, not dancing back.

I ended up beating her on the song by about 20 percent.

"Nice work, Maguire. Looks like you've been practicing."

"Don't mistake work for natural ability," I replied. "Helps when you go easy on me."

I nudged her with my guitar.

"All right, all right. I'll give you a fair fight this time." She dragged her fingertips through her hair. "Sorry, little distracted."

Same, sister.

"You'd better," I said.

When we were younger, Carter and Eliza could not have been more different—Carter loved sports while Eliza loved arts and crafts; Eliza liked reading and relaxing in Ms. O'Connor's flower garden while all Carter wanted to do was play soccer and video games. Carter always wanted to eat pizza and chicken wings, while Eliza wanted waffles and grilled cheese. On Friday nights, their fights over which movie to watch could last for a full hour.

Most of those characteristics hold true to this day—but the O'Connor siblings' similarities had evolved as well: they were total nerds who never scored anything less than an A-minus, they were absolute spitting images of each other with their blond hair and dark brown eyes, and their competitive streaks, however endearing, were absolutely never to be underestimated.

Elizabeth A. Seibert

She picked "More Than a Feeling" to be the next song. "Try and keep up, *pal*."

The power ballad's slow rhythm echoed around us, and she kept it closer this time.

"Slow songs make it harder to show off my mad dance skills," I said.

"Exactly."

"Oof."

Eliza's laugh mixed sweetly with the music, its falsetto register perfect for sarcasm.

The notes sped up as we reached the guitar solo. While that should have called for more concentration, Eliza decided to throw me for a big, fat roller-coastery loop-de-loop.

"Earlier," she started, "when you said you'd go out with me if my date with Josh was sub-par . . ."

The roller coaster plunged, deep diving straight to the ground, and my stomach dropped to my ankles like a complete wimp who'd gone on the ride only to impress the girl who'd never looked twice at him. *Abort abort abort*, my brain screamed. As if that would work.

"Yeah?"

"Did you mean it?"

I've been at a loss for words twice in my life: the first was three years ago when my dad decided I was going to start waking up hours and hours before school every day, and the way he said it made me realize nothing I could do would get me out of it; and the second time was two years ago when Austin told me he drinks pickle smoothies to make his hair shiny.

This moment marked time number three.

The good play here would be to punt: "Why do you ask?"

"I don't know," she said. "Something Carter mentioned bothered me. About you making sure Josh didn't, like, give me a hard time. Just thought it would be weird if it were more than that and you weren't kidding."

"Well, us dating isn't really a possibility," I replied. My legs shook as they tried to contain my awkwardness. If it wasn't already abundantly clear to both of us, it felt like the time to clarify that I couldn't ever have a non-platonic relationship with Eliza. The Bro Code was quite clear about that.

Of course, I could not give a flick of the finger about the code or Carter or Austin or Josh and date her anyway; though to be honest, as much as I liked Eliza, I liked Carter more.

"Carter was telling the truth, then? Not that I thought he was bluffing, I mean, he would *totally* do that."

"What else would you expect from Carter?"

The song ended and Eliza's guitar hung off her shoulders. She stuffed her hands into her pockets. The abrupt silence coming at the wrong time.

"I'm glad it's you looking out for me and not someone else."

Eliza's whisper sounded like truth bubbling out of a cauldron of buried secrets. I'd left my phone upstairs, but if I could've made a bet, I'd have said it was around 3:00 a.m.—the time people tell only the truth.

Three in the morning was when Madison had admitted to me that she was sleeping with other people because she didn't want anyone to get too close. On another day, it was the time I'd told her she didn't have to worry about that with me. Three in the morning also was the time at parties when whoever is still there starts discussing the mysteries of space and someone inevitably asks, *Do you think we're alone?*

"Josh kind of seems like the clingy type," Eliza continued. "I might need you for an emergency."

"So you can avoid hanging out with him?"

"Yeah. Occasionally."

"To clarify," I touched my chin for dramatic effect, "you want me to help you avoid the guy you're dating."

Eliza busied herself by turning off the video game equipment. Her hair caught the blue glow from the projector screen, making me want to joke that she seemed possessed. I didn't.

"It's just . . ." Her voice emitted waves of anxiety. "I don't know. He kept trying to make out with me all night, and he wouldn't leave me alone after I asked, and he didn't seem to want to take no for an answer."

"What?"

"Don't tell Carter," said Eliza. "It wasn't exactly that I didn't want to . . . he got a little f'ed up and I didn't want to, you know, take advantage."

The gigantic room began to feel too small. "Are you . . . okay?" Giving her a hug felt appropriate, but we'd had that weird conversation. And now this. And I had no idea if she wanted me to.

"Yep. Thanks, Nick." She yawned, solving the situation for me by brushing it off completely. "I'm glad we can be friends."

"Me too." Staying friends meant taking the pressure off whatever it was I felt when I was around her. Which was nothing important. Or plain nothing? Friends was something I could do.

"Hey," I said as she turned towards the door, "is your shoulder okay? I could give you some stretches—I'm pretty much a stretching expert."

Whatever happened to her shoulder couldn't have helped how she felt about tonight.

She put a foot on the bottom of the stairs and leaned against the railing. "That would be awesome, thanks, Maguire. First, sleep."

"You got it, *pal.*"

"Smell ya later, then."

Friends.

RULE NUMBER 5

A BRO SHALT NOT WAKE UP BEFORE 11:00 A.M. ON A SATURDAY.

The clock read 10:07 a.m. Somehow, my legs felt relaxed and my mind felt as if I'd chugged six iced coffees—the main coffee a bro subscribes to.

A whiff of cinnamon goodness drifted into my room, followed by the heroic scent of casually cooked bacon. I headed downstairs to find Carter and Eliza already sitting at their dining table.

The O'Connors' dining room matched the rest of their house in the sense that it was *nothing* like the rest of the house. While the kitchen was deep blue and filled with shiny metallic baking supplies, the dining room was a pale pink, with tiny teacups and artificial flowers scattered around the surfaces, as if it were straight out of one of those English country novels I was assigned in literature last year but didn't read. (Austin would know what I meant.)

I pulled out the dark wooden chair across from my best friend, but Carter kept his head parallel to his plate and shoveled in the golden-brown pancakes that his mom had whipped up before that gender-reveal shindig. She was flippin' (ha) good at pancakes too. Her banana pancakes were award-winning, if you count the certificate Carter and I gave her as a legitimate prize.

Today's were blueberry pancakes, some bacon links, orange juice, a fruit salad, and some variety of muffin that, as I sniffed it, made my mouth water and forget to care about what kind it was.

Eliza wore her leggings and a plain long-sleeved shirt, with her hair in a messy braid thing. She frowned at her plate, which housed an architectural masterpiece of a syrupy waterfall and a bridge made out of bacon.

"I forgot," I said, "about your breakfast designs." A few years ago she'd managed to build a replica of their house out of bananas and oatmeal.

"Sound the alarms," said Eliza, "Nick Maguire got up before noon."

"Don't get too excited; I'm still trying to decide if I like this world."

"Maybe getting up early isn't that bad." She balanced some orange slices for a second bacon bridge.

"Sleeping late means I will never run into morning people." Grabbing an empty ceramic plate, I piled on the delicious foods and inhaled the treasure. *If every morning were like this, I'd become a morning person.*

"What about you?" I said. "How did you sleep?"

"I was having a good dream. I'll take it." She balanced a blueberry on top of her bridge.

"A good dream? Do tell."

"You weren't in it."

I leaned back in my chair, making the front two legs scrape and lift off the floor.

"That's too bad," I said. "You were in mine."

She opened her mouth for a comeback, but her almost statement was interrupted by Carter choking. Eliza clapped her brother's back until he caught his breath.

"You really shouldn't say things like that," said Carter. "It's too early for me to tell if you're kidding."

He rested his back against his chair, finally looking up from his plate, and had calmed down to his usual relaxed self when the doorbell rang.

"I'll get it." Eliza abandoned her syrupy mess.

Carter poked her bacon bridge.

"She's gross," he said. "It's 'cause you're here. Our mom's gone and she's showing off."

I took a forkful of blueberry pancake, reveling in its buttery fluffiness. I continued with my mouthful. "I mean, girls are great and all . . . but *wow* these pancakes. "

"Ew," said Eliza, rejoining us.

Austin casually sauntered in behind her, dressed in his soccer pants and his favorite hooded sweatshirt. Carter gave him a nod. The three of us always hung out on Saturdays, sometimes to play video games or sometimes to roll around town to see what trouble we could get into.

"'Sup, boys?" Austin sat next to me, grabbing a muffin.

I elbowed him hello. "Hear anything from Jamal?"

"Oh yeah. He can't get a beach permit until middle of September, so we gotta wait until then."

"Damn," I said. "Better late than never." I held out my hand for a fist bump. Austin, being a bro, of course returned it within the socially acceptable two seconds.

"Jamal's bonfire?" Carter's plate clanged as he threw down his fork. "About that . . ."

"You're not bailing on us, are you, O'Connor?" Austin asked as if Carter were the only O'Connor in the room.

"I can't go back to BB. You guys know that."

Every year, our friend Jamal Sanchez threw this huge bonfire on the nearest beach. He usually timed it with the beginning of school, but we'd still have plenty to celebrate when the time finally came. Carter and that party, however, had a mixed relationship.

With my mouth stuffed with pancake, I said, "Austin, did you hear something?"

Austin looked about the quaint, pink room, cupping his ears. "It sounds like . . . can't be. Is that whining about a party?"

"Can't be," I said. "'Cause whoever it is must know we're going to drag their sorry ass there anyway."

Austin shook his head. "That guy must be a real idiot."

"Probably thinks the sky is blue too."

"It's clearly orange."

"More of a clementine today, in my opinion."

"Excellent point," said Austin.

Eliza sat back with her arms crossed, the tiniest trace of amusement on her lips. I made it my mission to make that bigger.

"That guy's probably such an idiot, he went to the dentist to get a Bluetooth," I said.

Austin's chair scraped the floor as he tipped it back to match mine. "That guy's probably so dumb, that when the judge said, 'Order, order,' he said, 'Diet Coke, please.'"

"I heard he broke his finger and tried to call Dr. Pepper."

"Oh no," said Austin, "that wasn't the same guy who asked his eye doctor for an iPhone, was it?"

"Yep, and then he went grocery shopping at the Apple store."

"You're both idiots," Carter muttered.

Eliza coughed. "Probably still thinks Bruno Mars is a planet."

I stood up. "That was *one time*."

"One more than the rest of us." She took a long swig of orange juice, her shoulders shaking with laughter.

"What's the plan for today?" asked Carter, tired of us ganging up on him.

"I'm free till like midafternoon, then I have to do homework," I said. "Some stuff from AP bio I want to read, even though our boy here is doing an awesome job with the h-w." I gave Carter a high five.

Normally, a bro would never talk with his mouth full in front of a chick, but I had to make sure the guys knew my priorities for the day. Before, like, Austin could sketch up some five-hour plan to haze a varsity freshman with condoms and glitter glue that I wouldn't be able to turn down.

Not that that's ever happened. Because hazing could get us kicked off soccer. This is purely a hypothetical, very specific prank that has definitely never been pulled off by me, Austin, or Carter. Perhaps by three guys who *looked* like us. They must have been handsome bastards.

"Nick Maguire? Doing extra studying?" said Carter.

"Yeah. I need at least a four on the AP test for Clarkebridge so—"

"Same," Carter said.

"When's your tryout?" Austin asked.

"End of October," said Carter.

I groaned. Clarkebridge was the one college that Carter and I were both applying to. He wanted to do pre-med and I wanted to do something with exercise—still had a little bit of time to figure out what, exactly. We were both trying out for its soccer team.

A fun hobby of ours was to try to not think about whether Clarkebridge had room for both of us, because statistically, it didn't.

"Want to take some cupcakes for studying? I think my mom left a couple," asked Carter. It was a well-known fact that Carter was the best of us. Sometimes how big of a bro he was still caught my cold, sarcastic heart off guard.

The answer to whether I should take mouthwatering, somehow still low-calorie cupcakes, was always yes. Of course, calorie counts didn't matter to us bros, unless a bro was on the wrestling team and had a weigh-in to obsess over. No, the low-calorie mattered because it enabled a bro to be a flirtatious hero when he delivered a chick (or another bro, if he swung that way—a bro supports all bros) with a much-needed, flawless dessert. Naturally, the cupcakes were vegan, organic, and gluten-free.

Just kidding, cupcakes can fit two of those categories. Please not all three. Brownies? Sure. Actual cake? Maybe. Cupcakes are where we draw the line.

"Okay." Austin's phone vibrated on the table. "I made us plans. We're ballin' at noon." He addressed me specifically. "Which means you boys have fifteen minutes before we have to leave."

I eyed the stack of pancakes still left on my plate. "Is that like a hard fifteen or . . ."

"We can't let those sixth graders get the courts first." Austin grabbed one of my bacon slices, crunching loudly. "And Joshy can't get there till 12:15. It's on us, gentlemen."

"Daley's joining?" Carter did nothing to hide his dismay.

Eliza stood and gathered the empty dishes, starting to carry them into their kitchen. My mouth went dry.

"Yeah, two-on-two," said Austin. "Try not to fight over being on my team."

"That's cute." Carter rose, stretching to remind us that not only was he an inch taller than Austin and me, but he was about fifteen pounds of solid muscle heavier. As bros with extremely fragile egos, that gesture was 100 percent like throwing down the gauntlet.

I stood up too. "Peace out, Girl Scout," I said to Eliza. "See ya in gym Monday, bright and early."

"*Super* looking forward to it," she replied, flipping her braid to keep it out of the syrupy plates. She vanished into the kitchen and I exhaled.

Stop, Nick.

■

Besides Straight Cheese 'n' Pizza, North Cassidy embarrassingly lacked in the entertainment department. On the nice days, however, we could use what the town leaders, or whatever they're called, referred to as "the concourse," but the cool kids knew as "the intercourse."

I mean c'mon, they totally set that one up for us. Dared us, even.

The con-/intercourse consisted of overmanicured grass, metal bleachers, and plastic turf that caused more ACL tears than it was worth. The recreational area sat beside the high school and the town's athletic track, football fields, softball fields, soccer/lacrosse fields, basketball courts, tennis courts, and swimming pool. The space had one asphalt basketball court, with smelly, mosquito repelling lights to illuminate it at night. The closest courts after that were a twenty-minute drive to the next town over—and those didn't have mosquito lights, so you'd get a lot of bites playing there, though maybe reduce your risk of cancer.

Unless there was a school event, the fields and courts were first come, first served—especially for tennis. (Not really; I just wanted to make that pun.) We dribbled onto the basketball court minutes before a gang of rather large middle schoolers was dropped off by their parents.

"Sucks to suck," called Austin.

"Your mom sucks," one of the sixth graders shouted back.

Carter and I merely listened to the soothing swish of sinking our basketballs into the net.

"Maguire, your elbow's out," said Josh as he approached us. "Balance, elbow, eyes, follow-through. You know how it be."

"Thanks, but I don't need your help scoring," I replied. *Not ever.*

Josh's stupid lifted pickup sat in the parking lot, the sunlight illuminating its true doucheyness. His lift kit suspended the truck high above its larger-than-normal tires, which was a good indication of his manhood situation and, conversely, made girls somehow more into him.

"Your ride's looking pretty clean," I said.

"Thanks," Josh replied. "I'd been meaning to take it to the wash. Thanks to y'all I don't have to."

"Our pleasure," Carter muttered.

Honestly, why Austin had invited him was beyond me. Normally, Josh hung out with us as the result of someone else hanging out with us and bringing him. Although, after his grass business took off (and I don't mean landscaping), Josh had become the guy who could get you things.

"Want to do Carter and Josh versus me and Mags?" said Austin, throwing his sweatshirt on the ground. "Seems fair."

The twang of Carter's basketball hitting the half-court line answered him. Josh's sub-par ball skills, matched with Carter being too good at everything, made for a pretty even game.

After an hour of sweating, Austin getting called out for traveling too much (someone get this guy a passport, am I right?), and us trying to dunk on Carter every chance we got, which *did* happen— Scout's honor—Josh and Austin flopped on the moist grass beside the court, gulping from their water bottles.

The afternoon sun baked the asphalt like rocks in a desert. Heat had started to scald the bottoms of my sneakers, but I'd gladly have put up with that over sitting and braiding each other's hair with Josh.

"You guys doing anything tonight?" Josh asked.

"Obviously," said Austin, "we're on a mission to end Carter's dry spell. How long's it been since you had a date?"

Carter replied with a clean swish of the net, shooting from the three-point line. We had absolutely no plans for the evening, especially since I'd be studying, but Austin took every opportunity he could to make fun of Carter.

"Nah," I said, "unless its first name is text and its last name is book, Carter won't be giving it the time of day."

Josh snorted.

"This is true," admitted Austin. "I heard that if you don't get all hundreds on your high school quizzes you can kiss graduating college, getting a good MCAT score, being accepted into med school, winning your dream residency, passing your boards, and becoming a surgical attending good-bye."

"Assholes," said Carter. "Without me you'd literally fail biology." He lined up another three-point shot. It banged against the backboard.

Austin mimed bowing down to Carter, stopping when two sophomore girls strutted by us, tennis rackets over their shoulders. The basketball's synthetic leather felt good against my palm, but even better when I whipped it at Austin's head.

"You'd all be failing b-ball without me," I said.

Carter tossed me his ball and grabbed his empty water bottle from the sideline.

"I'm filling these up. Had enough of your smack, Maguire." He plodded across the neighboring grassy field to the water fountains.

Austin waited exactly four seconds for Carter to be out of earshot. "How'd it go with LOC? What'd you guys talk about?"

LOC, or Little O'Connor, was Austin's code name for Eliza. Another rule of the Bro Code is that a bro always kisses and tells. It was time to hear Josh's side of things. If he didn't exaggerate the deets anyway, which a bro also tends to do.

A warm bead of sweat rolled down my cheek. I wiped it away, but a salty scent still lingered in my nose. With insincere indifference, I aimed at the net for an easy two-pointer.

Josh smirked. "Didn't talk that much, if you know what I mean."

I intentionally missed my rebound. The ball bounced at Josh and slapped against his head.

"Oops," I said. Josh waved me off.

"You give her enough jungle juice . . ." Josh continued. "Isn't that how you guys have added, like, ten girls to your lists? Legend has it that you guys can mix some pretty potent drinks."

"Yikes. Def hope not." Austin stood, gesturing for me to pass him the ball. His sudden restlessness signaled that he was 100 percent done with this conversation.

"Hope not what?" Carter jogged back with his water bottle.

"Oh," said Austin, "Nick and I were giving Joshy pointers for being a perfect gentleman."

"Josh, do me a favor," Carter said. "Whatever they tell you to do, treat Eliza the opposite way." He pulled out his phone, studying it in a quick moment of distraction. Josh took it as an opportunity to mime a crude act of romance.

"Don't worry," he said, "She's in great hands."

I forced myself to give him a thumbs-up. The leftover taste of sugary blueberry pancakes churned in my stomach.

Carter's phone thunked as he tossed it towards the grass. "You guys want to play again?" he asked, "Nick's got another hour."

"Or we could continue to discuss the merits of date rape," Austin muttered.

"Wait, what?" asked Carter.

"Bro." Josh hit Austin with his snapback. "That's not what I said."

"Better goddamn *not* have been," said Carter.

"It wasn't," I said, though it pained me to side with Josh. I threw my basketball at Austin. What had gotten into him? Yeah, the Eliza conversation was weird, but playing the #MeToo card was a bit much.

"*Bros will be bros*," was a familiar saying among North

Cassidy's classiest, which Austin, Carter, and I had subscribed to until sometime last year when Carter, our woke hero, drew the line for our bro behavior. Josh, however, was unaware of this, and it seemed like Austin might have been taking it too far. Because with the kissing and telling rule of the Bro Code, also came the no-judgment rule, regarding how a bro earned his kiss. This rule was hard to reconcile with the line Carter had drawn for us.

But Carter didn't have to know that.

■

Around three in the afternoon, we drove our separate ways, which left plenty of time for me to take the packaging off my AP biology book.

Several things stood between current me, high school Nick, and future me, college Nick. First, there was the question of how, in the vast, ever-expanding universe, the Maguire fam was going to finance my journey to adulthood, since, like, my dad was a middle school teacher and all of my mom's earnings went to food and electricity and stuff. Then there were the college interviews, which caused palpitations upon hearing the word "interview." Finally there was that whole *picking a major* thing.

My dad's advice on choosing a concentration was this: "Whatever's the easiest to stay on the soccer team." But he was Exhibit A of how not having a backup plan can come back to bite you in the ass—or in his case, blow out your knee at twenty-two.

All the good sports science programs meant a good grade in Introduction to Biology. A score of four (out of five) on the AP bio

Elizabeth A. Seibert

test counted for that and would help with acceptance into most exercise-y majors. According to my guidance counselor, anyway.

Hence, me spending a sunny Saturday afternoon holed up in my twin-bed, no-desk, gray-walled bedroom, textbook thrown onto my Red Sox comforter, actually trying at school.

"You owe me some drills." My dad poked his head through the doorway. His coaching whistle knocked against the wooden frame.

He and I were spitting images of each other. Same five-foot-eleven, 135-pound build, same wavy brown hair. When his dark green eyes—*my* dark green eyes—stared at me, uncomfortably cool, it felt like having the future version of you travel back in time and tell you how disappointed they are with how their life turned out.

"I have to study."

"You have to get a scholarship."

The open textbook sat between us like a shield.

"You had all detention yesterday for homework," he said. "Put your shoes on."

Instead of good cop/bad cop, my parents liked to play mad cop/disappointed cop. Much less straightforward. Much more effective to get an admission of guilt.

"Fine." Hitting the floor with a *thud*, I rummaged through the duffel hanging on the bedpost and grabbed a pair of mud-caked cleats, their stench diffusing around my small room. The AP book lay forgotten with my unfolded laundry. "What are we doing?" I asked.

"What you missed at practice. One-on-one shooting and hill sprints for time."

Fantastic.

■

All the time, people ask if it's hard to have my dad as the high school soccer coach. Most people know him as their eighth-grade English teacher, but they didn't know he'd rather injure his other knee before coaching the middle school soccer team—boys' or girls'.

All the time, my answer changes. Sometimes it's good, because it makes me work a little harder. It brings an extra thing to prove.

Sometimes it's hard, for exactly the same reasons.

My dad sped through North Cassidy at the helm of a whale-sized minivan that shouldn't have been physically able to speed. Like most things in this world, it obeyed his every command. Despite having just one child, he'd wanted a minivan to transport me, my friends, and all our sports equipment to our travel games. He'd bought it when I was born, long before I could have even showed an interest in playing sports.

The brakes hissed a sigh of relief as he glided towards parking at the intercourse and a long, looming hill that overlooked the track and football fields inside it. It was my fault that my dad discovered this as a good workout hill; during a snow day in elementary school Austin and I had gone sledding on it, and I'd complained about having to run back up to the top.

I still complained, ten years later.

"All right," I muttered, "let's get this over with."

"Stop right there," said my dad. "Want to edit that statement?"

My fists tightened, the grass catching my cleats as they dug into the dirt.

"Going through the motions—" he started.

"—is a waste of everyone's time, I know," I finished.

Like your wife making you roast chicken, he liked to say, *it gets the job done, but at the end of the day, it's not really what you want. If you want her to make roast beef, you've got to work harder.*

"Let's go, Nicky." He clapped. "Three, two, one . . ." *Tweeet,* went his whistle, "This hill is yours."

My calves screamed as I shot to the top, pumping my arms like the finish line had bottomless root beer floats.

After ten reps of the 100-meter or so hill, I jogged down and crouched on the crunchy grass, dizziness pumping through my veins. My dad frowned at his stopwatch.

"How am I doing, coach?"

"'Bout as well as any other nerd. Averaging twenty seconds. Next ten, I need you to beat that."

"That's a mile and a half of sprinting," my chest heaved with each gulp of air, "and we didn't warm up."

"That *was* your warm-up," he said.

"Gee, thanks."

"Ready? Set . . ."

As the blood pounded in my ears, the hill seemed to laugh at what was to come.

My dad loved to call us nerds during practice. Carter had invented our unofficial name, Lords of the First-Strings. (The other options were Dribblers of Catan and Star Scores.)

"Pick your knees up!" he shouted as the top of the hill neared. "You're running like your mom."

My teeth clenched. If my mom knew he said things like that, he wouldn't have a throat left to say them with, but I couldn't exactly defend her honor when my delicate butt was being kicked into pristine shape.

After my next mile of sprinting, Coach Dad threw a soccer ball into the mix, running me for another hour. When he finally escorted me back home, I trudged up the stairs, in need of either an ice bath or fifteen hours of sleep.

Despite my moans and groans, and making my dad into the bad guy, the running had felt *good*. For the first time all week, thinking about the Clarkebridge tryout didn't make me want to throw up and immediately change the subject.

About time.

RULE NUMBER 6

A BRO SHALT NOT SWIM IN 'STREET CLOTHING.' IT'S TOO RESTRICTIVE AND YOU LOOK RIDICULOUS.

The next few weeks were a repetitive yet stressful whirl of extra practices with my dad, looking at my textbooks and then doing anything I could to procrastinate studying, cleaning more whiteboards in detention, hanging out with stupid Josh in my electives, and trying to ignore the fact that he was still going out with Eliza.

Austin, Carter, and I could hardly keep up with how quickly senior year seemed to be flying. Luckily, one evening in the second half of September, the party we'd been hyping up like it was to celebrate the end of the world finally arrived.

And it would change everything.

■

I drove to Jamal's party wearing an old shirt and jeans. It was Saturday night, and the last official summer night before fall and darkness and gross cold. The rusty orange sunset gleamed above my steering wheel like magic. The evening had my absolute, full permission to go wherever it wanted.

Austin sat shotgun in my Mustang and our pump-up playlist blasted. The two of us had put it together when we were fifteen, and we played it on the way to every party, sports game, and general awesomeness we attended. It had become a sort of, you guessed it, tradition.

My Mustang rattled over several potholes during the drive to the O'Connor's residence, and Austin cranked our music to cover it. No matter how much crap Austin and I had given him the last few weeks, Carter still stood firm that he wasn't coming to the bonfire. There was no way, however, that we'd let that happen.

"I'll make the call." Austin put his phone to his ear. This was serious business, which required, gasp, an actual phone call. Misconstrued texting would make the situation worse—when it came to bros, of course. A bro would never talk to a chick on the phone unless she called him first. Even then, only after two dates. Before that? Straight to voicemail.

"We're here. Yup. Nope. Um, bullshit. Totally. Of course we would never force you to wear a bikini, who do you think we are? Okay. Sure, here he is." Austin handed his phone to me, clicking it into speaker mode.

"Dude," I said, "you're three whines away from Taylor Swift status."

Taylor Swift status *n: petty, whiny, and all things unnecessarily dramatic.*

"Nick," Carter spoke slowly and shortly, "I can't go back there."

"And I can't parallel park. Oh, snap. Looks like we're both going to be doing things we can't tonight."

"Think I should go in there?" Austin cracked open his door.

"Carter," I said, "what's the worst thing that can happen?"

"They call the cops like last time and I have to wear a coconut bra all night in jail."

"If that happens again, you know we'll be sitting in the cell with you. Sounds fun. Now get your butt out here, man. I need to get gas." The phone beeped as our call ended.

Austin honked my car's definitely loud, definitely-not-dorky horn. A minute later, Carter strode down the front entrance's steps, pulling his arms through his plaid overshirt.

"All right, your wish is granted." Carter slid into the backseat. "This had better be some bonfire."

"It will be now." Austin reached for a fist bump.

"We have ignition," I said, as my car sputtered and coughed. "Ready for takeoff. Dude, why were you giving us such a hard time? It's going to be awesome."

In the rearview mirror, Carter shook his head. "Freaking Josh Daley. He's like, asking me all about how he's doing with Eliza, and whether she likes him. And I'm like, read the room, man, I'm not talking to you about this stuff. Now she's going to this with him, and he told me not to tell people about it, even though they've been going out for like a month and they went to the movies last night. I can't deal with his crap."

"Eliza's coming tonight?" I asked. Before this year, she'd barely hung out with us. Now it felt like she was everywhere. Or maybe she'd always been everywhere, and I'd finally started to notice.

Austin coughed. "What Nick *meant* to say was, that's B.S. You can't take the same girl out twice in one weekend and then say not to tell everyone." Yes, Austin considered himself and me "everyone."

Carter grumbled in the backseat. Austin looked from me to Carter then back to me. Then he reached for the stereo dial and turned our tunes all the way up.

Bro points for Austin.

■

Finally, we arrived at Bonfire Beach.

Bonfire Beach wasn't its actual name, but Austin, Carter, and I like to invent new names for things. The parking lot by the beach's boardwalk was already packed, and it looked like Jamal had invited almost all the upperclassmen from Cassidy High. The boardwalk was about a half mile from the actual party, but after the heat from the fire had melted Robert Maxin's tires a few years ago, far away was the best place to park. We heard faint sounds of someone strumming badly on a guitar before the fire was even in view.

"Is it too late to turn around?" Carter asked. He shoved his hands into his pockets. "I don't think I can stand people singing right now."

"Bah humbug," I replied. Whenever a bro starts complaining about general happiness and joy, *bah humbug* is the appropriate response. Unless none of us are in good moods, in which case the response is *yippee-ki-yay*.

At the top of the boardwalk stood a short policeman. Beach bonfires require a permit, which requires a police detail. He was there as a formality, however; he knew that he was no match for hundreds of high schoolers or anything involving the strength of a raging fire (or the swiftness of a great typhoon, for that matter). Still, him being there probably stopped teenagers from doing activities they wouldn't otherwise do—like streaking across the pier wearing nothing but a coconut bra.

"Boys," he looked at Carter for a moment longer than was necessary. Austin saluted him. Carter ducked inside his shirt.

We came to a stop on a sand dune overlooking the fire. It was already enormous and the heat radiating from it could have warmed a small army, a.k.a., my classmates.

"See you on the other side, gentlemen," I said.

Anything that happened from this point forward was every bro for himself, unless there was some kind of emergency, in which case the other two bros were to abandon everything they were doing to assist the third bro in said emergency.

The three of us trudged through the refined sand to where Robert Maxim and Madison Hayes drank out of totally-not-suspicious paper bags. Across the fire, some guy in a denim jacket and jeans lazily strummed a meek ukulele that was about the size of his forearm. A gaggle of girls surrounded him, creating the howls Carter hated so much. Next to their group, Jamal Sanchez— *the* Jamal—manned one of the beach's many red-oxidized grills.

The crowd contained a bunch of familiar faces, except the one I was looking for.

"Got this for you." Madison pushed a paper bag at me.

"He's our ride." Austin intercepted it. A hiss and pop came as he cracked the tiny can inside.

"Yo!" Jamal waved from the grill. "You guys bring the speakers?"

"Duh." Carter pulled a tiny Bluetooth box from his pocket. A bro is always ready with tunes, and Carter's were the best, reason number six hundred that it was mandatory for him to come to this. That tiny box was like Captain Kirk on the USS *Enterprise*—or, I mean, something relating to a coach and his locker room pep talks—the thing could command a room.

As soon as Kelly Clarkson started blasting, the girls flocking around the guitarist made a dance floor closer to us. Among them were Hannah Green and a few of Eliza's friends.

Where is—nope—you have a problem, dude.

Austin moved first. He casually strode over to the girls and introduced himself to the few he didn't know, or that he forgot he knew. He gestured for me and Carter to follow. I shook my head.

"Nick, try to have fun," Carter said, joining Austin. "Don't be a turd."

"None of those girls is even a *maybe* on the bangability scale," I muttered. Plus, the barbeque called my name like football called Tom Brady. I couldn't not answer.

"Hot dog or cheeseburger?" asked Jamal. Six-four since freshman year and an expert in all matters of food (he'd watched every episode of *Chopped* and *Chopped Junior*), Jamal was one of the coolest people in our school, if not the country.

"Hot dog, extra ketchup," I said. "Definitely made the right choice coming over here." It was Jamal's party, but as with all his other parties, he loved to be on the periphery, making sure his guests had the most awesome time possible. Four fishing-sized coolers were parked on the dusty sand behind him, one with a package of paper lunch bags resting on its lid.

Her flowery perfume hit me before her hand touched my shoulder.

"Make that two," I said, turning to face her. "You hungry?"

"How'd you know?" Madison smirked back.

She wore tight jeans and a top that clung to her like it was a second skin, and the last of the sunset cast a rich shine through her loose black hair. As much as I told myself, and her, that I didn't ride with one chick, something about Madison had always been irresistibly exciting.

"It's my job to know," I replied.

"Yeah? What else do you have in my file—" she started, cut off by Jamal.

"Leave room for Jesus," he teased, handing us the hot dogs.

I waved my food in thanks, careful not to have ketchup fly into the sand. Another reason Jamal was a bro: he always knew what to say in every situation. That wasn't part of the code, though it for sure helped a regular dude achieve bro status.

"Want to get out of here?" Madison asked. She slid the tip of her hot dog into her mouth, making a show of licking off the ketchup.

Madison's expertise lay in color-coordinating her shirt with her shoes and always knowing how to make me pay attention to her. Next thing I knew, I tramped behind her, falling into the sand and a situation we knew all too well: taking a break from a full-out rager to have even more fun.

"How long has it been," I asked, once we had our own private slice of beach. "A week?"

"Wayyyy too long, handsome," she laughed. "This hot dog is really testing my patience . . ."

"Good."

We plopped down, elbows hitting each other as we inhaled our food, like a decadent, chocolate mousse dessert was waiting for us.

Madison finished first. The crashing of the distant waves was soon forgotten as she crawled into my lap, her legs digging into both sides of my waist. Instinctively, my hands pulled her hips closer, like we were picking up where we left off.

Her shirt was silky against my chin. It wasn't until she kissed me breathlessly that the adult beverage on her lips fully registered.

Sand flew into my shirt, my hair—everywhere—when she pushed me onto my back and fumbled with my jeans. Heat pulsed through the humidity around us, stirring my need for her.

"Don't they have a cocktail named after this?" she asked.

"Aren't you too young to know what that is?" I cleared my throat in an attempt to think straight. Something felt weird about this, but I couldn't . . .

"Older than you." She took her hands off my zipper to adjust her hair. "Can you imagine?" she whispered, moving my fingers down her legs. "Sand everywhere, hands everywhere." She practically purred over me.

A million out of a million times, I would have let her make that sentence come true.

But.

"I can't," I said.

Madison pulled back. "Are you serious? Maguire, we're by ourselves out here."

"I know."

The music had faded into the background of the ocean waves, and the firelight had disappeared into the starry sky. That wasn't it, though. *It* hadn't been there when we'd left the party together. A taut ache in my neck, an ache for her, still kept my grip tight on her jeans.

Elizabeth A. Seibert

But.

Sensing my hesitation, Madison wrinkled her nose, as if I were some nerd saying I loved her after we'd kissed once. Madison didn't do feelings. And didn't take uncertainty.

"Nick, what the hell?"

I wanted to say it was whatever she'd been drinking, which lingered in the air between us like Eliza's words from a few weeks ago had hung about when she told me about the horror of making out with drunk Josh. But Madison and I had both screwed in worse states and it wasn't her. It wasn't me either, or any of that cliché. And it wasn't that I would do anything to avoid being like Josh Daley—even though he was trying to be like me. It was—

My phone vibrated in the sand. Madison, still pouting, fished for it. It was Carter.

"Sorry." I sat up, sand cascading off my T-shirt. *Bros before hoes*, I wanted to say. "Hey, man, what's up?"

"Found that dustwad Josh, but I can't find Eliza. Could you look for her?"

Madison examined her nails, keeping herself admirably composed, like I wasn't worth the breath she'd waste with angry words.

"Right now?"

"Yeah, Austin and I are kind of in the middle of something."

"Dude," I hushed, "I am too." It should have bothered me that Carter was making me Eliza's official babysitter, especially when he could have easily looked for her. It bothered Madison more.

She stopped straddling me, dusting her cropped jeans. She flipped me off and stalked back to the party.

"Fine." I hung up. I shouted after Madison, "Are you going to be okay? Where are you going?"

"Wouldn't you like to know," she shouted back.

"Madison," I said. She put her finger in the air, signaling the end of this conversation. Whatever. She could be a drama queen if she wanted. This wasn't the first time I'd made her mad and she'd stormed away from me, and I didn't think it would be the last.

Whoosh. A low plane flying overhead pulled me back from my thoughts. A hollow reminder to rejoin the party.

"Nick Maguire," Robert called from the sand dune. He reached for a high five. "Dude. Madison again? You're the *man.*"

"Don't forget it," I said, giving him the obligatory shoulder punch.

Fifty or so more people had scattered around the fire during my brief intermission, and a sense of pride caught in my throat. This scene had every kind of student from all the senior cliques—the athletes, the smart athletes, the theatre kids, computer science guys and the one computer science girl, the princesses, the stoners, and even the stoners who had made the trek from other schools—everyone mingling and making memories.

This would be what I missed the most about high school: the rare moments of forgetting to pretend.

Eliza was settled in a camping chair a few yards away from Jamal's grill, roasting a marshmallow. By herself, her yellow hair caught both the moonlight and the fire, accidentally creating a gentle, mesmerizing glow. How had Carter not found her?

"Hey, dude." I plopped in the dirt next to her. "What's happening?"

"Hello, Nicholas."

A light tap touched my shoulder. "Let me guess," said Jamal, "two hot dogs, extra ketchup?"

"How 'bout some waters? And one with a lime. For the lady."
Jamal shot me a thumbs-up.

"Jamal knows your food order?" Eliza asked. "How often have you come over here?"

"Actually I think the line is, 'come here often?'"

"Duly noted." Eliza slid the marshmallow off her stick. Its gooey center oozed between her fingers, while its exterior was burned black. Just how I liked them too.

"It's truly an honor to have pick-up lines explained to me by Nick Maguire himself." She chewed her marshmallow, keeping her eyes on the bonfire's playful flames.

"What can I say, O'Connor. You're special."

Jamal approached with the waters, handing Eliza a plastic cup with a lime wedge in it. I had been *joking* about the lime—how Jamal had thought to bring limes to this bonfire was anyone's guess. That bro knew his way around a party.

"Tell Madison that too?" Eliza sipped. Jamal retreated to bro-ing the grill. "Can't have been what made her cry, though."

Not even the calming ambience of a roasting fire and Eliza's mellow energy could stop me from wincing. *Nope. Not talking about that.*

When faced with a question a bro does not wish to answer, a common strategy is to deflect and turn it back onto the asker. For instance, asking Eliza, "Why do you care?" In my experience, a different approach has a much higher success rate for avoiding certain topics: the classic change of subject.

"Where's John?"

"Nice try. *Josh* is by the pier."

"And he left you here all by yourself?"

"Whatever," she muttered. "If he wants to sabotage his shot

with me, he can go right ahead. And for the record, I hate limes."

She pulled the wedge out of her drink and hurled it at the flames. It splatted a few feet from the kindling.

"Pretty sure you bring it up every time your mom even attempts to bring one into your house."

"You're mean," she said.

"It was the perfect way to mess with you and Jamal. Two birds."

Despite the actual bonfire ten feet away from us, Eliza shuddered like her lime had come back from the dead and was now haunting her.

"Can we go for a walk?" she asked. "Starting to feel crowded."

"Let's do it." My sneakers slid as I jumped up. Sure enough, a wide group of hungry teenagers edged towards Jamal's five-star makeshift establishment. Among them were Josh Daley and Austin, but Eliza had booked it halfway to the ocean before I could ask if she'd seen them. Which answered that.

She didn't stop until she'd reached the waves. Her shadowy figure was barely visible in the moonlight, even in her white long-sleeved shirt and black shorts. The breeze blew her hair in every direction. She kicked off her flip-flops and threw her phone on top of them.

"In Australia," Eliza toed the Atlantic Ocean, "we swam every morning. My dorm room was right on the water. My roommate and I'd wake up with a quick beach run and hop in."

That explained the tan.

"Ever swim at night?" I asked, imagining how the city's bright lights would look over the water.

"Wanted to." She stepped until her ankles were covered. "Doing it alone seemed super dangerous, and my friends had studying to do."

"Nerds," I coughed, surprised Eliza herself had wanted to do something besides study.

"Like you even know what studying is."

"Ha. Ha. Everyone knows it's when you deeply mourn a stud for dying. C'mon, Eliza. Too soon."

"L-O-L." Eliza lightly kicked the frigid water. Her splashes vanished into the peaceful waves.

"That's pretty bold," I said, "spending so long in 50-degree water." *When, exactly, did Eliza get to be cool?*

It occurred to me that if she were a different girl, my move here would be to fulfill her wish of swimming at night and we would plunge, laughing, into the freezing water. Fade to black. Roll the credits. My spontaneity would totally sweep her off her feet, and the walls around her would melt away. It would be just us—no rules, no expectations.

Jesus Christ, Nick.

Her hair flew in tangles, her shirt was sooty from the fire, and coarse sand covered her legs. The textbook definition of a hot mess. Emphasis on the . . . *stop.*

"Hi, earth to Nick."

Just have fun. Carter's earlier demand popped into my head.

And so, I kicked off my blue foot-mobiles (sneakers), rolled my jeans above my knees, left my phone safe in the sand, and joined her in the great big pond (ocean).

"Ah, that's cold. Real regrets." The water lapped against my ankles. A chill had already shot my nerves.

"I did *not* think you'd come in," she said.

Eliza had ventured deeper, now up to her knees. Hopping on one leg (to keep the other safe from frostbite), I waded over.

"Phew." Holding her shoulder for support, I turned towards

the twilight horizon, overdoing trying to seem pensive.

"I mean," I said, "you should be swimming here with your boyfriend. Since he's not around, looks like I'll have to do."

"If you push me in, I swear to God . . ." she said.

"I would never."

"Nick—" Eliza gripped my arm as my body swerved, teetering from one leg to the other, purposefully off-balance.

When both my legs were safely back in the water, I gave her one last twirl, spinning her with our fingers locked together.

"*Nick!*" her shriek pierced across the ocean. She tugged on my T-shirt for dear life.

The moonlight sparkled on her lips, almost making me forget our impending hypothermia. She shivered against me as the calm waves crashed against our knees, the air filled with the salty ocean mixed with spicy cinnamon. Her loose hair tickled my face as it whisked in every direction.

Abort, abort, abort.

Somehow, my arm wound its way around her back, helping both of us balance against the electric weight of the other. Her waist pressed against mine, slowly swaying with her quiet breaths.

Eliza dragged her fingers through the water, swirling tiny ripples into my rolled-up jeans. I flicked a splash at her, well aware that she could have stepped away by now. Even more aware of how she was much warmer than I thought she'd be.

"Nick?" Eliza whispered. She relaxed her grip on my shirt and shook her hair into place. "Thanks, Maguire, but I didn't come here with you."

That statement was enough to throw anyone off their game.

"What are you talking about?" I asked, though we both knew

what she meant. Though my thumb remained loosely tucked through the belt loop on her shorts.

I didn't come here with you.

"Okay." She stayed put too. "You throw me in and I'm taking you with me," she said. "Mutually assured destruction."

"In that case."

Eliza yelped as I scooped her up, careful to keep my hands away from where they shouldn't be. She fit into my arms like a goddamn princess, her warmth mixing with the cool breeze to make a dangerous energy.

Rocking her in the air, I tried not to freak her out. Tried not to freak me out.

"One . . . two . . ." I reluctantly let go.

The shock of ice-cold water erupted through me as I swung her into the ocean. She'd grabbed my hand at the last second, true to her word. We plunged into the waves, heads-first into the rocky sand. My face prickled with water shooting up my nose. My lungs, unprepared, fought for a gasp of air.

But it was her shrieking laugh, right before we'd disappeared underwater, that had left me the most breathless.

A BRO SHALT SET UP ANOTHER BRO ONLY IF HE HAS ASKED TO BE SET UP.

Bros can talk about what happened at a really awesome party, but for a really *really* awesome party, a latency period applies. That was why, for the rest of the weekend, I had no idea what went on during the rest of the bonfire. I had heard a rumor that Jamal taught everyone to do backflips, and Hannah Green's mom showed up with her supermodel friends . . . but I didn't know anything for sure until school on Monday.

Austin, Carter, and I had left early, and we didn't get to witness any of it. Right after Eliza had pulled me into the ocean and we'd returned to the beach, I dug out my phone from the sand to see I'd missed an emergency phone call from Austin. The police officer *had*, in fact, remembered Carter, even without the coconut bra. Dripping wet, I had to drive them home before we wound up in jail. Or worse, juvenile counseling classes taught by Mr. Hoover at 8:00 a.m. on Saturdays, which were what my parents threatened me with if I ever did drugs. They didn't realize that having to get through those would make me depend on drugs *more*, but I appreciated their efforts.

When Monday came, I stood in Cassidy High's freshly mopped hallway with Robert, trying to remember my locker combination. The faint scent of limes wafted towards me, which I tried to ignore.

It's the cleaning products, Nick.

"What about you, Mags? Was Madison telling the truth?"

I stopped. *Why would Madison want to tell anyone what happened?* Until I remembered that of course she would lie about it.

My locker's rusty dial squeaked with every twist. "Depends on what she said—"

I never found out, because the metal door of my locker swung open to reveal the messiest wreck in the history of the school.

"Holy . . ."

Robert's laugh filled the hallway. "Oh . . . shizzers, bro." He patted my head. "Hoover's gonna smoke your tunnel."

It didn't occur to me to ask for clarification. Mr. Hoover, and how many detentions he might give for ruining not only my locker but his self-esteem as the hall monitor who's supposed to prevent these things, didn't register in my mind at all. Nope. As I gawked at the twenty-ish cut-up limes, precariously thrown among my late homework and gym clothes, with a begrudging awe and respect for such a perfect prank, someone else invaded my every thought.

Eliza tiptoed towards us like she'd learned how to time an entrance from freaking *Mission: Impossible*.

"What's that?" she mused, pointing at what was no doubt her

handiwork. Lime juice dripped onto the floor, creating a sticky puddle smack in the middle of the senior hallway. "You're teaching everyone to make limeade? Ew. Maguire, didn't anyone ever tell you that show-and-tell is for third graders?"

"In that case, O'Connor, what'd you bring?" I tried to keep my eyes locked with hers, rather than check out her appearance. Because if I *had* checked her out, I'd have noticed her wearing a skirt that perfectly traced the curves of her hips, rather than her usual jeans. I'd have to wonder what the occasion was. I'd have to wonder if it was me.

"To be honest," I said, "I expected better."

"Dare I ask to what you're referencing?"

"This prank's been done before. Three years ago, when Carter and I filled Jenny Martin's locker with crickets."

"I dunno," she said, "I think it'd be pretty crazy to pick out eighteen of the juiciest limes available, slice them all into thirds, and then forgo precious sleep to get up early and stuff them in some rando's locker that happens to have Carter's birthday as its combination." She wiped imaginary dust off my shoulder. "I'd never have time for that. This is some serious dedication."

Yes, my combination was indeed Carter's birthday. A bro never forgets another bro's special day—that was my way of remembering it. Which, given how long it took me to open my locker this morning, wasn't going well.

Robert watched the scene in front of us, looking more dumbfounded than Austin had when he'd realized cupboards are called cupboards because they're literally boards you put your cups on.

"How'd you know there were eighteen limes?"

"Same way your mom knew it was your dad's kid growing

Elizabeth A. Seibert

inside of her." She hiked up the backpack on her shoulder. "Lucky guess."

She shrugged, turned, and walked away.

Our fellow students gingerly passed by, avoiding the sticky juice dripping onto the floor. I emptied my locker, not sure how to even begin cleaning this up. The lime aroma was overwhelmingly sour, yet sweet at the same time.

"Why is every girl on the entire planet and most likely the whole universe into you? I swear they are programmed to gravitate towards you," said Robert. "It's like you're the Earth and they're the moon; they revolve around you all the time. Except you'd actually be Jupiter because you have way more than one moon."

I wiped my fingers on the locker next to mine and closed the door. The mess was a problem for future-Nick. Not to be dealt with right now.

"Eliza likes Daley, bro," I said. "Try to keep up." Robert trudged next to me as we avoided the kids staring at us and headed towards our first-period class, AP history.

"I am caught up," he said, "And she doesn't. She dumped him after the bonfire. I thought Carter would have told you?"

My cheeks flushed. "What? What happened?"

"Dunno. All Josh said was that she didn't want to go out with him anymore. She didn't tell him why, though it's pretty obvious. She must have met some guy at the party. Guess it wasn't you."

We got to history and I slid into my scratched-up desk with its dumb, attached chair. I could've guessed Eliza would want to break up with Josh. I didn't think she'd do it right after we were together. If she were any other girl, I would be wracking my mind for the perfect line—some way to ask her out before anyone else did.

Even though she'd "made herself available" moments after

I could have kissed her, and even though I'd really wanted to, Eliza wasn't another girl. If there was going to be anything there it had to be real. Not little laughs or flirty sass.

Well.

Damn.

■

I didn't get a chance to talk to Carter until soccer practice that afternoon. He and I were the two captains (obviously) and one of our responsibilities was to lead warm-ups while my dad set up our drills. We had to do that, and then we had to make sure that all the underclassmen looked up to us for our charm and wit. As we jogged around the field, I panted next to him.

"I hear Daley is no longer a problem."

"Technically," Carter spat on the grass. "But I don't trust that guy."

"Eliza's a good kid, though. She's not going to let him do anything to her—"

"Josh doesn't strike me as the kind of person who cares about consent."

His tone crushed me as he picked up the pace. When Carter was upset, he ran. Sometimes, after a full soccer practice, he would even do a round loop from his house to my house, which was at least four miles away. I liked to shout at him out of my window, "Run, Forrest, run!" He usually didn't hear me. That was probably a good thing. Carter hated to be made fun of.

Which was exactly why I did it.

Tweeeeet. Coach Dad blew his shiny whistle and pulled us

into the center of the soccer field. I braced myself for what was coming. My dad had a strict attendance policy, and I'd been tardy to school again last Friday, which meant yet another detention from Mr. Hoover. I swear that guy just wants to be my best friend or something.

My dad's unwritten policy stated that if any player had to miss any practice for anything short of a family emergency, their punishment the next time they came was a full practice of sprints. Our goalie, Mike Dawson, even had to do sprints when he went to the orthodontist to have his braces fixed. As a result, people missed practice less often than I wear the color pink.

"Maguire," he called to me. He called us all by our last names. God forbid that he treat me any differently. "We missed you on Friday." My dad pointed at Austin. "Banks, what do we do when we miss practice?"

"Shuttle suicides for three hours, Coach," Austin mumbled. He had to wear contacts for soccer, which he hated. Even if he'd been wearing glasses, however, he wouldn't have been able to meet my eyes.

While he was coaching, my dad was Thanos-level no-nonsense. Even with the glaring knee brace over his track pants.

"Didn't catch that," Coach Dad shouted.

"Shuttles, Coach!" Austin shouted. "For three hours!"

Shuttles were an exercise that should really be called "run like you stole something and don't throw up." Three hours of it was really three hours of nonstop sprinting. It was the kind of drill that separates the men from the boys. Ten years ago, one of my dad's players had rolled his ankle during the shuttles. My dad made him finish the practice, *and* he made him do jumping jacks after every set to strengthen his bones.

"Where were you, Maguire?" Coach Dad continued to publicly stone me in front of team, as he would've for any of us. "While the rest of these ladies were finishing their first week of grueling hell? What were you doing?"

"Detention." At that point in time, I didn't *really* care that the man could have legitimately eaten me for breakfast and washed me down with a swig of unicorn blood. Sometimes he went too far to seem like a tough guy.

"And is that going to happen again?"

"Are you going to call us girls again?"

I was met with silent stillness. My teammates studied the soccer balls at their feet, while buses blew by, taking the more fortunate students home.

Not yet used to our Shakespearean soccer saga, the varsity freshmen huddled closer to Carter, who dug his cleats into the grass, soaking in the sun and waiting for the storm to pass.

One . . . two . . . I counted in my head the time it would take for my dad to answer.

"Gentlemen." He patted his clipboard. "Good news. Practice today is optional, apart from Maguire, who is going to do his punishment sprints right now."

Was he kidding? I hadn't even given him that much backtalk.

"Anyone else is welcome to join him, though I wouldn't recommend it. Tomorrow we're scrimmaging the girls' team, and it would be a shame to lose as badly as we did last year." At that, he turned on his heel like a middle school drama queen and headed to open the locker rooms.

So, not kidding.

Thanks a whole dang lot, Dad.

Determined to complete the workout, I jogged to the other

Elizabeth A. Seibert

side of the field. The soccer field was next to the baseball field that was next to the high school, and it comprised part of the intercourse's facilities. The football team practiced a few fields away, as did the girls' team and the field hockey team. Lots of witnesses if I were to fall over, puke, and die.

"Yo." Austin hustled to catch up. I'd made it to the midfield line. "Thought you could use some company." He kicked the side of my cleat. "I dunno why you don't quit and stick it to him."

"Because screw him," I replied. Austin and I had had this conversation before, and I couldn't deny that it would be a power move.

I *had* threatened Coach Dad with quitting before. About two years ago, during a rare family dinner. My mom had even ordered a pizza.

You're not quitting soccer, my dad had said.

It's not fun, I'd said. I'd been eating broccoli, I remember, because my mom wouldn't let me eat the pizza until I'd finished my veggies. That night, it meant I didn't get to eat any pizza.

I highly doubt that. My dad had already finished his broccoli and was taunting me more with every bite of his pizza.

It's not. I don't like always getting singled out at every practice.

I embarrass you?

No one else has a dad who pushes them this hard.

That you've seen.

Other people's dads let them quit things. Like when Austin was taking Mandarin. Or when Robert was taking piano.

You're not quitting soccer.

I have to quit eventually, right? Not like I'm going pro.

Nicky—My mom had started to say.

I'm not. I'm going to get an overuse injury before that's even possible. Like Dad.

That had gotten them quiet. I'd patted myself on the back, happy to have perfectly orchestrated making my parents speechless—as is the job of any high schooler. I'd expected my dad to let me quit right then. We can all guess that's not what happened.

Okay, said my dad.

Okay I can be done?

Okay you can be done when you have an overuse injury.

Seriously? That's what it would take? Me getting a horrible injury so you'll listen to me?

We are *listening to you*, my mom chimed in, finally.

That's seriously what I'd have to do to get out of soccer?

Wouldn't recommend it, my dad had said.

Because then I'd have to live vicariously through my superstar son? I'd raised my voice, but my dad simply sat there, chewing his pizza, as calmly as ever.

Because you'd miss it too much.

■

Instead of quitting, I'd resolved to stick it to him by being better than he ever was. It wouldn't be enough, however, to break any of his personal records, like the number of goals he'd scored during his high school soccer career (138), or his percentage of completed goals (45 percent).

I had to *shatter* them.

"Ready to start? Where is Mags . . . ?" cooed Austin.

"Sorry," I said.

"You'd better be," said Austin, "Now we've got to do this stupid workout. You're such an idiot, by the way."

"Thanks."

"You're still an idiot."

"You're still ugly."

Austin hit me with his forearm. "Still an idiot."

That continued until we reached the goal line. I pulled my shirt over my head and tossed it on the grass. For the beginnings of fall, it was a hot, sunny afternoon. We didn't all have a Brazilian side of the family, like Austin did. Some of us had to work for our golden-brown tans.

Even though he was half Brazilian, Austin didn't call himself "black" or "brown," though he did have that tan during the summer. Austin's mom had been born in the United States after his grandparents moved to Massachusetts from Brazil, and she had given up trying to get Austin and his brothers to celebrate Brazilian traditions. Austin was super into tacos, which he considered close enough. Carter liked to remind us that Americans invented the version of the taco Austin loved so much, and that they were more Mexican anyway, but to be honest none of us really knew. Also, Austin had always resisted learning about Brazil because he didn't want to be one of the "token diversity" guys at school.

Austin threw his shirt on top of mine. "Too bad there aren't any girls around."

"I could call your mom," came Carter's voice.

More of the team jogged with Carter, coming to do the workout. The grass squeaked as they ran. Not one of them was complaining.

"There's no way you're running by yourself, man," said Carter. "Although if you ever get another detention, I swear on the lives of every single member of my family I will kill you."

"I will too," Jeff Karvotsky, a freshman on the team, called out.

"Piss off, Karvotsky," Carter said, "I already called dibs."

I looked between them. "Do you boys want to take this somewhere else?"

"Hell yeah!" Jeff shouted back. "I can take him."

Carter swatted at him like a pesky fly. Carter was about seven inches taller than Jeff, and he was, without question, the strongest person on our team. Not one of us could take Carter. Not even me.

"All right, boys." I placed the toe of my cleat on the white, chalk line. "Three hours of misery starts now."

The others tore off their shirts and lined up. The overwhelming scent of fifteen sweaty teenagers was in the air before we'd even started.

"If you need to stretch," I said, "stop and stretch. There's nothing heroic about a pulled hammy."

"Can we start now?" Jeff Karvotsky called out. "Faster we run, faster we're done, ya know?"

"Everyone can start except Karvotsky," said Carter. "Ready? One . . . Two . . . Three . . ."

For the next three hours, I focused on one idea: my dad's stupid *girl* comments. I had no idea why today of all days the comments had gotten to me. Was I being hypersensitive? Maybe. Sprinting until I puked would be way easier than figuring it all out. No contest.

■

We finished the workout and clapped each other on the butts, as bros do. Carter and I led the stretching circle that followed, making sure the guys were thoroughly taking care of themselves, from stretching their heads, to their shoulders, to their knees, to their toes. Knees and toes.

On the way back to the locker room, Carter, Austin, and I each took turns throwing blades of grass at Jeff's sweaty back. It could have been the endorphins, but I felt more content than I had in a long time, including being with Eliza. Something about soccer stirred that up.

"Thanks, dudes," I said. "Glad I didn't have to do that by myself."

"You'd have done the same for us," said Carter.

"By the way," Austin added, "you're still a total idiot."

"Um," I feigned confusion, "that's not what your mother said last night."

Austin kicked my ankle.

Carter gave me a fist bump.

Jeff Karvotsky still didn't notice the garden on his back.

And that contented feeling, like I truly belonged somewhere, lasted until I got home.

■

The stench of the messy kitchen hit before I walked in, and not in the good way, like when you overfill your blender and your peanut butter protein smoothie explodes into the heavens and you try to make a fun game of catching it in your mouth as it drips from the ceiling. Super fun.

Both of my parents sat at the kitchen table, surrounded by

take-out boxes and soy sauce. There were two Chinese places in our town. One of them was pretty good, and the other was cheap, deep fried, and just the right kind of salty. My parents ordered from the cheap place in one situation: they were stress-eating.

"Hi," I said.

My dad sat with a pile of bills in front of him, which he read in between bites of crab rangoon. My mom held her head in her hands, with a full glass of white wine in front of her. An actual calculator—like real-life, not on her phone—was next to the wine.

"This why you ditched us at practice?" I asked.

"You're lucky we saved you dinner," my mom said.

"Are you guys going to tell me what's going on?"

My dad kept his focus on the stack of papers while my mom shook her head. "Everything's okay. Your college applications are going to cost more than we expected."

"Quite a bit more," said my dad, "though Clarkebridge will totally be worth it."

I eyed the greasy take-out boxes. Long brown noodles sat in a puddle of oil with some squashed green beans.

"So, yes, this is why you left us all at practice?"

My mom pointed to an empty plate and chopsticks, under the bills she worked on.

"Easy, tiger," she said. "We're doing this for you."

The lady should really get an award for her ability to guilt-trip me. Then again, maybe that's what moms are for.

The other take-out boxes made the oily noodles look gourmet.

"Do we have any other food?"

"Not really," said my mom. "Want to take a trip to the store?"

She had her wallet in her hand about five seconds later, already ushering me out the door.

"Get bread and whatever you want. Not anything too crazy."

"Okay," I said.

She closed the door with a loud click.

Interesting . . . my parents didn't usually try to get rid of me. Nor did they let me buy whatever I wanted for groceries.

Chocolate chip cookies for dinner it would be.

■

Knee-deep in the bread aisle of the local grocery store, I searched for the perfect loaf. Bad timing. Parents and nine-to-fivers filled the place with their evening shopping and jostled into me like it was Black Friday. A guy who was five inches taller than me and easily twenty pounds heavier studied the bread beside me, and I almost lost it. I could only imagine having to wrestle him for the cinnamon raisin kind.

"Hey, handsome." Her voice dropped its trademark line. Madison looped her arm through mine and tapped her chin. "Hard decision, isn't it?"

"What do you want, Madison?" She wore tight jeans, a leopard-print tank top, and a black leather jacket. The heels of her combat boots clacked against the linoleum floor. "Kinda dressed up for picking up eggs and milk, huh?"

Madison pretended to look offended, even as the dads pushing around kids in unnecessarily big, space-hogging strollers swung past us.

"Who said I wanted anything? Maybe I'm happy to see you."

"If that's what you're going with . . ."

"I need your help with something," Madison whispered. "I'd call you about it but now that we're here . . ."

Restless anxiety crept into my lungs, as if she were about to deliver the news I feared most. "Did you take a test?"

"No. Maguire, I'm not *pregnant*."

Her hushed whisper got more than a few looks from the parents that passed by.

"Okay . . ."

"Is there a girl you like?"

"I haven't liked anyone since the second grade, Madison. You know that."

"Nice try."

"Joke's on you," I avoided her answer, "'cause I'm actually trying to focus on myself right now. You know, find myself before going off to college. I'm thinking of taking a gap year with the monks."

Madison started to protest my sarcasm but was interrupted by my bro from another hoe.

"Whaddup, Mags?" Carter's grocery cart squealed down the aisle, followed by Eliza. Because apparently the entire town had received an exclusive invitation to buy groceries at the same time, which was now. I stepped away from Madison and she took her ringed fingers off my shirt. Carter, like me, still donned his sweaty soccer clothes. Eliza had on her volleyball sweatpants.

"'Sup, man." I pounded Carter's fist.

"What's up, Madi?" he asked. Good call. Madison loved being the center of attention.

"Stocking up your lime supply?" I said to Eliza while they chatted.

"Maybe. I've heard having a citrus-scented locker is the thing this year."

She *still* wasn't going to admit to it.

"I heard that too."

Eliza leaned back against their shopping cart and put one of her sneakers on its bottom rim. Even under the flickering fluorescent lights, she still looked pretty cool.

"You know, for a moment there, Maguire, I'd almost forgotten about *your reputation*. You certainly know what you're doing, don't you?" It wasn't a question. And it didn't come with the usual admiration or praise that other guys, or even girls, gave.

"Comes naturally."

"Good for you." Eliza crossed her arms defensively, as if protecting her heart.

"No way . . ." I smirked. "You're not jealous, are you?"

"You're not funny." *Oh. My. God*, I stopped breathing. *She is.*

Be cool, Nick. As casually as I could, I reached behind her to pick a bread loaf off the shelf. I didn't care what kind it was; I needed it to mess with her.

"Lucky me," I said, trying not to get caught up in the light-headedness from standing a breath away from her.

Eliza's fingertips brushed against my arm, warning me not to get too close. I instinctively glanced at Carter. He had his back to us.

"You wish." But she wasn't pushing me away. If only Carter were not, literally *right* behind us.

A little old lady somehow managed to shove herself into the middle of the action. "Damn kids," the woman swore as she reached for the shelf between us. "Move out of the damn way. It's not rocket science."

Eliza took that as an opportunity to step back. "Whatever, Maguire." She flipped her ponytail and pushed their cart into her brother. "Let's go! Olivia needs her chocolate chips."

Whatever, Maguire. If there were a Chick Code, this would be one of the rules: at all times, a chick must be harder to read than *War and Peace* written in Dothraki.

When it came to the secret language of the Chick Code, I liked to think I was an intermediate. Not a total novice, but there were things I'd never be able to understand. Such as the obsession over pumpkin spice. I mean, it's cinnamon, allspice, cloves, and sugar. Why is that so special?

"Lates." Carter clapped me on the back. As quickly as they'd appeared, the O'Connor siblings vanished into the crowd of dads with strollers and moms carrying two gallons of milk.

"Haven't liked anyone since the second grade?" Madison mused. "Yeah, right."

"That's correct." Suddenly the list of ingredients on whatever loaf I'd picked up to mess with Eliza (which turned out to be quinoa, tomato, and spinach—not my best cover) was the most interesting thing in the world.

"Liar, liar, pants on fire." Madison crossed her arms.

For half a second, I debated whether to play dumb. Even if Madison told the whole school, or performed whatever trick she was about to blackmail me with, everyone knew that Eliza and I were just friends anyway, and Madison was blatantly dramatic—there's no way Eliza would pick up whatever nonsense Madison was throwing down. Carter on the other hand . . .

"What do you want?"

Madison grinned like a cat trapping a mouse, plus extra Cersei Lannister vibes. Like, right now we were just shooting the breeze, but in a few moments she would burn the place to the ground.

"Spill," she said.

"Fine." I pulled her to the corner of the store where they sell flowers. The floral section? Not sure its technical name.

"You can't tell anyone."

"Not sure you get to set the terms here, Maguire."

"Madison."

"Fine, fine." Her dark hair perfectly framed her evil smile. "Fine. What's the deal with Carter's *little sister*?"

"Before you get any ideas," I said, "I'm not like—I don't."

Madison tapped her shoe on the floor, emphasizing every clack. She was going to make me say it.

"It's not a big deal. She's . . . cute."

Really stinking cute.

That was the whole truth and nothing but the truth. I wasn't going to admit to Madison any more than that, because I wasn't going to admit to myself more than that. Carter would . . .

"You're such a wimp." Madison frowned, bored.

"Thanks."

"I swear, you wouldn't know what to do with an emotion if it climbed into your purple boxers and bit you where the sun don't shine."

"Then why did you ask me if I like anyone?"

"Oh." She adjusted her top, as if she'd forgotten why we'd started down this road. "Because I like someone. Don't worry. I didn't catch feelings for you. *That* would be tragic—no, I need insider info."

Uh-oh. Heat rose to the tips of my ears. Insider info applied to two bros. *Maybe* it would include Robert or Jamal.

"Who?" I asked.

Madison made an act out of sniffing the flowers around us. "I can help you, you know. If you do really want to go out with her."

"I'd do fine on my own, thank you."

She moved from sniffing bouquets of flowers to a pot of something purple.

"One wrong move with that girl and you're toast," she said. "You're going to have to, what's that word . . . try? And there's even something you can do *pour moi*."

"Jesus, Madison, what is it?"

"Carter."

The blood drained from my face.

"He's the only guy in school who's never looked twice at me. I'm shooting for a perfect record. If you can help me get Carter, I'll help you get Eliza."

I couldn't believe I considered her proposition, even if only for a moment.

"I stand by my natural wit and charm," I said.

"In that case," said Madison, "I can't wait to tell Carter about your nighttime swimming adventure with his sister moments after you hooked up with me. Obviously, I won't get to tell him about it as soon as I'd like, but inevitably . . ."

She did *not*.

"It's not worth it, Madison, sorry. I don't like her as much as you think I do, and I don't need to do this." *Good talk*, I thought to myself. *You've got this totally under control.*

"No, Maguire," she said. "You do. You just don't know it yet. I gotta go get milk."

Madison saluted me, then sauntered off into the distant aisle seven.

I was caught in the crowd milling about, the loaf of bread heavy in my hand, but not as heavy as her ultimatum. The little old lady who'd interrupted Eliza before now examined flowers on the shelves opposite me. A little boy wrestled his sister for a box of cereal a few feet away.

It felt funny to imagine that, for these people, the most important thing for them to think about was whether to make spaghetti or burritos for dinner.

Whereas I'd completely lost my appetite.

RULE NUMBER 8

A BRO SHALT NOT BACK DOWN FROM SPICY FOODS.

My appetite came back for lunch the next day, however, when I sat with Carter and the rest of the soccer team at our usual super-long table in the back of the cafeteria, as far away from the teachers as possible. It was right against the dirty windows that bore a close resemblance to the back of my Mustang, that time I'd gotten three layers of mud caked onto it from that shortcut in the woods between Carter's and Austin's houses. We'd taken it after Austin got grounded for shoplifting deodorant and had broken out of his room to play the new Nintendo game with Carter. The hangout went later than we'd intended, and I'd booked him back to his prison. It ended up not saving any time, however, since my car got stuck in the mud and we had to push it out. The things we do for Nintendo and deodorant.

Most people at Cassidy High ate lunch in the cafeteria, but the

　　　　　　　　　　　　Elizabeth A. Seibert

geeky nerds and cool nerds ate in the library—probably the only rule they'd ever broken. All of the cafeteria's walls were windows, which meant the room was either megahot or wear-hats-inside-but-not-ironically cold, depending on if the sun came out. Since Cassidy High wasn't that big we had a handful of cliques, which, despite my classmates' extreme desires to be nonconforming, could be identified by a key clothing item: bros had hats, hoes had something neon, hipsters had flannels, overachievers had scrunchies or crazy-short socks, the people into anime had colored streaks in their hair, the freshmen had braces, rebels had faded jeans, cool underclassmen had black jeans, hot girls had leggings, the normals had Converse, marching band people had hoodies, artsy-fartsy kids had supercolorful glasses, theatre kids had business casual, geeky nerds had graphic tees, cool nerds had bad posture, and secret nerds had whatever name-brand quarter zip was in style.

See? A handful.

I approached my table, where Carter and Robert were diving into their peanut butter and jellies. The cafeteria buzzed with the usual mix of unsubstantiated yelling and tone-deaf gossip. Sweat had already started to congeal on my back from the sun's sadistic sheen, boiling the room and reminding me, yet again, of impending global warming.

"Hey, Mags . . ." Carter greeted me. "You in for the fashion show?" He pointed to a single sheet of paper under his peanut butter and jelly sandwich. It had two columns and a lot of lines with people's names on them.

"What happens if I say no?"

"Yeah, right," he said.

Every year, the Parent Teacher Association hosted a fashion

show to fundraise for their organization. Ms. O'Connor, as a hardcore volunteer, always enlisted Carter to get representatives of the male gender (me) to sign up. Super-not-optional.

"When is it?"

"Two weeks." He scribbled my name down. "My mom's getting the rental tux place to donate suits."

"Your mom is ridiculously on her game," Robert said from across the table. "She should run for president."

"She's overqualified."

Robert sighed. "And a woman would never get the votes. She should! But she won't."

"She will if you vote for her," said Carter.

I threw up my hands to mediate. "Guys, it's not even 12:30."

Luckily, my phone lit up with a new notification. Text message from Madison: *You first.*

I gulped.

She sat by the small (exclusive) table closest to the door with the other, overly dramatic senior girls, and held my gaze for three impossibly long seconds.

Fine.

"Oh hey, Carter," I said. "You still need tutoring hours?"

"Is the National Honor Society still up my ass? Yes. Yes it is."

"Right," I said. "The National Horror Society. So, Madison, you remember Madison, the girl you've known since sixth grade, talked to her yesterday—"

"Sounds familiar."

"She requested your help with trig." Maybe setting up a tutoring date was totally lame, but that was me thinking on my feet. Anything to keep her from flipping out.

Carter dug through his sandwich like I'd asked him for the

Elizabeth A. Seibert

time of day. Not good. If he wasn't even secretly into her, then this would take ten times longer.

"This week is kind of full," he said.

Uh-oh. If he didn't want to even tutor her then things were going off the rails before we'd even started.

"But I can do next week. Can I have her number?"

Phew. "Thanks, man." I texted him the details. "I hope she knows where the library is."

"Right?" he laughed. "Nah, it'll be fine. I think Madison's smarter than she pretends to be."

Okay . . . I picked at my school-bought lunch of watery lasagna and cold peas. The lasagna I could eat. The peas would come in handy for throwing at freshmen later. Carter stashed his phone in his pocket. Across the room, which was bustling with hungry students taking their seats, Madison smiled down at her phone.

Moving right along.

■

As expected, the day that Carter was finally set to tutor Madison was the day the real drama started. Unexpectedly, it involved me.

An unknown number called as I hit the locker room after practice. One time, Matt Damon called my mom anonymously to campaign for some senator, and I got him to say, "How do you like them apples?" Now I *always* answer spam calls.

"Talk to me."

"You have a really weird way of answering your phone," Eliza replied.

"How do I not have your digits?" I strained to hear her over the banging from the football team shoving each other into walls.

"There were a lot of creepers blowing up my texts. It was easier to get a new number." She didn't sound like she was kidding.

"Sorry about that. I told Carter the prank calls were a bit much." There was a long pause on the other end. "Did I lose you?"

The boys' locker room, with its stone walls and cracked tile flooring, basically needed a hoard of canned goods and it would be an instant bunker. The last time someone had good cell service there was when the school was built . . . somehow only a few years ago.

"Still here. Well for that, since you basically owe me, can you come help me make curry?"

Was I being punked? A quick scan of my immediate area turned up zero hidden cameras.

"Excuse me?" I asked.

"I started to make some, but I killed it and I dunno, I need someone's opinion."

And she was asking *me*. "The thing is, I don't know anything about curry." That wasn't entirely true. I *did* know that was it was usually way too spicy for me.

I mean, not spicy enough. I can totally, without a doubt or my eyes watering, handle absolutely whatever food is being served. No problemo.

So.

Yeah.

"You know what tastes good," she argued, "Never mind. Calling you was kind of a shot in the dark. I'd ask Carter but he has tutoring, and Hannah has too much homework or something. You were the next person on my go-to list. I'll get someone else."

The tallest guy on the football team, who was an inch taller than Carter, saluted me as they skedaddled. The stench of stale soap remained, however, especially with my mouth hung open, in pure amazement. She was simply going to hand me this opportunity?

"I never have too much homework. It'll take more than that to get rid of me, O'Connor. I'll come."

"Really?"

"No. I was talking to someone else. Yes, really. Need me to pick up anything?"

"Funny. Maybe some chicken? I kind of undercooked mine and, like, freaked out and burned the backups . . ."

"Chicken?" My pulse quickened, like I'd been informed about a pop biology quiz, where the questions were pictures and the answers had to be made from silly putty. "Like what kind, are there different kinds of chicken? How does one pick out chicken . . . ?"

"Just get a pound of whatever's cheapest. It's chicken. Bawk bawk." She hung up.

I paused over the locker room sink, reflecting on what was happening. Lukewarm water (the hottest the sink would go) helped me get my game face on. I was going to cook with Eliza O'Connor. Cooking. Eliza.

I couldn't tell which of those made me more nervous.

■

Twenty minutes and one successful quest for chicken later, I found Eliza O'Connor fretting about her kitchen as if the queen of England were coming over. She flipped between three pans on her stove and two cutting boards with a mismatched array of tomatoes and white vegetables I didn't recognize. Later, when they left a sad, forgetful impression on my taste buds, I discovered it was cauliflower.

"Thanks for coming," she said.

"Cooking together? This is a big step in our relationship."

"I'm impressed you know the *r* word." Eliza stirred a sizzling pan, which smelled like too much garlic and watery tomato sauce.

"Really? See, I know two." I set the grocery bag on the kitchen island.

"Olivia's catering some fancy thing at a law firm," said Eliza, "And apparently got four new clients out of it. They make her ninety-seventh, ninety-eighth, ninety-ninth, and—"

"She got her hundredth client?"

"Hashtag girl boss."

Eliza wanted to celebrate in style.

"Is this chicken okay?"

"It's great," she answered without looking. Eliza flitted around the room, throwing ridiculous amounts of vegetables into one pan and slicing her newly acquired chicken for the other.

"How can I help, Chef? Usually the parentals have me stand out of the way."

"Don't think you're getting off that easy. This recipe is a monster. I need like ten extra hands."

She passed me her huge, plastic cutting board with the chicken, gesturing for me to continue.

"Okay. Here I go. Cooking. Yup."

"Nick Maguire, intimidated. And by a *breast* no less . . ."

I wagged my eyebrows. "What's this? Smack talk from Eliza O'Connor?"

She cranked open a can of tomato sauce, tossing the top towards the sink, where two more empty cans sat, patiently waiting to be rinsed.

"Third time's the charm, huh?" I said.

Her pan hissed with the addition of the sauce, its odor going from old onions bad, to old onions and old tomatoes worse.

"I needed that chicken yesterday . . ." She clomped to the other side of the table, leaving her concoction to start boiling out of the saucepan.

"Oof. Bossy too."

"Hey, thanks." She stretched towards me, her torso longer than I'd imagined, and grabbed the chicken.

"Don't mention it. Now what?"

"You can make the rice." She rescued her pan with a stir, just in time.

"Yes. I'll make the *rice*." The cat-sized bag of rice perched securely on top of Ms. O'Connor's massive cupboards. "How can two thousand tiny grains take up this much space?"

"Want me to do the rice? You can stir the pan."

"And concern yourself with this trivial task? Not today, Chef." I made a show of how easy it was for me to carry the giant, enormous, heavy (seriously cannot overstate how big it was) bag of rice.

"Hey, these are things you're gonna have to know next year. When you can pull off a three-course meal for your college girlfriend, you'll have me to thank."

My mouth went dry. In my experience, girls mention the existence of a bro's real or future girlfriend for two reasons: one, they want to pry into the relationship, look for flaws, and find a way to feel like the superior female; or two, the girl wants you to subconsciously link the word "girlfriend" to them instead.

Eliza's comment gave me further proof that I had a fighting chance here.

I leaned against the marble island, trying to look as suave as possible. "Yup, I'll call you up in the middle of my date to let you know."

"You'd better."

"Can't wait to tell you all about the meals of your sweetest dreams." She kept her back turned to me, and my head started to spin. Before this year, things with Eliza had always felt easy. Why was I now overanalyzing everything she did? Every stupid thing I said back to her? *Was I being?* No. Definitely not. *Pathetic?*

"Be right back."

Trying not to panic, I bolted to the O'Connors' downstairs bathroom and paced between the shower and the cupcake-shaped hand towels. Maybe Madison was right, and I'd need more than my charm for Eliza. Perhaps, an honest-to-gosh real connection?

Speaking of Madison, a solution to my troubles was a text message away.

Am I really going to do this? Yup. This is happening.

I grabbed my phone. *Ready for advice*, I sent, *ASAP plz, making dinner with her now.*

Time to wait for a response. For how long? I didn't want Eliza to think I'd abandoned helping her, but I couldn't read

Elizabeth A. Seibert

Madison's answer in front of her. I decided to count to one hundred and then go back.

Sixty-three . . . sixty-four . . . the phone buzzed in my hand.

I'm sad you never made me dinner ☹, Madison had texted. *Hope you lovebirds are having fun. What you want to do is . . .*

I skimmed the rest. Madison's Eliza tips were things I'd never have thought of and made me uneasy, like there was a tarantula in the bathtub I didn't know about. Then again, maybe a new approach was what I needed.

You're the man, Maguire. You got this. You can do it. Go talk to her. Come on. Go go go go.

Recovered from my trip to Losertown, I found Eliza exactly where I had left her: throwing the last ingredients into the saucepan and making a sizzling sound that was less like cooking and more like burning.

My stomach growled. Uh-oh. No one in the history of forever has performed well when they were hungry (maybe food-eating-contest winners, but we all know those people are really glitches in the Matrix).

I sat at the island in a tall bar stool. It matched the other counters in the room, which were now filled with either Ms. O'Connor's mixers and decorating tools or elements of Eliza's curry production. All around, this was a very creative family. Minus Carter.

"Everything okay?" she asked.

"Yeah, thanks. Oh hey, um . . ." Heat caught in my throat as I tried to keep this casual, "How's Hannah doing?"

Eliza shook a green spice jar into her concoction. "Robert can't ask her himself?"

I studied my hands. *Here comes the hard part.* "Not asking for Robert," I said.

"Nick . . ." she warned.

Well you've certainly got her attention. "Can't I ask how Hannah's doing without it being a whole big thing? She likes me more than him anyway."

Honestly me dating Hannah would have been a service to both of them.

"Are you serious? You'd really do that to Robert?" She gave me the kind of stare my mom had trademarked. As if I had let her down, but she wasn't invested enough to be disappointed.

"Do what?"

"Okay then." Her cooking was no longer the spiciest thing in the room.

"Is there a problem?" I said. Madison had instructed me to make Eliza jealous by asking about her best friend. Which upon further consideration, might have been backfiring.

"No." She turned off the stove and threw a cover over her pot, steam pouring out from under it. "I didn't expect you to break the Bro Code for Hannah Green."

"The Bro Code?"

"Yeah, like how Robert has dibs on Hanns and stuff. Not that any guy ever, like, *has dibs* on a girl. And it's not as if your guys' holy commandments are some big secret."

She still wouldn't look at me.

"What'd you think I would break it for, then? Someone one of my buddies had already hooked up with? Someone's sister?"

Come on, Eliza. I could not have been more obvious, right?

"Whatever," she said.

Without Carter as a buffer, her forced indifference felt like flames without a heat shield. Carter always mediated between our differences of opinion, and I always mediated between

Elizabeth A. Seibert

theirs. So far, Carter and I hadn't needed a mediator. Hopefully we never would.

"Now you *have* to tell me," I pushed.

Eliza sighed. "I don't have to do anything, Nick. That's the difference between you and me. You play with your friends like you're an All-Powerful Bro-Emperor, and I just . . . get to be Carter's kid sister and watch it all unfold."

The table between us suddenly seemed like Antarctica, but in size and climate, and without the cute penguins.

"You know you're more than that," I said.

"Leave me out of it."

I remained seated, dumbfounded, completely losing track of this conversation. The subtext, or lack thereof, or some combination of hidden meanings made it seem like we were speaking in different languages.

"Any girl would love to date me." That made her look at me.

"Why? Whenever you wanted, you'd find someone else."

"What do you mean?"

She folded her arms across her chest, with her back against the sink. "I, for one, would be scared. Dating you. Like you hooked up with Madison last week and are now suddenly into Hannah? That's not just kind of rude. It's a selfish way to treat people."

Her words washed over me like I'd found the Antarctic penguins and was playing on their favorite waterslide.

"Thanks for the help," she continued, starting to tackle the stacks of dirty pans and cans. "I can take it from here."

I didn't move, my legs weighing like bricks on the floor. "You do know I care about my friends, right?"

And you.

"Sure you do. Today."

"Then I look forward to proving you wrong tomorrow."

∎

I left her house with the aroma of burned garlic on my clothes. *Whatever. If Eliza wants to be honest with me, let her.* Although I hadn't exactly been honest with her.

Something had to be up. Her attitude about this wasn't really about me, was it? My AP psych readings about Freud said that strong emotional responses were conflicts you were having with different parts of yourself. (Would you look at that, I learned something!) Maybe, on some level, it was about her dad leaving them for a new family. About anyone except for me.

My phone buzzed for the millionth time that day.

How'd it go?

"Go 'way," I muttered. Madison could go fall off a bridge. *Did she give me bad advice on purpose?* I should have known, that would be a total Madison move.

I'm going to take the silence as a good thing☺, she pinged.

Stomping hard on the brake pedal, I wrote back, *Go fall in a river.*

I forced the car into gear and blasted the country radio station. Maybe the drive would help me forget my idiotic decision-making skills.

A second later, my *Mission: Impossible* ringtone sounded. Incoming call from Madison.

I tossed my phone onto the passenger seat, and the screen lit up. *What happened????*

Elizabeth A. Seibert

When I didn't reply, Madison called again.

"What, Madison?" I yelled as the phone slid on the seat.

"What a way to greet someone," she sounded as silky as ever. "Did you do exactly what I told you to?"

"More or less."

"And she isn't fawning all over you?"

"Why are you messing with me? I got you a 'date' with Carter, Madi. I thought we were square."

"Yeah . . . I know. This was supposed to work, though . . . ."

I swerved around a tight corner, narrowly avoiding colliding with a cop car. Holding my breath, I waited to see if they'd pull me over . . . nope.

"How?" I shouted, "When has making people jealous ever worked?"

"Usually in that sweet spot where they might barelyyyy kind of like you and then see you're actively looking for potential new friends, shall we say?"

"She obviously doesn't *barelyyyy* kind of like me. Kinda the opposite now. Actually."

"I'm sorry, Nick, this never happens, swear to God."

"Thanks." I practically spit onto the steering wheel, braking hard into the standstill traffic. "I'm gonna go—" The light we'd all been waiting for finally turned green, and the cars in front of me were off to the races.

"Unless," she cut me off, "she . . . okay, Nick. Imagine this: suppose you are minorly into, like Taylor Swift."

"Why would I be minorly into Taylor? She's a straight-up babe." I tried to keep up with the cars in front of me. Ignoring Madison made it easier.

"Bear with me. You're minorly into T-Swift, and she tells you she likes Justin Bieber. How do you feel?"

"Taylor would never go for the Biebs," I said, "but fine. I'd want to do everything I could to turn her off Justin. I'd want to spend more time with her and gradually fulfill her wildest dreams. Which I would, because I'm more of a man than Justin will ever be."

"There's the Nick we all know," she teased me. "Right. Okay. Now imagine you're like, super, secretly in love with Taylor Swift and she tells you she likes Justin. Now how do you feel?"

"After everything I've done for her?" I joked. "She goes and crushes on Bieber?"

"Exactly," said Madison. "Nick. We're talking your top-secret crush like from when you were a kid. Like honest-to-gosh, ride or die."

I finally reached my driveway, the stones gently rolling as I turned in. Shutting off the engine, I slumped down until my legs were on the dashboard.

"How'd you know I feel that way about Tay?"

"Nick, what would you do?"

I'd pretend I'd never liked her in the first place. I'd overcompensate as hard as I freaking could.

"Crap."

"If she more than barely liked you, which I had no way of knowing, then what happened makes sense."

"And if she didn't like me at all?"

Madison paused. "Then why would your Hannah comment bother her?"

I considered this. Whether to trust or distrust Madison was still a coin flip—either way, this was interesting.

"Now what am I supposed to do?" I asked.

"What you do best," said Madison, "Go get the girl. Oh, and tell Carter to meet me again tomorrow. Thanks, Nicky."

"Madison—" I started. She hung up before I could ask anything else.

I punched the steering wheel, feeling as if I were at the center of a female-revenge plot. That's what was happening here, right? The girls were trying to teach me a lesson for being a player?

If only. Because then I'd at least know what to do: an Instagram story and livestream of some Lloyd Dobler–level apology. When did girls get complicated? It wasn't like all of them were *easy . . .* but Eliza was next level.

My neck ached with stiffness and pent-up stress. *You need to get out of your head, dude.* The best way to do that?

Every bro's favorite pastime: video games.

RULE NUMBER 9

A BRO SHALT NOT SHOP.

Eliza ignored me for the rest of the week, and even for a few days into the next week.

Not that I was keeping track.

Things weren't going much better in the Carter/Madison fantasy land either.

I heard about it from Carter as we camped out in our regular booth at the back of Straight Cheese 'n' Pizza. Last year, going there had become a regular Wednesday night thing. It served the dual role of a top-notch, greasy dinner, and a place where we could swap homework answers inconspicuously. Gone were the days of being able to use the library—ever since Austin sent a virus through their computer system after illegally downloading *World of Warcraft*, he was on some unofficial library watchlist. The librarians had it out for him, and any less-than-savory activities he participated in there would be reported to the school.

Elizabeth A. Seibert

Austin being Austin, he wouldn't have minded trying to pull off a homework heist under their noses. But Carter wouldn't take the chance.

Straight Cheese 'n' Pizza's bursting booths and little kids playing in the arcade made a great cover for our homework swap—we looked like students studying, and there were too many screaming children for anyone to detect otherwise.

"How's the tutoring going?" I asked Carter. "Madison a good student?" They had been on two more tutoring dates since my chicken fiasco. Madison moves fast.

Carter flipped the page in his math textbook, too in the zone to hear me. I was putting the finishing touches on our Freud chapter outlines for AP psych. Austin had blown through his AP history responses and was now playing against himself at air hockey.

"You would know." The wink in Austin's voice was evident without even looking up from my notebook.

"Haha," I replied. "You know, Freud says humor is a way to deflect repressed thoughts." I tapped my psychology book. "Maybe he'd say *you'd* want to 'tutor' Madison."

Austin threw the air hockey puck in the air, spinning to catch it behind his back.

"Isn't he the dude who said we're all in love with our mothers?" said Carter, because *that* got his attention. "Do people still take him seriously?"

"Oh, I can wholeheartedly agree that I'm in love with Carter's mother." Austin grinned, giving the air hockey table to the two kids waiting.

Carter swatted him with his notebook.

"How'd you finish history so fast?" Carter said, "We're going to fail again, aren't we?"

Austin slumped into our booth, his back squeaking against the leather. "You know what they say, man: Cs get degrees."

Austin held his hand out for me to fist bump, which I half-heartedly returned. Something else that Freud, the outdated genius had written, intrigued me.

"Oh yeah?" Austin took my textbook, intrigued that I ignored him. "What now . . . oh. *Interesting.*" He cleared his throat and read, "*Unexpressed emotions will never die. They are buried alive and will come forth later in uglier ways.*" Austin gave me a funny look. "Something you want to tell us, Nicky?"

"Shut up," I took the book back, looking anywhere but at Carter. "Like Carter said. Dude's weird."

"I don't hate that point, though," said Carter, "about not being able to express things. Especially when it's because of some trivial social norm."

"Please. Explain. I love a good debate," said Austin.

"Nah," said Carter.

"Jerk off."

"Well, like, what about the Bro Code?" I asked, my hands starting to shake underneath the table. This was it—maybe my one chance to bring this up organically and get their reactions.

"Exactly," said Carter.

Oh no. Exactly? I continued, "Suppose one of us was super into Hannah, right? Except we can't try anything because of Robert. Or the whole dating Eliza thing. Like did you feel repressed by that rule, Austin?"

Two theoretical, non-topical examples. (Not that I was into Hannah. But continuing with my theme . . .)

Austin yawned. "I ain't got no time for no rules."

"I can't talk about this," Carter muttered.

The two kids playing air hockey, a boy and a girl, began to jump up and down, arguing about whether a point counted.

"You guys have never felt stifled by the Bro Code?" I pushed.

"What does that mean?"

"Probably means you're gay," Austin deflected.

"Aaaaand Austin's buying," said Carter.

"Every freaking time," Austin groaned. Coins clinked onto the table as he pulled his wallet out.

"CBR, please," I said.

Austin gave me a thumbs-up and trotted to the counter to order our chicken bacon ranch (a bro's favorite pizza after pepperoni). A few years ago, Carter decided it was his civic duty to get us to stop making homophobic comments as jokes. Whenever one of us used one they owed the rest of the group food or game tickets or whatever. Austin still had them in his arsenal for when he couldn't think of any better jokes. I basically never paid for food.

Carter gulped from his water bottle. "So, Madison," he continued. "Girl is a Piece. Of. Work. She spends the whole time talking about you. Legit, I feel like some kind of Nick Maguire expert witness and I'm being interrogated or something."

"Sounds about right," I said.

Austin rejoined us with a neon table number. He resumed his position of slumping as far down as he could go.

"Last time," said Carter, as if the conversation could, in fact, take another turn, "she asked about *my* dating life and what it would take for me to grow a pair and ask her out already."

Austin startled. "Wait what?"

"I know. I do not understand that girl."

". . . did it work?" Austin asked.

Carter shrugged. "If anything, it made me feel sorry for her. Like I should help her more."

He was sorry for her . . . I could work with that.

"Good job doing community service," I said, "We can't all be like you."

"My sister needs a ride soon," said Carter, "if you're offering." He frowned at the math textbook. "I've really got to do this."

"I could use a ride," Austin joked.

"Now you owe us mozzarella sticks," Carter said. "Chop chop." He turned to me.

"She needs to go to the mall to pick up fashion show dresses for Friday. Pretty sure they close at nine."

Another babysitting task from Carter. Thank God for the fashion show.

"Sure, no prob." I went back to my homework like it was nothing, and my knee wasn't bouncing against the table leg. "Tutoring must've been awesome, though. Spending three hours talking about me . . ."

Standing up to order more food, Austin stole the Red Sox cap off my head and threw it across the room, near to where Chef Pizzeria was giving us the hairy eyeball.

"If I'm not allowed to make dick comments, neither are you," Austin declared, though I knew he'd just been looking for an excuse to throw my hat. Austin hates the Red Sox more than I hate the Yankees, and we'd developed a sort of hat rivalry.

"You want to die, Banks? You'd better watch it. Remember, I know where you live."

"Be still, my beating heart." He pretended to check his phone, disinterested in my threat.

"Yo, what time is it?"

"It's 6:21," said Austin, "If you want to get Eliza, you're officially running late."

"Ah." I grabbed my soccer jacket and threw my notebook in my backpack. "Sorry boys, time to bounce."

"Later, bro." Carter sent me half a wave.

I was about to walk out the door when Austin called out to me, "Hang in there, handsome," his interpretation of Madison was spot-on. "Call me, okay?"

I laughed. "Keep it in your pants, Austin, Jesus."

"I can't, it's too hard."

I heard him let out a whoop and the last thing I saw before I went into the parking lot was the appalled look on an older couple's faces, passing me through the door. "Sorry," I said, "I'm sorry."

■

My shopping excursion with Eliza started off okay. The nice part was that we got to drive through the unparalleled, yellow and orange autumn foliage. The not-nice part was that she gave me the cold shoulder most of the way to the mall, only speaking to ask why Carter wasn't driving her, and to tell me I didn't really have to come.

"I wanted to," I told her. "Shopping is my favorite." Though we both knew that was extremely far from the truth—I avoid malls like the plague.

"Awesome."

Honestly, how sarcastic she was made me like her more. Ten minutes later, I walked through the hordes of middle school girls, right beside Eliza, matching her stride for stride. She seemed to know exactly where we were going. Good. The last time I'd been to the mall was in the eighth grade, and I hadn't really been there to look at clothes. Unless, of course, they were already on a high school girl.

Everything was exactly how I remembered it—sociologically, anyway. There are three kinds of girls who go to the mall: girls who look like they came from the gym, girls who stare down every boy they see, and girls who look like they can't wait to get out of there. With a bright blue running jacket, Eliza fell into category number one. It happened to match the shirt underneath my black windbreaker. Color coordination-wise, we went well together.

"Let's start here." Eliza stopped in front of a bright store that was all windows. "This is my favorite place." *Really?* I followed her into a loud, crowded room. Upon entry, my olfactory senses were struck by the overwhelming smell of candy apple perfume. *And this is why I never shop.*

I made a mental note to ease up on my spray deodorant.

"Hey, Eliza," a deep, masculine voice said.

Eliza waved towards the manchild working as the cashier. "Hi, Dylan!" She shot him my favorite of her smiles and gestured to me. "This is Nick."

"'Sup?" Dylan gave me a nod. I returned it and took in the cashier with one, swift glance. He was about Eliza's height with jet black hair, and he looked too old for high school.

I watched the way Dylan was watching us, and how a few (only a few, but a few nonetheless) of the females among us made sideways glances at him and not me. For once in my life, I didn't have a perfect record. That Dylan manchild-person had game.

Eliza's fingers grazed my jacket. "Before you say anything, Maguire, yes. I come here often."

"I can see that. What're we looking for?"

Eliza perked up. I guess she liked that I wasn't lingering on Dylan. "I need a long dress and a short dress. Formal wear. I'm going to pick some out, and you can tell me what you think."

"Cool."

Eliza started at the rack immediately beside us and did that thing every girl does when they look for clothes—walk past something, feel it, take a few steps, feel something else. Honestly, no one should ever take the first thing on a pile of clothes. Everyone and their mom has touched it.

I could not figure out how the store made its money. The outfits on mannequins looked like wedding dresses in a horror movie, and the colors reminded me of the leftover lollipop flavor that no one wanted. Wait a second . . . a really short, slick black thing hung in front of me. I smirked. I could picture Eliza wearing only that.

"Yo!" I called across the store and held it up for her. Eliza and two other women shook their heads at me.

"That's a slip, Nick. No."

"Your loss. That would have been great." I immediately spotted another. "Hey, what about this one?"

Eliza came over. "Nicholas James Maguire. Behave. That dress would leave everything hanging out. But you already knew that." She wasn't scolding me, though. More like wishing it had been anyone other than me who'd driven her that day. "Nick," she added, "If you do a good job, I'll buy you a treat later."

"Like a prize?" Smart girl. "What kind of prize?"

"Anything you want." At that, she turned and went back to looking for dresses. Anything I wanted. *Outstanding.*

However, she could not have been clearer: she didn't trust me to pick out a good dress. Challenge accepted.

When Eliza found me again, purple, gold, blue, and red fabric dripped over her arms. Those were supposed to be dresses?

"Ready?" she asked.

Was I ever. "I got you some more. I didn't know your size, though. I got a couple of different ones." I handed her the hangers I'd collected, with short, sparkly dresses and long, dark ones. I'd clearly stuck to a theme.

"These are actually . . ." She thumbed through them, nodding with appreciation. "These are great. Thanks, buddy. Nice work."

"It was nothing, really."

Eliza punched my shoulder. "Get over yourself."

"Never."

She led me to the dressing room, and I sat on the bench outside that dug into my butt.

"This is like one of those scenes in a rom-com, huh?"

"What?" I didn't know what any of those words meant.

"A rom-com," she called back. A rustling came from inside the dressing room—the sound of a woman struggling with her clothes. All of a sudden, the nearby flyer about food court smoothies seemed especially interesting.

"Like either the girl tries on stuff with her supernerdy, wacky best friend to get ready for some dance, and there's a pop-song montage over it, or she tries on stuff with the future love interest, and there's nothing there yet, but it's the exact moment when he falls in love with her.

"You know." The door clicked open. Reading about

mango-pineapple deliciousness would have to wait. "*27 Dresses, A Cinderella Story, The Duff...*"

She wore a long, yellow dress that followed every curve she had.

Oh boy.

"I'd be like the nerd, right?"

Eliza laughed. "You think you'd be my best friend?"

I put my hand on my heart, pretending to be wounded. "Right in the chest."

She twirled.

"I like it. Final verdict: a solid seven out of ten."

Eliza studied her reflection. "You know, you're right. This is a seven." She stalked back to the dressing room.

"How do I sign up to judge *Project Runway*?" I called. "Think I have what it takes?"

"I don't think anyone has what it takes," she shouted.

The next time she came out, she wore a dark blue dress with some lace stuff and straps that wrapped around her shoulders.

"The other one was better."

"Really?" She smoothed out the wrinkles in her skirt. "I guess. This is something my grandma would wear."

I nodded, drawing in a full breath of air. Honestly, that girl could wear anything, and that fact was making my job both easy and hard. The yellow one had been better, though.

"Try on one of the ones I found."

"So you'll stop asking."

She left me once again and I pulled out my phone. The geniuses at ESPN should win an award for coming up with score-checking features on their app—perfect for situations like these. As I was looking up which baseball teams had the best chances in the World Series, a string of shrieks and swears came from the dressing room.

"Ow, no," Eliza cried.

I jumped up, pausing, unsure if I was allowed to go in there and help her. I guessed not . . .

"Eliza?"

"It's my shoulder," she shouted. "Lifting dresses over my head popped it again. Damn it. Oh, gosh, ow."

What was the appropriate move here? From my self-taught obsession of how to prevent shoulder injuries, I—in theory— knew how to fix it. Did I volunteer to help her? Or would she think I was being a perv?

Luckily, she answered that for me.

"Would you be able to help? You can stretch it out, right? Nick, please, I think I pulled something."

"Sure, but you should probably go to the ER. In case it got dislocated."

I entered the women's dressing room the way a burglar robs a jewelry store: you know you shouldn't be there, and you're afraid of accidentally touching something and setting it off. I hadn't been in many dressing rooms in my life, other than the occasional trip to buy new jeans or whatever. From what I'd seen of men's dressing rooms, this place was comparable to the Four Seasons. It had white saloon-style doors into each room, and was decorated with tall orchids, smelling like them too. Bottles of water stood on a gleaming white dresser, below a picture of that lady from that movie.

One dressing room door was closed, which I knocked on.

"Do you want me to come in?"

"Yeah. I still have that dress on. Couldn't get it off."

She opened the door and I rushed in before anyone, God forbid, *saw me*. Her right shoulder had swelled to the size of a softball, double her left shoulder. Her dress swept the floor.

This dressing room was not meant for two people, and it made a series of me bumping into either Eliza or the wall. There was only enough space for her to flail her arms around and try to get the clothes on. Which meant we were back to standing too close to each other. Again.

If Eliza was thinking about that, her face didn't show it—at least not from what I could gauge from my occasional glances in the mirror. Mostly she winced, probably thinking about how much pain she was in, not about my hands on the bare skin her dress had left exposed.

"Has this happened before?"

"Couple times. Carter usually just pops it in and I ice it."

I traced the bump on her back. Her inflamed shoulder was peppered with goosebumps, but relaxed where I touched it. This was no "pop it back in"–looking injury, but if that's what she wanted, I could try.

"Lift your arm, like you're trying to touch the ceiling." She stretched it and I pushed down. The curve of her back tensed, then flexed. Getting there.

"I really shouldn't be doing this," I said. "You should get a physical therapist. I don't want to mess anything up."

"No," she said as I started to release her arm, "this is helping."

"Can you reach your arms behind you? Interlace your fingers." I pushed the top of her back away from me. "I'm going to pull."

Eliza followed my directions. I'd hardly touched her arms before she gasped, wincing. I let go, but she shook her head.

"Keep going. It's starting to feel normal, hold it there."

"Fifteen seconds," I said, rubbing her hand with my thumb.

Eliza nodded. Her cheeks flushed as I counted.

After about six seconds came a tiny *crack*.

"I think that did it," she said.

Her arms shook back to her side.

"That was awesome, Nick. Thanks."

I examined the tops of her shoulders. Less swollen, but her right shoulder was still dangerously contracted. I slid my hand from the base of her neck to the small of her back, checking to see which part of the shoulder might be her issue.

The more lightly I touched her, the more still she stood, until it didn't seem like she was breathing.

"Sorry," I said, "my hands are probably cold."

"That tickled."

I brushed the arc of her back, testing her tight muscles, trying to ignore her cinnamon scent. Trying to ignore what I wanted to do.

"You *really* should get that checked out." I finally stepped away. "I'm not sure if the swelling's going to go down before the fashion show either. Forty-eight hours of rest can do a lot, but not if you're really injured. Also ice and keep stretching, yadda yadda."

"Thanks. I guess we'll see." We locked eyes, her reflection watching mine. I had to restrain myself from tucking a strand of hair behind her ear.

"I have one more dress to try on."

"Right. I'll be right outside."

"Thanks, Nick."

When she came out the next time, she wore a red dress with a decoration thing-y on the front. And without any straps. It made her shoulders, which had just been uneven and injured, look like they'd been painted and airbrushed for the cover of a magazine.

"That's the one." Heat flooded into my cheeks. Stupid rom-whatever-they're-called.

I forced myself to stay cool as she looked at me, trying to decide if she believed me. "Dude, if you don't get that for yourself, I will."

She gave herself another twirl in the mirror, and I wondered if she'd heard the sincerity in my voice.

Dial it back, Nick. Stop trying so hard.

"You're getting closer to my nerdy best friend by the minute, Nick," Eliza called, back in her dressing room. I rubbed my jaw to hide my goofy smile.

■

Finally, she picked her dresses and left her selections at the desk with *Dylan* for her mom to grab the next day. We walked through the mall and back towards my car.

"Wow, good job, Maguire," she said.

"Oh, with the dresses? Yeah, I know."

"No . . . we passed a Victoria Secret and you didn't try to look in."

"Oh, shit, we did?" I spun around. And so we had. I'd been too distracted thinking about certain proximities to certain other people to notice. With the mall almost closing, the hallways were empty except for the few shoppers inside the boutiques. The smell of oversalted pretzels and greasy sushi hung in the air. "I mean, shoot."

"It's okay, Maguire. You can say 'shit.'"

"Nah. I have a strict policy of not swearing in front of girls."

"I'm surprised." Eliza said, her voice filled with disbelief and something else. Darn that Girl Code.

"How do you mean?"

"I don't know. I guess I really didn't think you, like . . ." she searched for the perfect phrase, "cared about other people?" *Other girls.*

As if it had never gone away, the awkwardness was back. "I deserve that." After a breath, I continued, "I shouldn't have said anything about Hannah last week. I didn't really mean it. I was trying to gauge how you thought she stood with Robert."

And then I said something bros hardly ever need to do, since the Bro Code clearly states that a bro is entitled to his convictions and should never feel the need to defend them: "I'm sorry."

"Thanks," she swallowed a lump in her throat. "Me too. I know you care about me and Carter. And that you're not, like, a terrible guy."

"Not a terrible guy. I'll take it."

"Don't get me wrong," she continued. "You're still *the* cockiest kid I have *ever* met . . . though maybe you're not *totally* immature."

I laughed and threw my arm around her, careful of her shoulder, pulling her into me like I've wanted to do a thousand times. "Thanks. Means a lot, O'Connor."

She didn't shrug away like I'd expected her to, even as we passed stylish middle school girls searching kiosks for the perfect phone case. Walking beside her, arm around her, felt all kinds of thrilling: like sneaking out, being wide awake, and like I could accomplish anything. That was what I liked most about her—how exciting she could be, even when she was totally chill.

Elizabeth A. Seibert

"Yeah, no problem," she said. "Actually, you did a really good job today. You can have your prize if you want."

"You know what I'd ask for if this were a rom-whatever, right?"

"Don't be gross."

"Can we keep this PG, Eliza? Please? There are kids." I gestured around the empty hallway.

She took a step to the side, leaving my arm to hang.

"All right, what were you going to say?"

"Well," I said, "I was *going* to say if this were a movie, it'd be the part where I said you owed me a kiss. But then I remembered that I'm your nerdy best friend now, so I'll have to ask for, I dunno, like a non-fat almond milk pumpkin spice latte or something."

"Oh my gosh. I don't know if I should start by unpacking that stereotype or the part where you know my coffee order."

"Nah, it's fine, though. You don't owe me anything. You know, pal, you're a lot different from how you were two years ago."

"What is that supposed to mean?"

"You didn't used to be cool."

Eliza punched me in the side. "Thanks. Thanks a lot."

"Anytime." We stepped out of the mall and into a chilly, early October evening. "Am I dropping you off at your house?"

"Duh," she replied. "Where else would I go?"

"Dunno. I can't keep up with your boyfriends these days."

"Neither can I." She swung her arms, dance-walking across the street with entertaining energy. I matched her dance moves as we traveled through the empty parking lot, keeping her same invisible rhythm. Eliza kept it up until we reached my car, where she clapped at our performance. I bowed, unlocking her door.

She curtsied in return, pushing me away before she slid into her seat.

In no hurry, I walked to the driver's side, taking in the freedom of escaping the mall and soaking up how it felt to be out and about, just the two of us. Lights from the moon and parking lot glinted off my car. It sparkled almost as much as the girl inside it.

RULE NUMBER 10

A BRO SHALT MAKE THE FIRST MOVE.

Finally, it was Friday, the second-best day of the week, the best being Saturday, obviously. I waited in the busy, stuffed-full senior hallway of Cassidy High on my way to fifth period biology. Some dude's backpack had exploded everywhere—pens rolling into students, highlighters shooting under lockers—which led to a giant traffic jam. I was going to be late. As usual.

Something thorny tapped on my shoulder. "Hey, handsome." The one and only Madison Hayes walked behind me, looking somewhat normal in her long-sleeved shirt and jeans.

Ding dong, went the bell. Several of my classmates still shoved through the line, and probably half the class wasn't seated yet; however, Mr. Kendrick, my sadistic teacher, wasn't the type to care.

"Madison Hayes. The girl I wanted to see. What class do you have?"

"Study hall."

"Last period on a Friday. Rough." I rubbed my forehead, dusting off the dirt blowing around from everyone's sneakers. Apparently, filth could accumulate on you by standing still.

"Torture. Between us . . ." she grabbed my flannel shirt's collar, "has Carter said anything about me?"

What?

"Honestly I think you'd have better luck with Austin," I said. "Carter's really focused on college . . ."

"Wondering if he mentioned stuff about last night. Something, like, happened."

Even if Carter had said something about Madison, which he hadn't, the Bro Code stated that drama between a bro and a chick was not to be discussed between that chick and a different bro. I wouldn't have been able to tell her yes or no, even if I *had* had the faintest clue of what she meant.

While it's hard to pinpoint the true origins of any of the Bro Code's stipulations, that rule in particular was solidified by Keith Richards and Mick Jagger, two OBs. In the 1960s, Richards allegedly cheated on his girlfriend with Jagger's girlfriend, and Jagger then allegedly cheated on his girlfriend with Richards's girlfriend. The ladies took their revenge by discussing the rock stars' allegedly below-average endowments with the media and entire world.

To avoid repeating this travesty, third-party bros no longer get involved with their bro's relationship drama, or else their manhood could end up on the front cover of a tabloid. You never know.

Madison hiked up her sparkly book bag as the students began to move again. "Get Carter's side, would you? Who knows, maybe I'll take that tip about Austin." She blew me a kiss good-bye and forged ahead. *"Come on, people!"* she shouted. *"It's not that hard. The sooner we get to class, the sooner we can go home!"*

Cheers erupted. I clapped along. The girl was straight-up drama, but no one could deny that she got things done.

I arrived fashionably late (for people who are fashionably late) to my AP biology class, where Carter already sat at our long, black lab table with his safety glasses secured.

The classroom smelled like an animal had stuck its whiskers in one of the power outlets, had been electrocuted, and had been there for an entire month. Fairly on par for Cassidy High.

"You're in a good mood," Carter said. "Great, you'll need to be for this lab. It sucks all the joy right out of you."

"Oh no," I said. Arranged on the table were latex gloves, scalpels, scissors, sticks, cutting tools, little poking tools, and some paper towels. On a separate pan, a dead rat soaked in stinky formaldehyde. Which meant my dead animal smell analogy for the room had been fairly accurate.

"Rat dissections again? We did these last year." In Introduction to Biology, our teacher had taught us basic human anatomy by having us dissect rats to uncover their muscles and tissues.

"Mr. Kendrick wants us to do the brain," said Carter. He pointed to a packet titled *Advanced Placement Biology, Laboratory Exercise IV.*

"Cool." The slimy rat rested before us as a hero among his people—a warrior who'd sacrificed his life for scientific pursuits.

"Do you think Stuart Little was a registered organ donor? Or are we performing brain surgery against his will? I, for one, am not comfortable going against his wishes."

"Me neither." Carter shook his head. "Poor guy probably had a wife and kids."

"I refuse to be a homewrecker."

"Gotta draw a line somewhere."

"Speaking of drawing lines . . . Madison asked about you. Like two minutes ago. It was weird."

The pan clanged as Carter dropped the scalpel. "Awesome," he said, with the tone of someone who did not think it was awesome at all.

"Why?"

Carter jotted something in his notebook.

"Oh, come on, Carter. She's hot A.F."

Checking to make sure Mr. Kendrick wasn't coming over, Carter pulled out his phone and called up his recent texts.

He'd received a string of about twenty. From Madison. Each insinuating how hot she thought Carter was, and each insinuating *exactly* what she wanted to do about it.

"Why didn't you respond?" I asked.

"Are you kidding? None of these have my name in them. She probably sent these, unsolicited, to other guys too." Carter strapped on exam gloves. "I'm surprised you didn't get them yourself."

I scrolled through them again. "The detail in these is impressive," I said. "I'm jealous. I can confirm I've never received romantic texts from her that were this vivid."

"But you have gotten them from her."

"What's your point?"

"Never mind." Carter skimmed our instructions. He picked up the scalpel and gave me a pinky-sized pair of forceps. "It wants us to see how the brain affects this little guy's organs and stuff too. We're going to have to do a full dissection."

"Goody."

"And we need the intestines to stay intact. We can't blow through them like last time."

"I don't recall that being my fault."

"Mags."

"I don't recall that being *entirely* my fault."

Carter sliced through the skin on the rat with one fluid movement. Future surgeon, everyone. I got to help him cut off the parts that would get in the way. This was usually the part when the people who were going to faint, fainted.

"Ewwww," chorused around the room as our classmates performed the same part.

"I have a better angle," I said, taking the scalpel. I had to be careful to keep the rat's muscles intact. That had screwed us over before.

This was serious business.

"That, like," said Carter, "made me want to take a hundred showers."

"I'm actually doing okay with the scalpel."

"No," he said. "Madison's messages." Carter drummed on the table. He reclaimed the scalpel, unable to stay still. "Was that sexual harassment? I think I'm going crazy."

Uh-oh. Carter broke.

Well, not totally broke. Was scratched. It would take something much bigger than Madison sliding into his DMs for him to really lose it.

The other tables continued on, not a care in the world but the dead animal slowly rotting before them, already accustomed to the smell. Mr. Kendrick, our six-foot, washed-out teacher, hated sunshine and joy and had put up light-blocking curtains. He claimed they would keep important equipment from being affected by the sun. Mostly the curtains made biology class a perpetually somber affair.

Of course, students knew the truth. I'd originally heard it from a senior on the soccer team when I was a freshman, who'd heard it when *he* was a freshman. Mr. Kendrick, a legendary vampire, actually guarded the school at night and protected it from the other vampires of North Cassidy. It wasn't an easy job, and many students are sacrificed, but someone had to do it.

Carter dug through the rat, coughing each time he accidentally inhaled toxic fumes.

"I've never been objectified to my face before," he said, still on Madison. "It was weird, dude. I dunno. Made me nauseous. Trapped in my own skin." He shuddered.

"Sorry, dude."

"It's not your fault."

Oops.

"Let me know if there's anything I can do."

"Thanks, bro. You can start by taking pics of all these. Need to label them for our notebooks."

While Carter performed neurosurgery, I played with my camera's lighting settings. I was up for anything, though, besides fessing up. I couldn't tell Carter about why I was helping Madison date him without getting what was in it for me.

"Let me make it up to you," I said. "How 'bout neither of us walks out with girls at the fashion thing tonight. We can do the catwalk together."

I reached for a fist bump. Carter returned it. "Nothing you have to make up for, though you got it, buddy."

"Maybe all the times Austin and I have objectified you behind your back," I joked.

"That's okay," said Carter. "I know you guys are jealous of my fire bod."

"Who isn't?"

Carter focused back on the rat and I snapped pics of him operating, ready to make a killing when he became a famous surgeon.

I knew I had to make it up to Carter with more than jokes, since he did genuinely seem really upset by this. I didn't really get why, but that was beside the point. From the air in my lungs to my below-average heart rate, I didn't want Eliza to ever feel like Carter had. It would be all or nothing with that girl. I was going to have to commit. Especially if we were ever going to get Carter's blessing. It was my senior year, but I vowed that if Eliza O'Connor were my first high school girlfriend, she would also be my last.

■

Despite Carter's pushback about objectification, at 7:00 p.m. sharp, I posed outside Cassidy High's auditorium, ready to debut my tuxedo to a live audience. I had a black jacket, white shirt, and yellow everything else. Straight fire.

"Selfie time!" Hannah Green grabbed me out of nowhere, sticking her pink phone in my face. Other fashionable participants passed by, also taking selfies, which I actually can't remember ever not being a thing.

"Nick Maguire, you are unbelievable. Do it again without sticking your tongue out."

A sunny laugh came from behind us. Tingles flared on my skin—I'd have known that laugh from anywhere.

"I want one." Eliza placed her hand on my back. My arm rested around the waist of her long, yellow dress, the fabric softer than Carter's favorite fleece blanket. I flashed Hannah's camera a rock star smile.

"Sure, *now you do* a normal one," Hannah teased. "Hey, you guys match!"

Eliza gave me a high five. Our yellows were exactly the same color. Which I had maybe, maybe not, done on purpose. "Represent."

"Oh good, there's Carter. Carter!" Hannah shouted towards where he was visiting the water fountain. "Come here! You and Nick need a pic."

"Shades," I said. Since we were modeling together, Carter and I both brought sunglasses. A bro needs his accessories!

Carter slid his on and positioned himself with his elbow casually on my shoulder. Iconic.

"You guys should model dress shirts," said Hannah. "Seriously. You could do it."

"I don't know if the magazines are ready for our good looks," Carter replied. "They could cause a lot of *issues.*"

I bumped his fist.

"Carter and Nick!" Ms. O'Connor called from the stage entrance. She organized most of the show, which involved waving at us like we were about to miss the last flight home while telling someone's grandma to enjoy the show.

"You guys are up!"

"If we're not out in ten minutes," I said to Eliza, "you know what to do."

"Bring the camera for evidence." Carter tapped Hannah's shoulder.

Ms. O'Connor led us to the searing stage lights.

Cassidy High's stage wasn't anything fancy: a classroom-sized wooden rectangle, like most high schools had. All Carter and I had to do was escort each other to the middle, strut to opposite sides, turn around, and strut back. The auditorium was about three-quarters full, and my parents hadn't come. No pressure at all.

Then why were my hands clammy?

Hannah and Eliza waited in the wings on the opposite side of the stage. They both clapped when we walked, as the lights began to blaze like uncomfortable July heat. The crowd whistled as Carter and I made our entrance and their applause doubled when we donned our shades. At the middle of the stage, we removed our sunglasses, making confused gestures to have it look like they were malfunctioning. We swapped them, nodding satisfactorily when they worked. If Austin were there, he would have yelled out from the audience for us to kiss already (and he would have had to buy us some pizza later), but apparently, he had better things to do, leaving our routine to be pretty straightforward.

Next, Eliza was escorted by some freshman I didn't recognize. Since we'd already gone, Carter and I got to sit in the front row, still in our tuxes, and enjoy seeing our classmates be fancy. I loved that she was the center of everyone's attention, so I had an excuse to take her in. Her shoulder was in line with the curves of her hips and seemed much less swollen than it had been yesterday. I wasn't really looking at her shoulder anyway. Her face lit up the entire auditorium. Her curled hair perfectly framed her dark eyes, with her glossy smile the highlight of her ensemble.

"Work it, girl!" I cheered when she walked in front of us,

knowing she would've hated a whistle, no matter how much I wanted to give her one.

■

An hour later, Hannah and Eliza joined us in the front row while Ms. O'Connor presented a speech on what the Parent Teacher Association meant to the students and the world, or something. It was hard to concentrate with Eliza sitting on my left and Carter on my right. I scrutinized every single movement Eliza made—every shift of her legs, every tap of her finger—I couldn't help it. That made me hyperaware of Carter's shifts and overall presence. And how his movements restricted mine.

Ms. O'Connor's speech marked the beginning of the reception. The parents milled about, ate some cupcakes, caught up on the latest gossip, and complimented the students who'd put on the show.

I leaned to Carter to make a sarcastic comment about what Ms. O'Connor had said, about how *the students here couldn't function without the PTA* and how she should have said PDA, to see that he was already in the middle of discussing it with Hannah. I couldn't see his expression, but Hannah's read like He. Was. Dazzling. Her.

I turned to Eliza, moving close enough to whisper, "*Now* I get why you didn't like me asking about Hannah."

She twiddled her thumbs. "Ya got me."

"Impressive . . . how much you seemed to care about the Bro Code when you knew Carter would break it anyway."

"A few weeks ago, she mentioned a sort-of interest in him, and he's had this little crush on her basically since we moved here. You have no idea how annoying it's been having to watch them figure out that they like each other. Especially since I've known for a while and I couldn't tell either of them."

I know exactly how that feels.

"What's funny?" she asked as I chuckled.

"I, um."

You could tell her, Nick. She gave you a good opening.

"What?"

"It's nothing," I said.

Someone's kid brother ran up to the stage. Even though the microphone was off, he stood on his tiptoes and tried to sing.

"Little dude bailed you out, dork," she said.

"Did you just call me a dork?"

"Huh?"

"Ha. Okay." The amount she stared at me was apparently inversely related to how articulate I could be. *Figure it out, Maguire.*

Maybe I was being a dork.

Before I could recover, she smoothed out her dress and said, "You want to get out of here? I sure do." She pointed towards Carter and Hannah, who were still deep in some random conversation, probably about math or something.

"You got it." I offered her my arm. She looped her hand through it so gracefully that I almost felt like a proper Englishman.

"Thank you, Nicholas."

"Of course. Where would milady like to go?"

"Anywhere it's not so hot." She fanned herself with her hand, kids now crowding around us to each get their shot at the microphone.

"Have you ever been to the roof?" I asked.

"Our school has a roof? Weird. I never noticed."

"And you made it to junior year? I don't know, Eliza. You might not be ready to see the roof. It's kind of a secret. I can't take just *anyone* up there."

We bumped against each other as I led her out of the auditorium, away from the microphone spectacle and (sadly) away from the cupcakes. The cooler air and emptiness outside the auditorium were worth it, however.

She squeezed my arm. "No, I take it back. Can I see the roof? Please?"

"You have to use the magic words."

"What magic words?"

"It goes like this." I cleared my throat for theatrical purposes. "Repeat after me: Oh wonderful and handsome Nick, who smells better than a rose in the summer, will you please show me the roof?"

"You're weird."

I released my arm and shoved my hands into my pockets. "Do you want to go to the roof or not?"

"How about *please*?"

"Perfect." I smirked. "Right this way."

Eliza looped her arm back through mine, and I tried not to get too caught up in how natural it felt to be close to her. I led her to one of the secret ladders inside a [details redacted].

"How did you even find this?" she asked. "Actually, never mind. I don't want to know."

The ladder whined as I pulled it down. I steadied her as she climbed on.

"You gonna be okay in those shoes?" I asked, her high . . .

whatever they're called . . . seemed dangerous. But what do I know about shoes?

"Don't patronize me."

"Fair enough."

I climbed close behind her, ready to help if she slipped, which she didn't. Not even close.

We stepped onto the roof, which overlooked the intercourse fields as well as the student parking lot. Eliza went to the railing overlooking the fields and leaned into it, resting. The only light catching her was a slim shadow from the parking lot and the starry sky, hanging over us like a blanket.

She shivered—my cue to give her my jacket. Girls go crazy for things like that. Also, she needed it, and I wanted to be nice. "Here." I draped it over her bare shoulders.

"Really, Ni—"

"It's all right. You can have it."

"Thanks." She wrapped it around her, wearing it way better than I ever did. "And to answer your question, it's surprisingly gorgeous up here. I thought it would be mostly parking lot, and I didn't think there was anything nice about this school. Clearly, I was wrong."

"What's that like?" I joked.

"Ha." Eliza pressed against the railing, which was a yard's length of cement around the roof. "Hey, can I ask you something?"

"You mean another thing?"

"What?"

"Asking if you can ask me something is asking me something."

"Smartass."

I bowed. "At your service."

A helicopter flew overhead, casting a green glow over us, and making our hair go everywhere. Eliza attempted to comb hers back into place, eventually throwing down her hands in defeat, giving victory to the tangles. I settled against the railing, a few inches away from her.

"What did you want to ask?" I said.

"Oh, right. Why haven't you ever had a girlfriend?"

A sudden jolt of hot air filled my lungs, making it hard to breathe as I realized how much she was initiating here: leaving the auditorium, brushing against me, asking this . . . those weren't all coincidences, right? Unfortunately, presuming with this girl would be fatal.

"Can I phone a friend?"

Do it, Nick, I commanded myself, dragging my fingers through my hair for the millionth time. *Just tell her.*

"Kidding." I patted the railing, dizziness buzzing in my brain. "I mean, there is this girl I like a lot, but it's socially unacceptable for me to date her, since she's my best friend's sister and everything."

"Good one," she said, and I couldn't tell if she thought I was kidding. Either way, she leaned against my shoulder like she wanted to be close to me.

"Can I ask you something?" I said.

"You mean another thing?"

With the way the moonlight shone on her face, it was impossible to look away.

"Why did you break up with Josh?"

She paused. "Remember at the beach, when we were in the water?"

I nodded. I liked where this was going.

"I couldn't stop thinking about that." She turned around so

her back was to the dark fields. Her fingertips lingered on my forearm. "I broke up with him, because I realized," her voice softened, "he wasn't the boy I should have been dating."

"I see."

We looked at each other in the way we hadn't ever allowed ourselves to. Eliza fidgeted with my sleeve. I brushed the sides of her dress. My heart hammered harder with each of her slight movements, especially as her glimmering brown eyes vacillated between mine.

"I've been trying to figure out how you felt for such a long time," I admitted.

Her laugh illuminated her face. "Same here."

"Except this isn't some—" I caught myself. *Easy, Nick.*

She tilted her head. "Not some what?"

Ordinary crush. I shifted from the railing until I stood before her, a mere step away. I couldn't take my eyes off her ever-so-slightly parted lips, or ignore my fingers, trembling with anticipation as I touched her cheek, about to ask the question I'd had on my mind all night.

But she got there first. "Nick, will you please just kiss me?"

"That's the best thing you've ever said." I tucked a piece of hair behind her ear and drew her into me.

I closed my eyes, making sure I'd remember this. The texture of her lips, and how slowly we started, testing the waters until it was clear that neither of us would pull away. I cupped her chin and pulled her closer, and Eliza tugged on the collar of my shirt, pushing things deeper, beginning to explore.

I grinned into the kiss, making her giggle and grip me tighter.

We eventually came up for air, but she stayed where she was—my arms locked around her, her dress flapping against my knees.

"If I'd known kissing you would be like that . . ." she said.

My fingers traced her collarbone. "Definitely worth two hours of shopping." With Eliza's knees woven between mine, I could not have asked for a better moment.

Unfortunately, a second later, voices came up from the ladder. We had company. Eliza slid out from under me, dusting herself off. It seemed like she understood we'd have to keep the last five minutes a secret. For now.

"Hey guys!" Hannah exclaimed, followed by Carter. "How is it up here?"

Eliza shot a shiver up my spine as she answered. "It's amazing." Her face practically glowed in the dark.

Something about her tone startled Carter, and his head whipped to us, eyeing the distance between me and his sister. Satisfied, seeing nothing off, Carter came over with Hannah following.

"They're almost out of cupcakes," he said. "You guys should go if you wanted any."

"Are you trying to get rid of us, Carter?" asked Eliza, putting her hands on her hips.

Hannah's ears turned pink, though it was hard to see *how pink* in the dim atmosphere. Carter shuffled to the railing, hiding his reaction.

"I, for one, would love another cupcake," I said.

"Another?" Eliza caught my subtext. "*Oh*. Right. Another. We should hurry."

"Definitely." I led her to the ladder, climbing down first, ready to help her if she needed. She didn't, but it gave us another few minutes to look at each other—really look—before it was time to go home.

RULE NUMBER 11

THE FORTY-EIGHT-HOUR RULE.

Eliza. It took me ten minutes to drink my orange juice the next morning because I kept zoning out, unable to focus on anything but her dress, her hand on my shirt . . . what it was like to be near her. To breathe her air.

Gross.

The best part of kissing her wasn't how natural it seemed or the way her long legs had pressed against mine. The best part was that she'd kissed me back.

I duct-taped my phone to the underside of my bed so I wouldn't call Eliza or even text her. Every bro knows that after he hooks up with a girl, he has to wait forty-eight hours before he can ask to see her again. A long forty-eight hours. It would be worse than watching reality TV shows with my mom, which she'd made me sit through more than once.

When I was done, the job I had done on my phone was

probably more effective than the security system in Fort Knox. It would take some serious work if I ever wanted it in my hands again.

A knock came on my bedroom door. "Nick?" my mom called. "Time to go."

Really? What time is it? I reached to pull my phone out of my pocket.

I am an idiot.

"Coming."

■

Twenty-five minutes later, my mom sat in the passenger seat of my car. Something had happened to the brakes in hers, and she had had to drop it off at the mechanic's for who knew how long. Our town had one car mechanic, and we drove a few towns over to her client's place where we'd get a discount. That was the town with the mall, three ice-cream places, the bowling alley, and the movie theater, which I used to go to before Carter got his own giant screen. I got to be the lucky chauffeur who'd escort her back to reality. My mom seized the twenty-minute car ride home as an opportunity to help me prep for my upcoming admissions interview.

"Don't forget, first impressions are everything. It starts with your shirt being tucked in, combed hair, and a good handshake. No one likes a flabby one."

"Got it," I said. Without any traffic on this fine Saturday morning, it was actually pretty easy to listen to my mom. For better or for worse.

Elizabeth A. Seibert

"Your suit still fits?"

"I sure hope so."

"Nick. If it doesn't, we still have time—"

"Yes, it still fits."

"Give an example in every answer. When they ask you what your strengths are, don't only say leadership. Talk about a time you showed leadership in soccer."

"Okay." My mom looked straight ahead and gestured with her hands. She was in her element and I was another one of the people that she coached.

"Don't say 'um' or 'like.' If you think you're going to, slow down."

"Okay."

"And don't 'up-talk.' That's making sentences seem like questions? Like that?"

"Okay."

"Don't mention your GPA."

Because mine's not good enough. "What should I mention?"

The light ahead turned to red, and my mom's lecture stopped when my car did. "What do you think you should mention?"

I tapped my foot against the brakes. "Maybe balancing school and soccer? How I like helping other people with injuries?" Those were the realest things I could think of. I could only hope they would be enough.

"Great," she said. The light turned green and I sailed through. "Make sure you ask them questions."

"Okay."

After ten more minutes of that, I pulled onto our street. "You're going to do great," said my mom.

"Okay."

We arrived at our house to find none other than Austin Banks sitting like a garden gnome on the front lawn.

"Go ahead," Mom said. "I can take it from here." I hopped out and she drove up the driveway.

"Hey, man." The too-long grass scratched my ankles as I approached. "What's up?"

"Are you okay?" he asked. The overcast, cloudy backdrop emphasized his worry.

"Yeah . . . why wouldn't I be? Are the Red Sox losing because last time I checked—"

"Unfortunately, no, they're not," he interrupted. "You weren't answering your phone. Which, if you were anyone else, I wouldn't come all the way to your house for, but you told me that if there is ever a girl fight, and I text you about it, and you're not there . . . I should come to your house immediately."

"Ah crap, sorry, I drove my mom and didn't have my phone on me. Who was in it?"

"Sophomores. I don't know their names. It wasn't that good, though. You didn't really miss anything. That's about it. Want to chill?"

"It is Saturday."

He followed me to my room. It was a little small for hanging out, with an old-school 1980s TV.

"Haven't been up here in a minute," said Austin. He flopped on my bed as I clicked on the TV. "Still have your Legos?"

"Check the closet." Playing Legos at my house had been a staple of our elementary school experience, before Carter and his toys moved to North Cassidy.

I flipped through the channels, searching for basketball or soccer. Watching football or tennis would have been okay, still

Elizabeth A. Seibert

second choice. Austin checked out my closet but sharply spun around, squinting hard.

"What?"

He pressed a finger against his lips. "Do you hear that?"

"Hear what—"

"There it is again." He scanned my few pieces of furniture. "Hang on, dude, why is your bed vibrating?"

I rubbed my neck, unsure of how to explain what I'd done with my phone.

Austin dropped to his stomach and crawled under my bed, prying my phone out of the makeshift fortress.

"Well that's just sad." He tossed it to me. Fully aware of exactly what I'd tried to do. "If you had plans tonight, forget them. What you need is an intervention."

"I'm fine."

Austin had the same expression he'd had when he told me that the pickle smoothies he drinks to keep his hair shiny were more than marketing crap—as if he were the sole authority on such matters.

"You're almost eighteen, Nick. No girl is worth taping your phone at eighteen."

There would be no arguing with him. I couldn't risk him asking who the girl was. If Austin knew I liked Eliza, he would definitely tell Carter, and that was something I wanted to do myself. Eventually. If I wanted to keep Austin from finding out about her, I'd have to humor him.

"Sure," I said.

"Great. I'll tell Carter."

He paced across my bedroom floor, texting. Seconds later, a reply buzzed in his hand.

"Carter doesn't want to leave his sister home alone tonight so we're going over to his house," said Austin.

"Why not? Eliza's a big girl."

It was too ironic that my "intervention" would happen at the O'Connor residence, but I'd never point that out. Not in a million years.

"Dunno. Do you need to grab anything?"

The AP bio textbook lay unopened and abandoned on my bed. With a big quiz next week, I considered putting it in my backpack.

"Nah. Let's go."

■

I lounged, fully outstretched on Carter's queen-sized bed, while he and Austin took turns driving each other off the road in their racing game. It was a two-player, which meant the winner of each race got to keep playing and the loser had to sub out. Which meant that Austin and I got to take turns against Carter.

"See, Nick," Austin said. "No girls, no drama, no stress. Pizza, video games, and music."

"Taping your phone to your bed?" said Carter. "Tragic. I mean, if that's what you have to do to wait forty-eight hours, fine. Still, who's worth not having your phone for two days?"

If he only knew.

"Thanks for helping me see the light, guys." Four days ago, I would have agreed with them. Amazing how things change.

"Hey, is your sister around?" I asked, trying to stay cool.

"Yeah, why?"

"She mentioned something about Josh Daley last night. Thought I'd check up on her, long as I'm here." The lie was too easy.

"I think she's in her room. Be nice about it, though, I don't want her running back to him." More and more often, Carter slipped into the role of the overprotective brother, not that I blamed him. Carter would do literally anything for Eliza. He'd probably even die for her, which may seem surprising, considering all the pranks and crap we'd put her through over the years. With their dad gone, Carter was the one left to make sure guys didn't break her heart.

As I was about to jump off Carter's bed, the faint scent of cinnamon wafted into the room.

"Carter, did you want—" Eliza stopped short. "Hey, Nick. Austin." Her cheeks flushed, matching her red volleyball T-shirt.

The race cars came to a halt as Carter paused the game. "Sorry, forgot to say they're coming. We still eating here?"

"Sure." She entered. "Olivia left us frozen pizza. I put only one in. Guess I'll do another." The only thing Ms. O'Connor loved more than cupcakes was frozen pizza—she left their freezer stocked full of it. That way, when she was at an event or with her friends, Carter and Eliza could fend for themselves.

Carter's comforter bounced as Eliza sat next to me. Already in her gray sweatpants, it appeared that she did not have plans for the night. Carter pressed play on his game and a second later went back to schooling Austin.

"What's happening?" she asked.

"We're throwing Mags an intervention," Austin answered as if he were talking about the weather.

"You don't say. What kind of intervention, if I may inquire?"

"You tell her," said Austin. "Acceptance is the first step, Nicholas."

"You sound like one of those self-help videos." I turned to Eliza. "There's this girl I can't stop thinking about, and these two idiots claim it's going to ruin my life."

I managed to keep a straight face. Eliza did too.

"Yeah, who's the girl by the way?" Carter asked. "You never actually told us. Not Madison, is it?"

"Her name's Ms. Banks or something?" I said.

"You *wish* you were her type." Austin flipped me off.

Eliza swung her legs off the bed. "I'm gonna start the second pizza. You guys are starting to sound hangry."

Hangry was Austin's worst mood. It was necessary to keep him fed before he reached that full-on Incredible Hulk situation. The last time Austin had been hangry, he'd called Robert a green turd, and I ended up driving to every burger place in a five-mile radius to find one Austin would eat at.

"I'll come." I followed. "Since these guys aren't sharing their *game . . .*"

"Darn," said Austin. "We were hoping you wouldn't notice that I was supposed to switch with you two rounds ago."

"Now I get first dibs on pizza. Fair trade."

Once we were out of sight and on the way down the stairs, I snuck my arm around Eliza's shoulder for a quick hug. Her arm wound around my back, and that same, energizing warmth from the night before caught in my throat.

I'm definitely in trouble.

"An intervention? Was that real?"

"They're reading me letters after dinner." We entered the hot kitchen and Eliza pushed the door until it quietly clicked closed.

"Gotta let the guys know the sitch is under control," she stated.

"Definitely."

She shook her hair into a loose ponytail, heading towards the fridge. I pulled my foot back to stretch my quad. That helped bring me back to the present moment, and out of thinking about what we could do with no one around to watch us.

Sneaking around with Eliza made the OCs' kitchen feel even bigger than usual—with hyperawareness of all the places we could get into trouble together. But her proximity also made the space feel much smaller.

The paradoxes of the female kind.

Eliza dug out the frozen pizza from the slews of ice cream, frozen hamburgers, and leftover cupcakes.

"I was wondering if you were going to text me. Forty-eight hours is a long time."

"It is a long time." I leaned against the wall. She didn't seem upset.

"That's probably the point of it, though, right? To try to wear the girl down until she thinks you won't call her and then when you do, she's overjoyed?"

"Something like that." Something most girls don't realize is that guys can play hard-to-get too, and it's almost always on purpose.

"Too bad your grand plan got ruined," she said. "Guess now we'll never know if I've thought about you as much as you've apparently thought about me?"

Eliza slid the pizza onto a pan and into the oven. "Can you get that please?" She pointed to a pitcher on the top shelf.

"My pleasure." Five or so inches taller than her, I was happy to help. The smell of cheesy tomatoes spread through the room, but she'd taken out the first pizza already to keep it from burning.

Eliza pressed her stomach flat against the sink, watching the pitcher fill. I moved to stand behind her.

When she turned around, we collided against each other and she let out a surprised gasp. "Well played, sir."

"Thank you." I trailed my fingers down her arms. Like the night before, her feelings were clearly displayed across her face.

I pressed my lips against her nose, pausing there. Teasing her with how close we were to kissing again. Then I remembered that Eliza knew how to play this game too.

"Nick?" she whispered, "If you want me to remember you when I'm eighty, you're going to have to do better than that."

"Are there other guys I'm competing with for that memory slot, sweetheart?"

"Maybe there are." She lightly bit her lip. Was that move in the Girl Code too? How did every girl know how to do that so attractively?

"I accept your challenge," I said. The pitcher began to overflow with water, and I reached behind her to rescue it. Her slippers slid on the hardwood floor as she adjusted to how close I was—stopping me from erasing all the distance.

"Is this okay?" I asked.

"I think so."

"You think so?" *What does that mean?*

The kitchen air, warm from the oven, felt heavy as I tried to figure her out.

"It's great," she finally said. Glints of joy in her eyes confirmed this, which made me happier than our school's once a year free-ice-cream Friday.

Moving glacially, so she could tell me to stop when she needed, I removed every inch of space between us.

She held my T-shirt tightly, keeping me close and letting me kiss her. She smiled against my lips and finally relaxed into my chest. Our legs pressed together, with her thumbs grazing my stomach, guessing at the muscles underneath. My skin seared under my shirt. Her kisses quickened as she surveyed more and more of my chest. Minutes later, our fingers found each other, and our hands laced together, resisting the urge to do much more.

She left me more out of breath than I'd care to admit. Not that I was complaining. "We don't have to tell Carter about this yet, okay?" Eliza traced the letters on my Cassidy High School soccer shirt. "I don't want to go through that yet."

Normally I would have told Carter and Austin about any girl I hooked up with. That's what we do. The three of us absolutely kiss and tell, per the Bro Code's rules. It's a good thing it didn't cross my mind to, in fact, tell him—not thinking about it meant I didn't have a chance to deliberately go behind his back.

I nodded and Eliza kissed my cheek. "Thanks, pal. You're the best."

She ducked out and pulled the pizza from the oven, before it could burn.

"Don't forget me when you're eighty," I said.

"Wasn't gonna."

Oh boy.

We started to carry the food and water up to Carter's room.

Bringing pizza to Carter and Austin was legitimately the only way they would eat something. "Wait . . . hang on . . ." I stopped.

"Oooh, good call," she said, on the same wavelength.

I put one of the pizzas back on the table and Eliza opened the fridge, which was plastered with test grades and upcoming events.

"What do we have here?" She tapped her chin.

I came behind her and wrapped my arms around her waist. Her heavily washed, cotton T-shirt felt coarse against my wrists. Apparently, Ms. O'Connor didn't believe in fabric softener.

"Hmmmm," I said, not really paying attention.

She pushed her head back, making it straight against my chest, and I rested my chin on her hair. She was the absolute perfect height for me.

"Hot sauce?" she asked.

"Call me Nick. But yes."

"Oh my gosh. Relish?"

I nodded against her head.

"Worcestershire sauce?"

"Is that how you say that? I never knew."

"Really—?" Eliza started, turning into me, stopping when she saw my wink. She stayed there for a few seconds longer than necessary. Kind of like she was as shocked as I was that this was happening.

I rubbed her hands, giving a soft pinch. "Don't worry, you're not dreaming."

"Ah darn. I'd hoped I was." She grabbed the ingredients. "Would you like to do the honors?"

"You're too kind."

I took my time drenching the pizza in jalapeño sauce. One of the things Carter and I had been doing for years was trying to trick Eliza into eating really disgusting foods. We would put onions in her milk, curry powder on her bananas, and once we'd even put asparagus in her chocolate pudding.

"You know, they'll probably still eat this." She crinkled her nose. The relish was kind of iffy, but there's not much that Carter, Austin, or I wouldn't eat.

"Good. I'd hate to waste a perfectly fine pizza."

"Race you." She took off before I could reply.

"Cheater." I carried more food than she did, and still caught her with little effort.

When we reached the stairs, she extended her leg and tried to kick me off-balance.

"Tsk, tsk, Eliza."

"What can I say, Maguire, maybe I like to play dirty."

"Oh God, I hope so."

She tore the paper napkins out of my hand and started running as I bent to pick them up.

"Want some help with that?" she called over her shoulder. "Too bad, I'm already way over here."

Seconds later, she tapped her slipper outside of Carter's room with one hand on her hip, pretending to be annoyed. "Took you long enough,"

I adjusted my shirt with my free hand. "Yeah, I mean, didn't want you to think I was *trying*."

She stuck out her tongue, grazing my hand with hers. Then stepping away. "C'mon, superstar, time to eat."

Austin and Carter were exactly as we'd left them, slumped low in their beanbag chairs, eyes glued to the TV screen, like pubescent zombies. I waved the pranked pizza in front of Austin's face, and he reflexively grabbed it.

Eliza looked over my shoulder to catch his reaction. More and more sweat beaded on his forehead. He'd eaten almost half of it before the hot sauce kicked in. When it did, he leaped out of his chair like his mouth was on fire. Unfortunately, calling 911 wouldn't do him much good.

Austin hopped over to Eliza and took the pitcher of water.

Spilling it on the floor but mostly on his shirt, he poured it into his mouth. When he finally calmed down, he turned to see the rest of us staring, startled at what had happened.

"What kind of pizza is that?" Austin gasped. Carter reached for a slice and Austin slapped his arm away. "You don't want to do that, bro."

Carter didn't listen. He ate the whole slice without any emotion, then shrugged as if it were a piece of cake. "It's better without the Worcestershire," he said.

I clapped my hands, laughing. I turned to Eliza for a high five, to find that she'd disappeared, having slipped out during the entertainment portion of the evening.

It was back to the Three Musketeers, as if nothing had changed. When, in fact, everything had. I went to sit on Carter's bed and lay back against his sheets.

"Make yourself at home." Carter raised an eyebrow.

I held up my hot sauce–free cheese pizza to say *I will, thank you very much.*

"Should we do this thing?" said Austin.

He and Carter spun around in their hamburger and Oreo chairs, their game forgotten. Carter cracked open a pineapple juice. "What's up, Mags?" said Carter. "Who's got ya all stressed out?"

"Honestly girls aren't even part of it." That part was a lie, but if they wanted honesty, I'd give them the rest as truthfully as I could. "I'm kinda freaked out about Clarkebridge coming up and I didn't want any distractions."

Low country beats played from Carter's speakers. His overhead light felt brighter than usual.

"Definitely understandable," said Carter.

Elizabeth A. Seibert

"What about it freaks you out?" asked Austin.

"The pressure, maybe. Not sure. My whole life is riding on this interview and tryout. Like I could be awesome, and still not good enough."

My shoes had dirt on the heels, I noticed, since I couldn't look at my friends. The three of us had never really talked like this before, though admitting this stuff helped my tense neck loosen and my breathing come a little more easily.

"The pressure on you is . . ." Carter began but wouldn't say it. "I'd be going crazy."

"Super unfair," said Austin, "Don't take this the wrong way, but your dad is kind of a dick."

"'Cause he cares," said Carter. "Gotta keep that in mind."

The comforter molded against my back. Even Carter's ceiling had basketball players on it, so every morning Carter would wake up to LeBron. On LeBron's jersey, however, Carter had redrawn his "23" to say "OB."

"Yeah," I said, "It's hard because he wants me to be him."

"No," said Carter, "he wants you to be *better* than him."

"Right. Like I get to do the stuff he couldn't."

"Because you're better than him," said Carter. "Nick, you're better than him, and he knows it."

"Own it," said Austin. "Work it, buddy. Plus, it'll probably be easier after you get a scholarship. That's what he really wants, right?"

"*If* I get a scholarship."

"You will," said Carter. "You're Nick freaking Maguire."

"Except that goes without saying," said Austin.

"Right," said Carter. "Plus, Clarkebridge isn't about him, dude, it's about you. You get to go there and play for *you*."

"Tell *him* that," I said. "I don't think he knows."

"Mags," Carter said in his cut-it-out voice that he used when the soccer freshmen thought they were hot shit and tried to wrap each other in toilet paper for *solidarity*. "It's about you."

"Yeah." He was right, that I'd been making soccer a lot more about my dad than about me. Maybe that was just a way to take the pressure off. Like if I failed, it wasn't really *my* fault. But then if I didn't fail, it wouldn't be because of me either. They were both right: super unfair.

"At least your old man gives a crap," said Austin.

"Seconded." Carter coughed through a swig of juice.

Like me, Austin lived with both his parents. Mr. and Mrs. Banks were really nice, but Austin was the youngest of four boys, and with five years between him and his next brother, as his parents described to the entire neighborhood, he was "unplanned."

"I need some air."

"Take as long as you need," said Carter. We were still getting used to the whole feelings thing. As weird as it was to really talk to them about my dad, some of the stress had definitely disappeared.

I strolled to Eliza's room. The *Wicked* soundtrack blasted on her speaker system. Her open door revealed her sitting at a steel, paint-splattered drawing table with charcoal in her hands. Maybe I was just using her as a distraction. But a distraction had never made my knees so wobbly.

"Yo."

"Hey, Nick. I hoped you'd make it down here."

Eliza's room was the same size as Carter's, but instead of filling it with movies and video game consoles, it had antique furniture with a lot of artwork: a desk with fancy drawers, a bed that matched her orange walls and held about a million stuffed bird-animals, and the drawing table. The latter wasn't supposed to be splattered in paint, though. That was the result of one of my and Carter's pranks gone awry—which was why we'd never pranked her art stuff ever again.

Sitting in the swivel chair at her desk, I leaned back and swiveled in fast circles.

"What are you making?"

"You'll see..." She frowned at the printer paper–sized drawing.

"Can't wait." My shoes tapped to the music while I rapped my finger against the chair. Eliza's bright orange walls were covered in her own artwork—mostly charcoal drawings with a few splashes of color, and abstract watercolor paintings.

"Finished." Eliza's sweatpants brushed against my soccer shorts as she came to sit sideways on my lap. "What do you think?"

If she'd been any other girl, I would've taken that moment to run for the hills. And given how much hill-sprinting practice I did, I could've been out of the house and two towns over in minutes.

Because it was her, my voice went weak, the drawing shaking in my hands. Each line she'd drawn, just for me, mesmerized my eyes. My arm wove around her back.

I really hope Carter and Austin are still playing video games.

Etched in black and white were a boy and girl. They stood on a dark roof that overlooked a grass soccer field. Dressed formally, they were masked by shadows from a cloud-covered moon. Still, the stars lit up the field and the girl's long dress.

Wow.

"Do you like it?"

"You sure your name's not Vincent?"

"I'll have to check my birth certificate."

A new feeling decided to enter my arsenal of emotions. It flashed through my fingers, swelled in my legs, and even made my jaw feel weak. I yearned to take her all in: the fact that I sat beneath the sweetest girl.

Eliza placed the drawing on her desk. She laced her arms around my neck, and I held her so close that the chair teetered on the edge of flipping over. *Three . . . two . . . one . . .* I leaned in and kissed her with everything I had. *Remember me.*

RULE NUMBER 12

A BRO SHALT NOT TALK TO A CHICK ON THE PHONE UNLESS SHE IS HIS RELATIVE OR GIRLFRIEND.

The next couple of weeks flew by in another whirlwind, but not a stressful one. Or, not an *entirely* stressful one, thanks to how much I got to see of Eliza. Which turned out to be a lot, given how often Carter, Austin, and I play video games at the OCs'.

Then that morning at the end of October came—that morning so early it was still dark out, the sun a distant memory to the shedding trees. The morning of the long drive to Clarkebridge University.

"Snacks?"

"Check."

"Tunes?"

"Double check."

"Dorm address and that guy's phone number?"

"Yes, Mom," I said to Carter.

"Perfect." Carter climbed into the passenger seat of my rusty Mustang. "Six hours of driving start now."

He set my phone in the holder on my dashboard and played with my GPS. "Clarkebridge University. Arrival: 12:03 p.m."

Our suits hung on the back windows, our soccer bags were in the trunk, and the rest—snacks, portfolios, other clothes—lay in a packed reusable bag at Carter's feet.

The dark-gray morning sky taunted me as my engine sputtered. Not even the birds were flying around yet.

"I still don't get why we have to leave before sunrise," I said, as I pulled out of Carter's driveway, "Tryouts aren't until five."

"Don't want to hit traffic, okay? We can't miss this."

"Yup. Traffic." I gestured to the empty roads.

"We're gonna hit it once we get to New York," he said.

Carter smoothed out his track pants and played with the window opener, either nervous or excited.

"Can't believe we both might get to go there," he said.

"Might? Bro, you're basically in. Isn't this interview, like, a formality?"

"I guess. Double alumni doesn't hurt either."

Keeping my eyes on the road, I punched him in the shoulder. "Wish my parents had gone somewhere I wanted to go."

"Downside is it's kinda far away," he said.

I tensed. *Crap.* How was that only *just* occurring to me? I felt like I'd forgotten to do a class project worth 70 percent of my grade. The big project was being a decent guy for once, and the class was Carter's sister.

"She'll be fine . . ." I said, trying to convince both of us. "She has your mom and lots of friends. And Josh Daley would never

Elizabeth A. Seibert

let anything happen to her." I joked, though even I didn't think that was funny.

"Great. Thanks for giving me that image."

"No problemo."

"I dunno, I want to be there for her."

The plan, since we were fourteen years old, had always been for Carter and me to go to Clarkebridge together and play soccer. Carter had a next-level version of that dream where he'd be pre-med and on track to be a superstar doctor. I was still focused on getting accepted. Clarkebridge wasn't a "safety" school for anyone, especially me.

What hadn't factored into either of our plans was Eliza.

Brush it off, bro. This isn't about her. It's about you.

I almost believed it.

The drive to upstate New York consisted of seeing how many gummy bears we could fit inside our mouths, listening to sports radio, heatedly debating which video game was the best, and of course, girls. Thirty of forty times, Carter had tried to text, inconspicuously, when he thought I wasn't looking. Carter texting a lot was normal—but the messages always popped up in our group chat. So far, all I'd received were reminders from my mom about having fun and reminders from my dad about keeping my legs warm. Carter firing quick messages every time I changed lanes on the highway was both totally hilarious and completely sad.

"Who dat?" I tried to keep it casual.

He hesitated. "Hannah."

"Booty call?"

"You're jealous because you can't get any."

My jaw dropped to the absolute floor of the car, and then

through the floor to the highway and earth's outer core. He didn't deny it, which meant one thing.

"*It was?! Dude!*" I held out my fist, but he declined to pound it. "Ouch. Why you gotta leave a bro hanging?"

"I don't know yet," he said.

"You're not exactly, like, staving her off," I said. "Isn't that the stuff you always call Austin and me on?"

"I'm not leading her on," Carter groaned.

"Why aren't you going for it? Hannah's great! Robert knows it'll never happen anyway, and he'd understand if she got with you."

Carter slid down in the seat. The car jolted as I pumped the brakes—not realizing we were going 92 mph due to my excitement. Luckily, the road was clear and speeding hadn't been too dangerous. Of course, with a clear road it's almost a given that cops will pull you over for doing 60 in a 55. I flicked on cruise control, just in case.

"Look, man," he said. "You're my best bro, so don't take this the wrong way."

I turned down his pop-hits playlist to give him my full, undivided attention—as much as I could while keeping us in a straight line.

"So, Hannah is my *sister's* best friend. And my dating her would mean that I'm dating my sister's best friend. Obviously, I told you that . . ." he mumbled, "I'm trying to say that me dating Hannah would be kind of hypocritical because I don't know if I'd be okay if it worked the other way around, with my sister dating my best friend, which," he said quietly, "would be you."

It took me a minute to work out what he'd said, *my sister's best friend . . . what?* When I got there, it hit me like a sock to the red zone of my manhood.

Not a great time for Aretha Franklin to be ripping us a legend in the background.

"Bro, I'm not saying I necessarily want to date your sister, but what's the issue? I'm a great guy, we all know that. Purely hypothetical situation here . . ."

"You know, Nick, I can't really rationalize it. I think part of it is that she's my sister, and I wouldn't really want her to date anyone at all, and then there's that track record you have . . ." He didn't need to say it.

"For crying out loud," I said, my foot pressing back on the gas as my distraction grew, "this *Nick Maguire is a player extraordinaire* thing is really starting to get annoying."

"Why?" asked Carter. "You usually take that as a compliment."

We flew past a cop car, and I held my breath. Seventy in a 55 would be an expensive ticket. After a few seconds and no sirens, I exhaled.

I understood why Carter wouldn't trust me with his sister. For whatever reason, his sister wasn't another girl. Even I knew, however, that being trapped in the car with him for another million hours wasn't the place to divulge that information to him.

"Sure is a lot of traffic for six in the morning, eh?" I sighed.

"Asshole."

By the time we'd driven through all of upstate New York and arrived at Clarkebridge, I'd mostly succeeded in pretending the tension between us no longer existed. As far as I was concerned, what to do about Eliza was a problem for future Nick. And before I could get to that, there would be tryouts for the Clarkebridge team, a campus tour, and our admissions interviews. Big things on the horizon, to put it lightly.

As potential soccer recruits (fingers double crossed), we were set up to bunk with two current freshmen on the team: Luke and Tyler. Since we got to Clarkebridge well before the tryout, Luke and Tyler were happy to show us around. Their recruitment tour started with the dining hall (very important) and ended with the science center, since Carter had specifically requested it. The campus hosted about fifteen thousand students and was filled with high-rise dorms and towering academic buildings. It looked new, it looked legit, and it looked like it had one heck of an endowment.

Luke and Tyler were cool too. Luke was from L.A., had a man bun, and wanted to go into nursing; and Tyler was from Florida, had short hair like Austin, and majored in finance. Like us, they'd both been recruited to try out in high school and had wanted to go to Clarkebridge since well before that.

"Clarkebridge pre-meds have a 100 percent acceptance rate to med schools," Luke told us, but mostly Carter. "If you decide to come here, you'll be in good hands."

"We're one of the only universities that let undergrads research at the Cancer Center," added Tyler, "which is a big part of it."

"Wow, that's awesome." Carter snapped a picture of the center, like he'd snapped pics of every building we'd stopped at.

It was more than a center. It was an entire section of the campus, with three of its own buildings and its own courtyard. The crowning glory was a holographic statue of DNA in the main building. Luke and Tyler kept insisting that it wasn't a school for rich kids either.

"You go here to get rich," Tyler had said. "Lots of us come in on scholarships."

"Whoa," I said.

"What're these buildings?" Carter asked. "The map has them named after people."

"You've got your physical sciences right here." Luke pointed to the main building, which was made entirely out of glass and looked like it had four floors that consisted of only lab rooms. "Like chem, physics, et cetera." He nodded to the next tower. "Then you've got your life sciences. You know, bio, geology, environmental." The third tower looked identical to the other two but was the farthest away from the parking lot. "Then you've got your physiological sciences—we're talking neuro, kinesiology—this is where the PT program is too."

"Bunch of guys on the team are in that," said Tyler.

"Like physical therapy?" I asked. I'd known Clarkebridge had a robust sports training department. That was the extent of it.

Luke nodded. "It's kind of a weird one. It's a six-year program, where the rest of Clarkebridge is four."

"But you graduate with a doctorate, basically," said Tyler.

"Wait that's awesome."

Tyler chuckled. "There are some hard bio and physics classes," he said, "and anatomy is a nightmare. But the guys love helping other people move better. And recover from injuries or whatever."

Carter nudged me.

"Probably have to be at the top of your class to get in, though?" I asked, dreading the answer.

Tyler shook his head. "It helps, though the professors actually prefer students with a personal connection. Helps you not fail out."

"If you're interested," Luke said, "there's a separate app you can fill out. I think you need to pass the AP bio test too. I can send you the info if you want."

"Same thing for pre-med," Luke said to Carter. "So many people apply here, it's another way to show you're committed."

"Easy," I joked.

Carter clapped me on the back, his way of helping me relax. "Study buddies, bro." He held out his fist for me to pound.

■

To try out for the Clarkebridge soccer team, you had to be invited, but they didn't try out all the potential recruits together. Instead, Carter and I joined the existing team for a practice session, and we'd be evaluated at their caliber. Kind of like how Spider-Man got to join the Avengers *after* he helped them save the world. The stakes of this tryout felt just as huge. Two other high schoolers joined as well.

Rather than feeling the pressure, excited energy fueled my every breath. Since it was already starting to get dark, we played under bright stadium lights that made it hard not to feel like a celebrity.

Carter and I were each given Clarkebridge practice pinnies (white on one side, blue on the other) and paired with one of the team captains—our drill partners for the evening. Kyle Kohl, a six-foot-five senior from Ohio, started easy on me.

"You're usually a forward?" he asked.

"On my high school team. On club I played mid. I can do whatever." *Though I hate defense.*

"I like it," said Kyle. "All right, in a few minutes we're going to join the team for a dribbling drill. First, you and I will do agility."

He led me to a course of orange cones and I rubbed my hands

Elizabeth A. Seibert

to stay warm. Even with long sleeves under my pinny, the end of fall was no picnic to be outside. I could see my breath as I panted and had to put extra energy into staying warm so my legs didn't cramp. "We'll do it first for a warm-up, then for time, then a practice go with the ball, then with the ball for time.

I nodded. Around us, the Clarkebridge team was running a similar drill, but their coach didn't have a stopwatch out. On the other side of the field, Carter stood before an identical course.

"It's high knees to the first cone, backpedal to the start, then full sprint to the second cone, turn and butt kicks to the first cone, side shuffles to the third cone, other side shuffles to the last cone, then full speed back to the start. It's a different drill with the ball, don't worry."

"No problem," I said. I did a drill like this with my dad every morning. Kyle did the practice with me, his strides so big he finished in a few steps. He then held back to evaluate me from the sideline.

"Ready, set, go." Kyle clicked his stopwatch.

I sprinted through the cones, fast and agile on the college turf. I stayed light on my toes for the backpedal, and lowered my center of gravity for fast, form-perfect shuffles. When I hit the last cone, my legs pushed for the finish line like lightning flying through water. It had been, maybe twenty-five seconds?

"Eighteen, congrats," said Kyle, jotting it on his clipboard

With my hands on my head, I already started to catch my breath. "What do people usually get?"

"Recruits? Generally between twenty and twenty-five. Guys on the team? Around seventeen to nineteen. One guy can do it in fifteen. We think he's part android." He clapped my shoulder. "Let's do it with the ball."

■

After the agility course came a dribbling and shooting drill with the team. We lined up to dribble through another set of cones, then shoot at the goal—pretty standard soccer drill. Except this one had cones tighter than I'd ever seen, we had to shoot twenty meters from each goal, double what I was used to, and we had to shoot at a random angle, determined by the coach, who stood next to the goal.

Carter went before me. The team clapped for him as he started, clapping harder as he made the dribbling look easy, when even some of the guys on the team struggled with it. He breezed through the cones, and in a fluid movement, shot a hard 30 degrees towards the goal. It swished easily into the net, and he jogged to the back of the line.

"Damn, that kid is good," someone had said behind me when Carter was still tackling the cones.

"Wow," another had said after his goal, "we gotta get that guy."

At first, I thought it would be nice to go after Carter, and I could watch his technique and tell him about it later. Now, *I had to go after Carter*.

The coach blew his whistle. "Dude, you're up," said the guy behind me.

I took a deep breath, balancing my toe on the ball. *Three, two, one . . .* I counted. *Go.* I exploded from the line, trying to tear through the cones as easily as Carter had. *Go, go, go,* I pushed myself to run even faster. At the end of the cones, the Clarkebridge coach held his hand up and to his left.

Shoot for the upper left. I lined up my shot and it sailed safely into the net—on the center of the right side. *Oops*. The guys on the team didn't know where I was supposed to shoot, however, and cheered for me as I jogged to the back of the line.

"I dunno, I think that guy was faster," someone said.

"The blond guy had a nicer shot."

"They're both incredible," said someone else.

At Cassidy High practices, I was always the absolute man. It was my group of guys, and I truly belonged there. Playing with Clarkebridge's team was different. A new thrill. Like the impossibilities I'd always dreamed of were actually in reach. When I lined up my next shots at the goal, hearing the encouraging cheers from the hyperathletic strangers around me, I felt like I was taking a dare from my future, challenging me to decide if this was what I wanted.

It was the thrill of getting to see what my life would be like if I wanted the guys around me to be my new guys. At least, if I was up to the work it would take to succeed on the team here. And if I was up to the good-byes.

We finished the shooting drill and jogged to the sideline for water. Next would be a scrimmage with the team. Carter came up beside me, sweat in his hair and darkening his pinny.

"Pretty cool, right?" he said. "Picture this with a few thousand people."

Imaginary cheering came from the stadium as we took it in. Carter nudged me. "I hear we're doing way better than those other high school guys."

The two recruits trying out with us sat on the grass, pouring water over their heads. Their cheeks puffed red from the exhilaration.

"I have a good feeling about this," I said, "Just gotta nail the scrimmage."

"That's what we do best," said Carter. He swigged his water bottle, and as the light caught him at that exact angle, his blond hair shone like a trophy.

I couldn't wait to tell my dad about this.

■

The next day, Carter and I anxiously waited for our interviews, rocking full suits. Carter was up first, which meant I had extra time to psych myself out and feel extra uncomfortable in the Buckingham Palace–style admissions building. Why does basically every school make their admissions building all plush and stuffy when it's nothing like the rest of the school? Maybe to make the one percent feel more at home. Mostly it was hard to breathe.

We both sat leaning over our legs, hands clasped between our knees. I'd showered, smoothed the wrinkles out of my jacket, and banned "up-talking" from my known speech, like my mom had asked.

"You're gonna crush it, like those shooting drills last night," said Carter. Since between us, my interview was the one that mattered.

"Duh." I tried to pump myself up.

"Try not to freak out."

"You're the one freaking out, bro. I'm cool as a cucumber over here," I said, my right leg bouncing hard enough to shake the chair next to me.

"It's going to be fine."

"You sound like my mom."

"Totally fine."

"Say fine again."

Carter grinned. "F-I-N-E—" he was interrupted by his phone ringing. "Gotta turn that off." He looked at the caller.

"Hey, Eliza," he answered it. "Oh, really?" At the same time, a tall door down the ostentatious hallway opened and a short man in a pinstripe suit, looking exactly like that guy from that movie, headed towards us.

"Carter O'Connor?" he called.

Carter gulped. "Here," he said into his phone. "Talk to Nick while I interview."

He basically threw the phone at me in his attempt to rush off.

"'Sup, Gorgeous?"

Carter couldn't make a face at me with the interviewer watching. He powerlessly plodded down the hall towards the guy who held our fates in his hands. It was almost as fun to make him think I was fake flirting with his sister as it was to actually flirt with her.

"Well would you listen who it is." Her sunshiney voice made the stressful admissions building feel like a yoga retreat.

"It's fine, I know you really called to talk to me."

"Do you know where Carter keeps the antacids? 'Cause that's what I want to find out."

"No, I don't," I replied, "because that would be way too much information."

"Let's say I taste-tested one too many cupcakes last night."

"And by one, you mean twelve?"

"I mean however many Olivia notices are missing. How's it going down there? Must be pretty boring, if you don't have anything better to do than talk to your bro's li'l sis."

"Don't you have class? Last time I checked, it's the middle of the morning." The one thing that really kept me going about this interview was that I'd get to miss school for it. And since it was a soccer tryout, I wouldn't have to do sprints for missing practice.

"Free period," said Eliza. "Hence the quest for antacid."

"Right, right. Well, you know me." I relaxed in my over-cushioned armchair. The waiting room was completely empty except for me and the grad student who had checked us in. "Parties up the wazoo. Surrounded by 'em. Been here twenty-four hours and this school has no idea what hit 'em."

"Didn't expect anything less." Her voice fell, which, from my basic understanding of the Chick Code, meant she was unimpressed. My normal B.S. wasn't going to get me far with her. Instead, she pushed for authenticity. "Ready for your first, and hopefully only, college interview?"

"You ask all these hard questions."

"Thank you. You need help?"

Normally, I never would have admitted weakness to another human being, let alone a girl. But this was Clarkebridge. And this was Eliza.

"Yeah."

"I did not think you'd say that. Nick Maguire, are you asking for help?"

My shoes rubbed against the tile floor, bouncing with my leg. "Don't get used to it."

"I would never. I guess let's start with the easy one? Why do you want to go to Clarkebridge?"

"Um . . ."

"Good start, buddy."

I groaned. "I'm going to tank this."

"Why are you doubting yourself, Nick? I thought you were, like, Mr. Confident."

"Ha," I said. "I'm also, like, Mr. Almost-Failing-Bio. Which I'm going to need to not be if I want to get into any of the sports majors here."

"Maybe. Except when you go to college you can be anyone you want, right?"

"I guess."

"Supposedly," she said, "we're all, like, some combination of the five people we hang out with the most. Unless you go to college with, like, Carter, Austin, your parents, and Madison . . . you're probably gonna be different."

I considered this. "Maybe I want to be more like you."

"Then you're going to have to hang out with me more," said Eliza.

I grinned into the phone. "You want to hang out more?"

Eliza went quiet. I had to take the phone away from my ear to check that the call hadn't dropped.

"Do *you*?" she asked.

Despite the heavy air conditioning, my cheeks burned.

"How's Thursday night?"

"I think I can make that. Where are you taking me?"

"Where am I taking you?" I could imagine her biting back a smile. "You mean you don't want to watch a movie and chill?" That was a joke, since everyone knew that phrase didn't really mean watching a movie, and she knew I didn't mean that as a suggestion.

"Wow. You really are a hot date," she teased me back. "Every girl's dream evening right there."

"Oh, it's a date?"

"I know you might be unfamiliar with the concept," she said. "I think it could be fun."

I was glad she couldn't see me. If she had, she'd have seen how completely *not cool* about this I actually was.

"I don't want to spoil the elaborate surprise I have obviously planned for you. Pick you up at six?" I asked.

"Does that give you enough time after soccer practice? I know how long you spend on your hair."

"I'll make it work."

"You'd better."

For a minute, neither of us said anything. "So . . . why Clarkebridge?" Eliza asked.

Because it already feels like home, I thought.

Yes, but why? I could already hear Eliza prompting, in the imaginary conversation in my mind.

Because . . .

I still didn't exactly have an answer. Carter's interview door opened, and he came walking out.

"My turn to go in," I said. "See you, Eliza." I winked at Carter as he approached.

"Have you been talking to her this entire time?"

"Yeah, I asked for stories about you."

Carter took his phone and the interviewer came out of the room, motioning to me. "Nicholas Maguire?"

Because . . .

You can be anyone you want, right?

Feeling the most confident I had all trip, I nodded, fixed my blazer, and went to shake his hand. I knew that Nick Maguire wasn't perfect, though he wasn't all bad, either.

Hopefully the interviewer would see that.

Eliza was wrong about one thing, however: neither of us could be *anyone* we wanted. She would always be Carter's sister. And I'd always be his bro.

A BRO SHALT TREAT HIS MOTHER LIKE A QUEEN.

After our interviews, Carter and I grabbed pizza at the place on campus. It was Sicilian pizza, square and extra crispy, whereas Straight Cheese 'n' Pizza was thin crust, so we couldn't decide which was better. Apples and oranges, basically.

The car ride back consisted of Carter sleeping and me testing my luck with the state police: how fast could I go without getting caught? Turns out 95 mph, since that's the fastest I went (although I didn't pass any speed traps).

We did the six-and-a-half-hour drive back in under five.

Even though it was after dinner, none of the lights were on in the O'Connor's house.

"You sure you don't want dinner?" asked Carter.

"We have frozen food at my house too, bro."

"Gotcha. Later." The passenger door blew shut as he slung his duffel bag over his shoulder. The half-eaten bags of chips stayed with me, however.

The second I rolled out of his driveway, my phone started buzzing. I secured it in my phone holder.

"Nick?" came my mom's voice. "Are you back yet?"

"Almost home."

"I just finished at the office. My car's in the shop and your dad's still at the school board meeting. Could you give me a ride back home?"

Geez, Mom. Late night. Though a twinge of guilt hit me like an itch. The extra hours were for me. My parents wouldn't let me get a job and contribute to my college fund—because apparently, I needed all my spare time to practice. Given how prepared I was for the tryout, it seemed to have paid off.

"Be there in fifteen." My Mustang kicked into gear. Her car was perpetually at the shop, but my mom was determined to run that thing to the ground. For three reasons:

1. With my college coming up, new cars weren't exactly on the top of our expense lists.

2. She was too far above asking our neighbors and family friends for rides.

3. She has the lowest Uber rating the world has ever seen.

Everyone thinks their crazy, vomit-prone, foul-mouthed friend is the person with the lowest Uber rating: nope, it's Alison Maguire.

My mom approached the pickup curb as I drove up. She worked in an eight-floor building, where most of the walls were windows. All of them were dark. Her black suit blended in with the shadows, and her dark hair shone under the streetlights. Her weary face gave away her put-together façade.

My mom was amazing at her job for the same reason she's a terrible Uber passenger: she provokes people to prove their value to her. Oh, you're amazing at typing and spreadsheets? A computer program can do that. Oh, you have good communication skills? Let's see how many languages you can give me directions in. Think you can perform well under pressure? What about with me hollering at you to go faster, pushing you to run the yellow lights, saying there's a cat in the middle of the street making you brake hard and get rear-ended? (Real talk: my mom is rated as one of the most unpleasant passengers Uber has ever driven because she ruins self-esteem, picks tiny arguments, and has left both drivers and passengers in tears, saying she was just trying to help them with their life skills.)

She climbed into the passenger seat, tripping over her seatbelt. "Frick." She caught her balance. "How was Clarkebridge?"

I waited for her to be situated before crawling out to the main road. Driving my mom was tougher than my driver's test—and impossible to retake.

"Great," I said. "Tryout went awesome, interview went well. Feeling good."

"Good or pretty good?"

"Come on, Mom." While I always tried to hold a nonchalant attitude around her . . . well, *she started it.*

"Good will get you a scholarship. Pretty good means we might need some more options."

"Why?" Even though it was late at night, in our tiny town, and I was the lone car on the road, I flipped my turn signal on long before I needed to, to appease her. "I've got a great shot at getting in early decision. What's the big deal?"

"I'm trying my best," she said. "We got an estimate from the federal loan offices last week . . ."

My breath stayed sunken in my lungs. Here it comes, the amazing last week or so, crashing down.

". . . and we might need more than we thought."

I exhaled. What could I even say to that? "Is there anything else you can do at work?" I asked.

"I interviewed for a promotion today, actually. I think it went well. Watch where you're going, Nick."

Well or pretty well?

Cars honked as I turned a little too close into traffic. The more we talked about Clarkebridge, the harder it was for me to concentrate.

"They have a physical therapy program that I can apply to," I said, trying not to tailgate the car in front of us. "That gives some financial aid, in addition to whatever I might get for soccer."

"The six-year program? You really think you'd be accepted to that?"

"Gosh, thanks." Ahead of us, another car appeared and stopped at a red light. I slammed on the brakes, barely seeing it in time. The dark made it hard to see to begin with, and now I had extra to worry about.

"You know, Mom, maybe if—"

"Pay attention." We were moving again. She dug her nails into her seat so hard that her knuckles began to turn white, visible even in the night.

"If you guys hadn't put so much pressure on me for getting a soccer scholarship, maybe my grades would have been better."

"Stop sign coming up." She raised her voice.

"And maybe if Dad didn't wake me up at the crack of dawn every day—"

"*Stop sign!*" she screamed.

Too late, I shot through it, right at a car turning at an intersection. My brakes screeched as I pounded them, turning at the last second into the curb. The back wheels lifted off the ground and threatened to tip the car on its side. My eyes squeezed shut, bracing for impact. Our car slammed into the curb, followed by a loud *crunch* and the *clang* of a hubcap falling onto the road. My head bobbled into the steering wheel. Thankfully, we hadn't been going that fast. Just going when it wasn't my turn.

None of the airbags deflated either, which was bad because they should have, but good because it turns out we didn't need them, and they would've cost about three grand to replace.

We sat in shock. We'd hit the curb just past the intersection with no houses or buildings within the next twenty meters. Lucky.

"Are you okay?" I asked.

She nodded.

After a second to catch my breath, I swung the door open to examine the damage. It would be hard to know for sure until the morning, but for now a softball-sized dent stuck out on the side of my front bumper. If I could live with the aesthetics, it might not need to be replaced. My hubcap clanged as I threw it in my trunk.

My mom stayed silent when I hopped back into the car. Tense and guilty, I fully prepared myself for a lecture. I didn't get one. She didn't need to say it.

I told you so.

Slowly, my foot pressed the gas and we rattled along at a normal speed towards our house. My eyes glued themselves to the road ahead.

"It's your own future." At last, she spoke. "The fact that you even have a college fund should feel like a gift from God."

I know. I was lucky to have a mom who would put her arm out, like she had for me during a minor collision with a curb.

"I feel good about it," I said.

"Want to take another look at that bumper?"

"I mean the tryout. I don't feel pretty good. I feel great."

The car treaded up our driveway. "I'm sorry, Mom. I'll try to do better."

My feet slid on the gravel as I jumped out to reassess the bumper's wound. Other than the good-sized dent beside the front wheel and a long scratch along the bottom of the passenger side, nothing too bad.

"Did you get hurt at all?" my mom called. She climbed out.

"Little shaken up," I said. "I'm going to go to sleep."

"I think that's a good idea. And you're grounded."

I winced.

"Car accidents are a big deal, Nick," my mom said, with her scary mom voice. "They kill people."

"Okay, okay."

My car keys jingled as she held them up. *Darn.* They'd been left in the ignition while I checked out the injuries.

"You can have these back next week."

I deserve that. It seemed like she knew it had been an accident, but she wouldn't let me off easy.

Head hanging low, I shuffled to my room with my soccer and interview gear heavy in my hands. I threw myself onto my bed, pulling the thick pillows over my eyes and burying into the fleece blankets.

Might as well tell Carter.

It wasn't until my fingers hovered over the Send button that I remembered: I couldn't be grounded.

A chill caught in my throat. The phone slipped out of my sweaty palms.

Eliza.

Elizabeth A. Seibert

RULE NUMBER 14

A BRO SHALT NEVER HALF-ASS
A FIRST DATE.

Thursday afternoon, Carter picked at Sir Whiskerton (the name we'd given our sacrificial rat—for science) and I flipped through the lab directions. This brain dissection had already taken weeks and nothing we did made sense.

This did not bode well.

Our classmates shrieked as they dug further into their specimens, many of them now uncovering the, *crap* I had still had no idea what it was, even though Carter and I had gotten to it last week. Because Carter is a supernerd.

"I want to take the AP bio test," I said, "for that PT program. I know we were already going to, but now I really want to do well."

"You do know your class average is, like, a 71." Carter wiped a speck of formaldehyde off his safety goggles.

"Actually . . . 69." I was pretty proud of that.

Carter punched my shoulder. *That's the spirit.*

"Good thing I have an in with the best tutor Cassidy High has ever seen," I said.

"Gonna take some work, Mags," he said. "It's going to be more than putting labels on—" He squinted at the label I'd stuck in what I'd guessed was the rat's outer intestine. "That's the left kidney."

"Testing you. And I know. I want to do it. That program seemed like a great fit."

"You want to start tonight, then? Test is in February—practice tests start soon, though."

"Tonight . . ." I wracked my brains for an excuse. *Nope, can't, chilling with your sister,* wasn't exactly something I could say.

Then again, how exactly I was even going to go out with his sister was still TBD, as I was grounded, and sans transportation.

It seemed like I was down to three options:

A. Cancel my date with Eliza, risk looking like a total flake and loser for prioritizing Carter and biology over her, and risk losing her forever.

B. Tell Carter I was busy and somehow pick up and go out with his sister without him realizing I was there or that she was with me.

C. Ms. Doubtfire the situation and make plans with both of them in the same location, then switch back and forth between hanging out with each of them and lose a wig in the process.

D. Come clean and actually communicate with both parties.

Each option seemed selfish and unfair to both O'Connors. If I *acknowledge* that it's selfish, it means I can do it anyway, right?

Dracula came by our table, plopping down our latest pop quizzes: 105 percent for Carter; 69 percent for your boy.

"Hell yeah—"

"No, Nick, not anymore."

"Right." I needed to do better. "Six-ish work?"

"Sounds good." While our other classmates compared quiz grades and debated whether points were unfairly deducted, Carter returned to poking Sir Whiskerton with the scalpel.

Option C it was.

I needed to get a wig.

■

Coach Dad drove me home at 5:00 p.m. that evening. After I'd told him my tryout had gone well, he'd smiled the whole fifteen-minute ride.

"Atta boy, Nicky," he said as we walked into the house. "Who's the man?"

"Okay, thanks, Dad." I pounded his fist.

"Mm, smells good," said my dad when we reached the kitchen.

My mom stirred a pot of spaghetti sauce, basil and garlic taking over the kitchen. And here I was thinking she didn't know how to cook. Her pink bathrobe was already tied tight around her waist. "Light interview day," she said.

On the days my mom didn't have a lot of work, she usually spent her free time napping. I guess the rest of her life took a lot out of her.

"How was school?"

"Pretty good," I said. "But . . ." I explained to them about how I was doing in biology and that I could use some extra help. "I know I'm grounded. Is there any chance I could hang out with Carter tonight so he could help me?"

My parents exchanged a look.

"How are you failing biology?" asked my dad.

"Technically *not* failing . . ." technically that would be a 65.

The pot clanked as my mom stirred it more aggressively. "How about Carter comes here?" It wasn't a question.

I hesitated. When I lie to my parents, I try to lie by omission—the stuff I tell them is true, but not the whole story. I'd learned, in my years of having to tell girls what they want to hear, that trying too hard was a dead giveaway. They gave me no choice.

"He's hosting a study group at the library," I said. "Would going there be okay?"

"You can't be failing biology," said my dad, "We have the L-W game coming up, the school won't let you play."

"I'm not failing. I need extra help."

My mom gave a reluctant sigh. "Home by nine. How are you getting there?"

"I was thinking that I could drive?" Even though my parents had their mad-cop/disappointed-cop routine now stitched into their DNA, maybe, possibly, my dad *wasn't* disappointed? For once?

He put his hands up in defense. "Whatever helps you get there."

The garlic began to overwhelm our kitchen. The smoke detector *beep beep*ed in protest.

My mom fanned the stove. "Bike tonight. You can have the car back this weekend."

Sigh.

"Reward for good interviewing." My whole body jostled as my dad ruffled my hair. I caught my balance on the kitchen table.

"You can't fail bio," said my dad. "Need you for L-W."

"I'll be fine."

L-W meant Littleton-West, a.k.a. the most important game of the regular season, according to my dad, since our rivalry with them went back to before he'd even started coaching twenty years ago. Leave it to my dad to think of my school performance in terms of athletic eligibility.

Now the hard part. I took the stairs two at a time up to my room. Somehow, I had to get ready for my date with Eliza in a way that made it look like I tried for her, only in a way that no one else would be able to tell I tried.

A quick shower helped calm my nerves, though my razor still shook as I tried to do a light shave (though I wouldn't have been able to do more than that anyway). I threw on some musky aftershave, my favorite jeans, a relaxed T-shirt, and, at the last minute, my Red Sox hat. The majority of the times I'd flirted with Eliza, I'd worn my hat. Who knows, maybe it served the dual function of keeping me casual and irresistible.

At 5:30, I hurried down the stairs, with my bio notebook and a fleece blanket stuffed in my backpack.

"See ya at 9:30," I called. Carter's house was a ten-minute bike ride away, but I had to pick up some things first.

At 5:40, I reached the grocery store. Time to pick out the ingredients for a perfect first date.

At 5:52, my backpack was full, making it difficult to bike up the half-mile hill to the OCs' house. The sun was finishing its descent into the night, but the dark yellow and orange backdrop would still suffice.

At 6:01, I texted Eliza that I'd arrived. Ringing the doorbell was too risky, since Carter might have answered it. I paced at the bottom of their back porch.

"Hey!" Eliza scanned the driveway, to make sure we were alone. "Where are you taking me?" She hopped down the porch stairs, stopping abruptly. "I don't know the appropriate way to greet you."

"Come here." I grabbed her hand and led her to a thick, mossy tree on the edge of their property. Its trunk took eight people to wrap their arms around, and its sprawling branches provided great hiding spots (especially when playing with water guns). The last light was enough to see each other with, but not enough for anyone from inside the house to see outside.

Carter and I had spent many afternoons trying to see who could climb the highest in that tree without Ms. O'Connor seeing what we were up to. It would have given her a heart attack.

My backpack dropped onto the grass, crunching the leaves of fall. I pulled out the blanket, a few types of cheese, some crackers, grapes, bite-size brownies, and sparkling apple juice.

"Thought we could hang out here." I gauged her reaction.

"Who knew Nick Maguire could be such a romantic?" Her cold hand squeezed mine.

We leaned against the tree, with her head pressed against my shoulder. She skimmed my cheeks with her fingertips.

"You smell good."

My skin tickled where her warm breath touched it, and even more when Eliza lightly kissed my jaw. I stayed put, half hugging her, playing with the ends of her sweater. When she didn't pull away, I slipped my pinky under it, brushing her bare skin. I found the waistline of her jeans and had to stop as quickly as I'd begun. I didn't want to freak her out. And I didn't want to do this here.

"I need to tell you something," I finally said.

"M'kay," she bit her lip, as if she were teasing me for not kissing her.

"Okay, you need to stop that," I whispered. She stepped away, laughing lightly. She knew she had me.

"I happen to be tanking my biology class—" I started.

"Hang on. Tell me over fake wine and cheese." She took in the boss spread I'd arranged on the blanket. "We need plates and napkins."

She tore off, back into the house.

"Can you bring back some cupcakes?" I called.

A gate creaked in the near vicinity. It was hard to tell exactly where, as the backyard was shrouded by darkness.

"Cupcakes for what?"

I paled.

Carter came closer, dripping wet and wrapped in a Mickey Mouse beach towel. Right—sometimes he liked to swim in their heated pool after practice to relax and stretch out more.

Whoops.

Their back door slammed closed—Eliza must have gone inside without hearing him.

I rubbed the back of my neck. "Great timing, I was just coming to find you. Told Eliza I was coming over and she thought it would be fun to have a study-picnic. I thought she informed you."

"It's almost November, Nick. It's freezing."

I dropped onto the blanket so he wouldn't see me squirm. Cold had kind of been the point. Warm, cozy blankets, stars, Eliza . . .

"This is stupid," he said when I stayed silent. "We're gonna need some more light." He paused. "And I need a coat. Guess she forgot about daylight savings time too. I'm gonna go change and get some lanterns. Thanks for helping her set this up. This is a real fancy way to study."

"Only way I know how."

Carter left me to guard the charcutenanny—or however you say that word—and the distant chirping of bugs trying to mate.

"Don't rub it in," I muttered.

I don't know what I really expected; of course there was no way I'd have been able to pull off running between the O'Connor siblings without either of them figuring it out.

Now it would be a devil's three-way in purgatory: my date with Eliza, with Carter as the third wheel; my study sesh with Carter, with Eliza as the third wheel; and Eliza and Carter's sibling life, with me as the third wheel. Weirdness all around.

Carter found our picnic, I texted Eliza. *It is now a homework party and he is joining. Rain check?* 😕

∎

When the O'Connor siblings returned, we situated ourselves equidistant from the food. Tiki torches, left over from one of Ms. O'Connor's catering events, lit up our textbooks. Carter had decided to start teaching me about biology by teaching me about chemistry, and had his old chemistry textbook open to the periodic table. I was trying to make it seem like I was less stupid than I was. Eliza had her nose buried in her history textbook, sighing with boredom every two or three minutes.

I had to do something to get her involved, and fast, or this could be the last date I took her on. Girls probably don't give you a second date after their brother crashes your first one and you don't tell him to leave. As a guess.

"Carbon is the element that leads to life," said Carter, "which makes it possible to create organic compounds. That's kinda important, because we'll for sure have to take organic chem in college."

"Okay." I half listened to him and scanned the periodic table for a joke.

"It's important to know how many isotopes—"

"I have an idea for a compound," I said. "What it's called when you combine sodium, bromine, and, um, oxygen?"

"That's a new one." Carter flipped through his notes for the answer.

"No, like I combined the element symbols together."

"Na, Br, O?"

"Nah, Bro."

Eliza looked up from her book. She didn't give me a reaction. No problem, I was ready for her.

"Also," I continued, "copper and tellurium."

"Cu-Te," said Carter, "yeah, I've heard that one before."

I gave Eliza a high five, which she halfheartedly returned.

"Who's been calling you cute?" I asked Carter.

Carter coughed, annoyed that I was flirting with Eliza. Or rather, trying and failing. "Helium, helium, helium," said Carter.

"What?"

"He He He," Carter punched my shoulder. "Oof, he can dish it, but he can't take it."

Eliza stood and picked up her materials. The blanket tugged under her sneakers. "I'm cold," she said.

"I guess that's it for tonight," said Carter. "I think this went well. Hopefully you know more now than you did two hours ago."

"Sure."

Carter closed his notebook. Eliza shifted her weight from one leg to the other. At the same time they asked me, "You need a ride home?"

Talk about a Sophie's choice. On the one hand, I was blowing my date with Eliza. On the other hand, I had to overcompensate about this picnic weirdness and demonstrate to Carter the cardinal rule of manhood: *Bros before hoes*.

Carter looked at Eliza and she shrugged. "Figured I owe him from when Nick took me shopping."

When I didn't jump in, Carter yawned. "That's okay. I got it."

"Thanks, man," I said.

Eliza and Carter shared a minivan, which I'd ridden in enough times to know it would not only fit my bike but it would fit my bike and an entire store's worth of peanut butter cups. I speak from experience.

Carter helped us pack up the picnic, still assuming it was Eliza's idea to put it together. I waited for him to realize the blanket he'd folded up wasn't actually his sister's. Carter kept yawning.

"Who you staying up late with?" I asked, remembering too late that Eliza (who did know) wasn't supposed to know that Carter had a thing for her best friend.

Somehow, that made me think about my mom and her stupid, arbitrary rules.

Shoot. The library was supposed to be closing soon, she was probably looking for me.

Elizabeth A. Seibert

I checked my phone, which was lit up with notifications. *It's late. Plz come home.* Then, thirty minutes later, my mom called me out. *Nick.*

"Hang on," I said, as Carter handed his homework to Eliza for her to take in the house. "I need a picture of you and the book."

Carter looked at me like I was asking him to rake sand at a beach.

"My mom thinks I'm at the library."

"Why?"

"Yes, Nick," said Eliza, "why does your mom think you're at the library?"

"I'm supposed to be grounded," I admitted. One on one, I had a chance to defend myself—but not against both of the O'Connors at the same time.

"You know, I could have actually met you at the library."

"Then I wouldn't have gotten do to this," I joked, attempting to make it seem like I was kidding. Hopefully, Eliza would get the subtext.

"Anyways, thanks." My phone flashed at Carter and our homework. I'd need a way to explain the tiki torches. At least she could see that I was studying.

Used to me having to answer to my mom, Carter was already halfway to the car. Eliza gathered the torches.

"Look," I said. "I know this didn't turn out exactly the way we wanted—"

"It's fine. It was going to be super awkward trying to keep it from Carter anyway. Don't worry about it."

"No. I don't want to—"

"Nick, let's go!" Carter called.

"This isn't over," I told her, jogging away.

I didn't catch her reaction in the musky dark. Carter gestured for me to hurry up. I could only hope she felt less confused and defeated than I did.

RULE NUMBER 15

A BRO SHALT NOT TELL NON-BROS THE RULES OF THE BRO CODE.

Even though I'd promised Eliza I'd make it up to her soon, the AP practice tests were upon us and so was prepping for the end of season soccer games. Every spare second I had, I spent with my dad hovering over me, making sure I wouldn't injure myself before L-W.

A week went by and things got even worse. Ms. Johnson was absent from teaching our PE class and the school's sub bailed at the last minute, meaning our thirty-person physical education squad got combined with Mr. Hoover's health and nutrition class.

The good thing was that Austin was in that health class and he hadn't skipped today. The bad things were:

A. Mr. Hoover.

B. Mr. Hoover's eternal quest to punish me.

C. Both Eliza and Josh Daley were in my gym class, and I had to somehow manage all of the aforementioned personalities without coming off as an A+ a-hole.

"No way," Austin fist-bumped me as I dropped my backpack on the desk beside him. The desks were in clumps of four. Robert and Josh could sit with us too. "We've got all my faves," said Austin, "minus Carter. LOC will have to do." Whether or not Eliza heard his acronym for Little O'Connor, she didn't answer.

"Ms. Johnson's class will be joining us today, settle down, phones away, we have a lot of material to get through," Mr. Hoover droned.

I recognized a few others in the class, mostly from my soccer team.

Eliza sat with her cool-nerd friends on the other side of the room. I had my back to her. Still desperate to say my piece, I hid my phone in a notebook and texted her. *Talk after school?* I had no idea if her phone was secretly out too, though I guessed not, because she was the extremely studious type.

"Welcome to hell-th," said Austin. He passed around a pack of gum.

At the front of the room, Mr. Hoover started his PowerPoint for the day. It projected nicely onto his pristine whiteboard. You're welcome.

The first slide was titled *The Importance of Sleep.* It had a cartoon of a dude tucked into bed, counting sheep. This was going to be good. And by good, I mean horrible.

"Guess he won't mind if we sleep through this," I whispered, "since it's so important."

Josh snickered. Austin leaned across his desk. "Yo, I have to tell you something."

Mr. Hoover remained completely oblivious to the fact that almost no one was paying attention to him.

Josh and Robert hung off Austin's every word. With him, you never knew if he was going to say something like, "Your momma is so fat, when she went to space she became the ninth planet," or if he was going to spill some serious tea.

"I hooked up with Madison yesterday."

I blinked. Of all the things, that was the least surprising.

"I should have asked where you guys stand," he said, "and I get I'm the worst. She came—"

I shook my head, signaling for Austin to shut up. While I still could barely believe it, since Madison had said she was specifically interested in Carter, Madison and Austin *did* kind of make sense.

"Are you asking me for my blessing?"

Austin blew a big bubble with his gum.

"Go for it," I said. "Just remember . . ."

"Bros before hoes." Austin slid back in his chair.

I'd been about to remind him that Madison was a psychopath who lived for juice, but that rule—the cardinal rule—worked too.

"Bros before motherfucking hoes."

Maybe it was the sudden swearing, or because we'd been pushing the envelope since his lecture started, but Mr. Hoover chose to start paying attention to us at that exact moment.

"Mr. Maguire," he called me out. Because who else would he torture? "Would you care to share that statement with the class?"

I glanced around. My bored classmates had been tuned out of his lecture for so long that this conversation didn't interest them in the slightest.

"I said I want to go home." I made up.

"That's not what I heard. What did you really say? Please share."

"Jesus, why?" I asked. That got my classmate's attention. With more eyes on him than he'd ever had before, Mr. Hoover took full advantage of his opportunity to teach me whatever sadistic lesson was at the bottom of this.

"It seems a bunch of you have woken up from your slumbers," said Mr. Hoover. "And that Mr. Maguire would rather discuss toxic masculinity than the five stages of sleep."

The class groaned.

Mr. Hoover took the yellow detention slips from his pocket, poised to rip me one. "Mr. Maguire, please repeat your statement for the class."

"Bros before hoes," I said.

"This is dumb," Austin muttered.

"Does anyone wish to debate him?" Mr. Hoover asked. The class stayed quiet. No one was going to risk going against it in front of everyone.

There was one person, however, who I did want to push back.

Instead, she finally texted me. *Guess I already know what you're going to say.*

She'd thought that comment was directed at her. *Oh, no.*

I promise it's not that. Meet me after practice?

"What makes masculinity toxic?" asked Mr. Hoover, changing lecture topics. "Is it that men are convinced they will never be able to understand women? That society thinks men and women can never be friends? The idea that wearing pink and going shopping are emasculating?"

He paused, as if anyone were actually going to chime in.

Elizabeth A. Seibert

"Or is it the world's permission for boys to be boys, when they hit on girls, shove each other around, or refuse to discuss their emotions?"

"Excuse me, I feel attacked," Austin called out. Chuckles rose around the room.

"Why is that?" asked Mr. Hoover.

"Because being born with a dick isn't something any of us can help."

If people weren't paying attention before, they were now.

"That's it," said Mr. Hoover, "the 'any of us,' language."

"Now I really feel attacked."

Mr. Hoover ignored him. "Let's break that down. *Us.* Implies *us versus them.* And with that comes a need for power and who to take it from."

I zoned out. After sitting through a few more minutes of Mr. Hoover's lecture on his hatred of bros, I got her answer.

Meet you after practice.

■

'Twas the practice before my dad's most feared game of the season: Littleton-West. He coached us like it was the practice before the World Cup.

"O'Connor, your foot's 90 degrees on those corner kicks; you're showing us exactly where the ball's going. Karvotsky, bend your knee more on the push kick. You need stability."

Coach Dad would never straight-up tell us he was nervous. That would be like a doctor saying he was worried before performing open-heart surgery. Can you imagine? The last thing you hear before going under the anesthesia is *Nurse, I'm not sure about this.* Truly horrific. Instead, like the surgeon, he overcompensated by nitpicking every tiny thing he could. Even making up things to nitpick, if he couldn't find something legit.

"Banks," he called to Austin, who was supposed to be trying to steal the ball from me but couldn't quite keep up, "come on. Your mom can do better than that."

"How would you know?" Austin muttered.

"Don't," I said.

"I want him to share some emotion," said Austin, "gotta prevent that toxic masculinity." He pushed me to show he was joking.

"Dude."

"Fine. He's scary when he gets emotional anyway."

Austin continued to fail at stealing the ball from me.

"What time is it?" I asked, once we were back at the sidelines, hydrating after our first drill.

"Time to get a watch," said Austin.

"3:30," Carter answered from where he squatted on his ball.

Two hours left.

■

When practice was over, I still had about half an hour before I was supposed to meet Eliza. I headed for the intercourse's pool.

The pool was one of the coolest and most unsafe parts of Cassidy High sports. First, it was giant—the same size as what Olympic athletes compete in, but *way* warmer, since old ladies could get a swimming membership at our school, and they don't joke around.

The scalding temperature deterred the rest of us, except the swim team when they were in season. There wasn't even a life-guard on duty—only people with swimming memberships were allowed to use it, and you had to pass a swim test so they knew you wouldn't drown.

The lone person in the pool, I tore off my sweaty shirt and headed for the diving board.

Although I was supposed to, I didn't shower first. No one ever came to the pool building. Who would know?

(I realize I'm part of the problem.)

When swimming at Carter's house, we had this ongoing con-test where whoever got the biggest splash out of a cannonball won. Austin, bless his heart, was currently in first place.

He must come here for extra practice.

The water splashed over me, warming up my stiff back and tired legs. I held my breath as I kicked to the other end of the pool without coming up for air. Even though Coach Dad's soc-cer drills got me in the best physical shape I could possibly be in, swimming the entire length of the pool completely under water made my lungs scream.

I hit the concrete on the other side, dizzy and panting. *Geez, Maguire, you're such a wuss.*

A minute later, I was back at it. Pushing my body to its limit was a dangerous game, but the rush of my lungs panicking and knowing I had a breaking point made me feel alive.

When I came up for air for the fifth time, someone called across the water, "You trying to drown yourself? I think it might be working."

Eliza hovered by the shallow edge of the pool, wearing her maroon-and-gold volleyball uniform, etched with the outline of an owl, and flip-flops. Her hair was pulled back in a tight braid.

I treaded water and maintained a comfortable distance. "Practicing up for the new *Finding Nemo*," I shouted. "Apparently they want real actors instead of animation."

Eliza walked to the middle of the pool, which I took to mean that I could doggy paddle over. She crouched and dipped her palm in the water.

"If you get the part, let me know. I would pay so much to see you in a giant orange fish costume."

"I'm trying out for the shark." I played with my wet hair, spiking it up to look cool. "Are you coming in or not?"

Eliza shook off her flip-flops, splashing the water as she dangled her legs off the edge.

"I'll count it," I joked. She wouldn't meet my eyes.

"Um." Her face flushed.

Goosebumps sprouted on my exposed chest.

I tried to get there first.

"I'm sorry about our date that didn't happen," I said, "I know it's weird with Carter—"

"It's not that," she said. "Yeah, the date was awkward, but what first date isn't?" She paused, her fingers making smooth ripples in the pool. She had such beautiful hands. "What I want the most from you, as a friend or whatever else, is respect. And what you said this morning, when you guys go around the school saying stuff like that, people listen, and it catches on. And it doesn't feel good."

What? I felt like the world's greatest idiot for not being able to follow that.

"*Bros before hoes?*" she said. "It's offensive. It generalizes all women as *hoes*, and it generalizes putting women second."

Elizabeth A. Seibert

Oh, boy. "If you want more attention—" I started.

"It's not about attention," she said. Her long braid scratched her shoulders as she shook her head. *It's about respect*, it said.

"Of course I respect you," I said. "It's just an expression, Eliza."

"That toxic masculinity stuff that Hoover was going over this morning," she said. "*Bros before hoes* feeds into that. And it makes guys act in a way that's actually super scary for me."

"What do you mean?"

"Like boys will be boys."

My throat was scratchy as I swallowed. "What do you mean?"

The air ventilation took that moment to pause, which left a haunted silence for Eliza to fill.

"One time, at a house party in Australia, one of my friends disappeared in the middle with her boyfriend. Everyone thought that was normal, but he came back after a while and she didn't. The guys cheered for him when he sat with them, like he'd scored the winning home run. You know, all rowdy and high-fiving each other. I found her when I was going home, sobbing in the sand. She'd said he'd wanted to touch her in some new places, and she was uncomfortable with it, but she was drunker than he was, and he did it anyway.

"The next few weeks, she was super torn over what to do. Some of our other friends told her that he was her boyfriend, like if she cared about him why was it a big deal? She eventually broke up with him and couldn't be in the same room as him for the rest of the trip. Meanwhile he continued to be treated like a hero."

She looked at me. "That's why I'm being weird today, and I get that it looks dramatic. But that's what I think of when people say *bros before hoes*. Some totally generic dude at a party, supported by his loyal bros, who left his girlfriend feeling powerless. And stole an experience from her that she'll never get back."

The more she said, the colder the warm pool water felt. Blood rushed in my ears like hearing a bomb before it denotates, as if I were still waiting for the explosion.

She was scared of me.

She thought I might push her too far. That I might ridicule her to save face.

That my masculinity mattered more to me than her safety.

"Not all guys are like that, though," I said. *Right?*

"You mean predators?"

I paled. She was on a *roll*.

"The point is," she said, "*Bros before hoes* perpetuates a world where shit like that happens."

The chill washing through me boiled into a heat that filled my cheeks.

"How is your friend doing now?" I asked.

Eliza shrugged. "We didn't really keep in touch."

"Does Carter know?"

She nodded.

And that was why Carter had been dead set on being extra nice to girls since Eliza had come back from Australia, after he'd heard that story.

"I'll stop saying it," I said.

The water around her hands went still. "What?"

"*Bros before hoes,*" I said. "I didn't mean for it to offend anyone. I don't know about this stuff as much as you do."

"Thanks," she said, and then came the bomb. "It's hard to know who to trust."

"I'm really sorry. Whatever you need."

"Um," she started like she was going to tell me something else, but I had to keep ingratiating myself. I should have let her talk. I couldn't help it.

"Thanks for telling me," I said, feeling frantic. "Promise you'll keep telling me about this stuff?"

"The stuff that makes me uncomfortable?"

"Yeah. Like when I'm being an asshole."

"—that's okay, Nick. I know you're a good guy."

"Not sure I believe that," I said. *But I'd like to be a good guy.*

The water waved through the pool as I continued treading. "Are you coming in?"

She looked down at her hands, whatever she was going to say was gone. Then, finally, she said, "Not if there's a shark in the water."

"Fish are friends, not food," I said solemnly.

The water glided underneath me as I swam over and lightly splashed her shins. "Better watch out, Eliza, it looks like there's a storm coming."

"What are you doing?"

I splashed her knees a little bit harder than I had before. "Uh-oh, it looks like a big one . . ."

"Nick, no. Don't do it." She jumped up. I was a lot faster and held her wrists tightly, securing her near me.

"Can I still pull you in the pool?" I asked. "Or does that count as not okay?"

"I'll allow it this one time."

In she went, half laughing and half shrieking.

Eliza stayed under water for about five seconds.

"That was a big splash," I said when she surfaced. "You could totally beat Austin."

Water rained over me as she kicked it in my face.

She flipped her braid over her shoulder and started floating on her back. I lay on the surface with her.

"Did you know that otters hold hands when they're sleeping?" I asked.

"What?"

"So they don't drift apart."

"That's adorable."

So are you, I wanted to say. Instead I reached out to touch her fingers.

"Wonder what the chemistry term for that is."

"There's that smooth Nick Maguire we all know."

We stayed like that for a few peaceful minutes. Her volleyball jersey clung to her, lifting enough to reveal the fading tan on her stomach.

Things finally felt right enough for me to say, "I'm sorry. I'll stop saying stupid things I don't mean, I never wanted to make you uncomfortable."

"I know."

She stood. I hadn't realized we'd drifted to the shallow end.

"I didn't mean to make you uncomfortable either," she said. "I like when you surprise me and kiss me without asking."

Our bodies were dangerously close together, and she placed her fingers on my naked chest, one by one. We'd been this close before, but now it was skin against skin.

I kissed her nose, then dove underneath her, surfacing with her legs around my shoulders. I grabbed her ankles, water streaming down my cheeks as she shook my hair.

Her laughs echoed across the pool. My cheeks hurt from grinning like an idiot. The eerily fluorescent lights shone down on us. It was the least romantic backdrop ever, but also perfect.

All of that I knew.

And if I'd taken the time to look around me, instead of being completely distracted by the pressure of Eliza on my shoulders, I would have seen the person standing at the pool's entrance, looking through its glass windows. Watching us.

RULE NUMBER 16

A BRO SHALT ALWAYS CHECK HIS PHONE.

We played in the pool for a long time.

"Gotta get you home," I said, eventually, "before Carter kicks my ass."

"I'd definitely be worried if I were you."

"Great, thanks."

My triceps ached as I climbed out of the pool, and even more as I pulled on my sweaty T-shirt.

"Aw," said Eliza, "I was enjoying the view."

"Guess we'll have to do this again sometime."

After a quick detour to my locker for my spare sweatpants, I met her outside the girls' changing room. It was almost seven, and we were already enveloped by the setting sky and shifting seasons. A few cars were left in the parking lot, but Carter's minivan was long gone. Eliza curled into my passenger seat and crossed her legs, bobbing as we drove over manholes and little rocks. One Direction blasted on the radio.

"You're wrong," she said, "they're seriously good. It sucked when they broke up; they were on track to be the next Beatles."

"You did *not* say that. 'What Makes You Beautiful?' A song about five different guys creeping on one girl? *You* don't have a problem with that?"

"See? You've listened to them, Nick Maguire. Don't deny it."

"Last time I checked, Eliza, I don't live under a rock. You know, like with bugs and without any news." The car slowed as we reached the bottom of her street.

"That's good. I'm sorry, I don't think I could date someone whose roommates are fire ants."

"What do you have against fire ants? They're trying to provide for their families."

"They attack and eat dead worms. That freaks me out."

"Well that's rude."

"Hang on," she said, "you didn't correct me."

"About the friendships of underground species?" I tried to act casual.

"No." The scent of chlorine dripped off her as she scooched closer. "About the '*d* word.' Isn't it coded in your DNA to correct girls about that?"

"Um, do you know what's going on with Carter and Hannah?" I asked.

"I take it he gave you the 'I'm not going to date Hannah because that would mean it's okay for . . .'" she paused, "'other stuff to happen' talk?"

"Yup."

"Fantastic." She drummed her seat with her fingers. "I told him it wasn't his job to butt in on who I go out with. Like Josh. He didn't want me to go out with him and I did anyway. I don't have to listen to Carter. That little conversation isn't going to change my mind about you, Nick. Maybe for you, though, what Carter said hits a little different."

That little conversation isn't going to change my mind about you, Nick. I'd barely heard what she'd said after that.

"Wish we'd had this conversation before I totally wrecked our picnic last week."

"We were a little busy."

Her hand twisted in mine, shocking me with its smallness. A squeeze from her was all I needed.

"How to tell Carter, though . . ." I mused.

"Do we have to?"

We both knew we did.

With a tender clatter, my Mustang crawled up her driveway. The kitchen light was on and Ms. O'Connor's car was in the driveway. The vehicle the siblings shared was not.

"Interesting," said Eliza. "Carter's spending an *awfully long* time at Hannah's house."

Her red cheeks drew me in, but it was her whip-smart observations that kept me diligently staring at the soaking wet beauty beside me.

We both knew, deep down, that Carter was going to lose it. Then her pruned palm covered mine, making my heart thump so loudly in my ears that it drowned out everything else. And that was that. I was sold.

"You're cute, Nick."

I'd never been described as "cute" before. I had to wrack my brain for everything I'd filed away about the Girl Code. Was "cute" good?

"You know that thing you do with your eyebrow is incredibly sexy."

Sexy, on the other hand, I knew.

"Really?"

"Really."

"What about this?" I lifted her knees and slid to the passenger side, climbing underneath her so she was now on my lap, her back to the passenger door.

"Risky," she said. Our knees crashed together. She glanced over her shoulder at the dark house behind us.

"You love it."

"Yeah." Her breath felt cool against my cheek, like a raindrop in May. "If you combine sweat and pool water and basically shove that smell down my nose, you know, that really does it for me." Her arms laced around my neck. "Goodnight, Nick."

"Night, Eliza."

She rested her head on my shoulder and kept her legs draped over mine for a moment longer. Not long enough.

After Eliza vanished into her house, I sat still, trying to catch my breath. I couldn't tell whether it was Eliza or the thrill of sneaking around that made me feel so much joy, but I wouldn't know while everything inside me raced.

I pulled my phone from my pocket, coming back into reality. I had six text messages.

Two were from Carter:

Carter 5:30 p.m.: *Thx for driving Eliza. Leaving for tutoring now, not sure if I'll be there when you get back.*

Carter 6:30 p.m.: *Still at tutoring, won't be home.*

And then four messages from Austin:

Austin 5:34 p.m.: *Carter + Hannah . . . amirite?*😉😉😉

Austin 6:00 p.m.: *You still at the school? Think I left the history textbook behind, if you see it lmk.*

Austin 6:20 p.m.: *WYA? No one's in the pool rn, if ur still here want to do some c-balls? Gonna go change, be back in 10.*

And then I read my last message from him.

Austin 6:29 p.m.: *dude. You and LOC? We need to talk.*

I punched the steering wheel. My phone fell, banging on the dashboard.

Shit.

RULE NUMBER 17

A BRO SHALT ALWAYS KEEP HIS COOL.

I successfully avoided Austin for the majority of the next day. That's a legitimate accomplishment, since we're in most of the same classes and he knows where I live.

Neither of us could skip soccer. He cornered me in the locker room, moments before what would turn into probably the most important soccer game of my high school career. I took my cleats out of my grimy, stained duffel bag as he plunked down on the long bench behind me. Guys changed and ran around in every direction. Carter wiped off his shin guards a few lockers away and I really hoped Austin wouldn't start something between Carter and me right before the game. We needed a win for so many reasons.

"My house. Eight o'clock. Tonight."

"I'll be there," I said. He was giving me an ultimatum. Austin is a great friend, to both Carter and me. Either I would go to his house tonight and give him my side of the story before he told it to Carter, or I wouldn't go to his house tonight and he would tell Carter exactly what he'd seen.

"Good." He plodded to the other end of the locker room to begin his pre-game routine. Ever since Coach Dad gave us a two-hour long lecture on sports psychology, every player on the team had developed his own pre-game ritual. For some guys it was nothing more than wolfing down a candy bar or putting black lines under their eyes like we were in the NFL or something. For others, it was considerably more complex. Carter, for example, had a specific motivational quote for each piece of his uniform. He was really secretive about it, and I had no idea what most of them were, but once I heard him say, "You have a choice—you can either throw in the towel, or use it to wipe the sweat off your face," which I'm pretty sure was a Gatorade ad.

My routine was to drink one of those ten-ounce cartons of chocolate milk from the school cafeteria. I did that before every practice too. It helped me transition out of the school day. I knew that as soon as the carton swished into the trash can by the locker room door, it was time to play.

I washed down the chocolate milk with a mouthful of water and tried to focus. If I closed my eyes and exhaled, I almost forgot about Austin. *Think about soccer, think about soccer,* I thought. *Think about beating the crap out of Littleton. Think about playing striker. Think about shooting the ball. Think about that "swish." Hear the cheering. See Dad's face as he nods, and you jog back to the half-line. Feel the sweaty high fives. Think about soccer, Nick.*

Coach Dad thundered into the locker room for our pep talk. All my emotions had settled—the calm before a storm. I'd even replaced the cinnamon scent of Eliza's shampoo, stuck in my mind for hours, with the dank smell of wet grass and dirt.

I was ready.

And we were going to win.

"Gentlemen," Coach Dad began. A few guys on the cross-country team, who still lingered in the locker room, even turned to listen.

"Last year we beat Littleton 2–1," he continued. "We would have tied them if it hadn't been for O'Connor's last-minute penalty shot." A smattering of claps came. "This year, I want to score, and I want to score early."

That's what she said. I wanted to catch Austin's eye. That day, I couldn't risk it.

"Maguire," my dad boomed. "Today you're playing defense. Right side," he listed off some of the other changes in our formation. I didn't catch them. *Defense? Is that a joke?* I'd never been put on defense in a soccer game—not once in my thirteen years of playing. During practices, sure. Never for real. Scoring goals is what I did. Carter, Austin, and I were always the three starting forwards. Every. Single. Game.

"Sorry," I interrupted, "did you say I'm playing defense?"

"You're goddamn right I did." My dad didn't elaborate on the fact that he'd changed my position half an hour before the game. *Unbelievable.* My jaw clenched. Carter's forehead crinkled. Everyone was thinking it, but no one said anything: if I played defense instead of offense, we were going to lose.

■

Ten minutes later, we warmed up on the soccer field. Carter and Austin practiced their shooting techniques, and I was tempted to join them. Instead, I stood by the bench with Kevin Light and Paul Jones, two of the other defenders, and pretended I didn't care that I had to play beside them.

The school had built a sparkling bleacher section for the parents to sit on while they watched the game, but hardly anyone used it. Instead, the spectators had gathered near the sidelines and around the field's perimeter. Apparently, none of them thought the ball would ever go out of bounds.

I noticed my mom, deeply involved in a conversation with Ms. O'Connor, among forty or so of my classmates. It was a decent turnout, considering it wasn't a league title or state game. Eliza was stationed with Hannah and a few of the other junior girls who had brothers or boyfriends on our team. All of them wore our school colors: maroon and gold. Eliza looked good in those colors.

Go Owls.

Austin's texts flooded back to me.

I squatted on the dewy grass and laced up my cleats. That was part of my ritual—not to lace them up until game time. I threw my sweatshirt next to my water bottle and jogged to my new position on the right side of the penalty arc. Kevin Light, the next closest player, pounded my fist. It was time to play.

Carter did the ceremonial coin flip with Ben Johnson, the captain of Littleton-West, to see which team would start with the ball. Ben had a reputation for being a dirty player; not officially, of course, since he's never been called on it. Once he checked Carter so hard that Carter had to sit out the rest of the game because his nose wouldn't stop bleeding, and the ref, who

Elizabeth A. Seibert

was looking directly at it when it happened, somehow didn't see it.

Yeah, right.

After a quick check to see who was refereeing that day, my mood dampened. What were the odds it would be the same guy? He was still hairy, short, and wearing a faded white-and-black jersey that should have been taken off his back years ago.

Wonderful.

I jumped, trying to stay loose. I knew Ben's moves. Jeff Karvotsky, the new, standing center-forward, didn't have a clue.

"Maguire," my dad called. "You're on corner kicks."

Translation: *You're playing defense, and you're going to play it like your life depends on it.*

That was when I saw *them*. They wore Clarkebridge-color windbreakers—blue and white. Their clipboards hung loosely at their sides and they both chomped gum, like they'd been chewing when I'd tried out for them. They weren't the coaches but were the administrative coordinators. We'd had our tryout. Now the coaches would be conducting their due diligence to see if we really deserved the spots on their team. The team administrators go around to confirm scholarships.

They stood close enough to the half-line that they could have been scouting players from either side.

My fists clenched. Today was the day I was being scouted for my scholarship, and I was playing defense.

Was my dad trying to screw with me?

When other players whine about what position they have to play, I'm usually the one who tells them to man up and quit complaining, because there's nothing they can do or say to change the situation. Now it was time to say that to myself. *Focus on the ball, Maguire. You're going to be the best defender on the field today. No excuses.*

"How's the nose?" Ben asked Carter. Even from the penalty line, the smirk on that little slime ball's face gleamed.

"How's yours?" Carter answered. "I'd imagine everything smells terrible, considering all the asses it's been up today."

Atta boy. Then the ball was in motion. Carter immediately kicked it to Jeff Karvotsky. Jeff dribbled it a few feet and fired it towards Austin before Ben could take it away. It wasn't a good enough pass. Ben intercepted it and what do you know? The spinning sphere of black and white hexagons headed towards me.

Ben tore down the field while my team raced after him. He looked up while he was dribbling and sneered at me. I stood on the right side of the field, waiting for him. I knew he recognized me, because he passed the ball behind him. He knew that since I was the farthest back defender, I had to stay where I was and keep the ball from getting in my space, or risk having them take a shot.

Impressive.

When Ben's team caught up to him and passed it back, he made it all the way to the goal before we pressured him to pass to the winded kid heaving next to him.

Way to use your team, Ben.

Coach Dad would have benched any of us if we'd gone as long as Ben had without passing. Kevin and Paul descended on Ben and his teammate like flies at a picnic and I dropped into the space behind them. The gassed kid from L-W faked right to Ben, awkwardly attempting a shot instead. Our goalie, Mike Dawson, scooped it up and threw it to me. Mike was under a lot of pressure from the L-W kid guarding him. His throw fell short. Ben tried to catch it with his knee.

"Oh hey, Maguire," Ben sneered. He tried fancy soccer moves to keep me from getting the ball. "Almost didn't recognize you all the way back here."

Like I could do it in my sleep, I stole the ball from right under his foot and kicked it hard up the field, all the way up to Austin, who easily trapped it and passed it back to Carter.

"How about now?" I shot back. Ben flipped me off and jogged back up to the half-line.

"Prick," he muttered.

I stayed by my team's goal. Carter worked the ball up the field. He was doing some highly technical footwork, and I couldn't help but notice Austin gave him the ball every chance he got.

Keep on playing defense. This isn't about Carter. Except that maybe, it was.

Carter sprinted into shooting range and aimed. The ball sailed through the goalie's fingertips to land squarely inside the net. Carter jumped and crashed into Austin's side. They slapped each other's butts. The crowd erupted. Scoring against L-W ten minutes into the game was a big deal.

The scouts nodded to each other and scribbled on their clipboards. My blood went cold. They weren't there to watch me. They weren't even there to watch Ben. They were there to watch Carter. Carter, who didn't even need a scholarship.

When Carter came to high five me, I almost didn't take it. "You okay?" he asked.

"Yeah. Way to work, man." My cheeks stung from grinding my teeth so hard.

Carter grinned and we jogged back to our positions. It was

impossible to be mad at him. Carter O'Connor was my best friend, and he wasn't doing anything wrong. The same could not be said for me. I couldn't think *screw you, Carter*, without feeling guilty.

The hair on the back of my neck stood up—someone was watching me. I turned and found the Clarkebridge scouts staring back. *Think about soccer, think about soccer.*

Even if they were there to watch Carter, I would give them something exciting to see. I had to. In the next thirty minutes, L-W scored twice, and by halftime the score was 2–1, Littleton-West. I'd touched the ball three times, and in each I'd successfully taken it away from Ben. That was all I could do.

Tweeeeeeeet came the referee's whistle, signaling halftime. Barely having broken a sweat, my jog to the halftime huddle felt easier than ever. After everyone had taken a few sips (or in Carter's case, gulps) of water, my dad called us in.

"Good job so far, nerds," he said. "You scored early. That was nice, but I need you to do that two more times. And you must not, under any goddamn circumstances, let them score again. Maguire! Karvotsky! I'm switching you. Maguire, you're back on offense, Karvotsky, you're my new right-side defender."

My shoulder panged as Carter gave it a hard clap.

Oh, thank God.

Soon, I stood on the half-line between Carter and Austin, the way things were supposed to be. Ben waited across from me.

"Look who's back in the game," he said. "What happened, Maguire? Did they think you could win if they switched your position around?" His laugh bounced off us. "Yeah, that's going to work."

"They said the same thing about your dad's condom," I said.

"Guess the birth certificate was their apology letter."

"Nick, that was beautiful," said Austin.

"Bitch," said Ben.

"There's a big word," Carter interjected. "That what your mom calls you?"

Tweeeeeeet came the ref's whistle. Carter kicked the ball to Austin and I cut forward, making me wide open when he passed it. Ben caught up, breathing heavily as I maneuvered around him, passing back to Austin. Ben didn't leave me alone; he stayed right behind me, preventing me from getting open again. I checked to see that the referee wasn't looking (though to be honest, he owed us one) and then gave Ben a sharp elbow to the ribs, hard enough to make him move, but not hard enough to do any damage. He backed off, though barely.

My lungs thanked me for finally using them as I sprinted towards the goal, where Carter passed to me. After faking right, then left, then right again, I kicked it back to Carter. Carter took the shot. It hit the edge of the goal, right where the goalie was waiting for it, and bounced back. That was exactly what Carter had wanted it to do. With a slam loud enough our own goalie could have heard it, the ball bounced off my chest, seconds after I'd jumped for it. I punted it with my knee and heard the best sounds in the entire world: the swish of the ball against the net and the cheering of the crowd behind me.

Carter and I had worked on that play a million and ten times.

My arms fired into the air like I'd crossed the finish line in a marathon.

"This is how we do it!" Austin shouted, throwing his arm around me, like maybe things were okay between us. "Yeah, buddy. All tied up."

The scouts jotted something on their clipboards. My dad gave me the approving nod I always get when I score a goal. Eliza smiled back at me. The universe felt small in the palm of my hand.

The three of us walked back to the half-line, murmuring strategy and game plans. The referee answered a question from one of the scouts and Coach Dad called in a substitute for two of the midfielders. Ben Johnson had all the time in the world to egg us on.

"Looked like you were showing off with that victory wave, Maguire," he said. He scanned the spectators. "Who's your girl?"

"Now who's being ridiculous," Carter said, like I couldn't possibly have had a kinda-sort-of-maybe-almost-hopefully-girlfriend in the crowd.

"Shut up, Johnson," said Austin. "Don't be jealous that Nick can get some when you can't, pal."

Carter laughed.

As much as I appreciated Austin trying to help me, that comment made everything a lot worse.

"So there is a girl." Ben glanced to where Hannah, Eliza, and their friends waved at us. "Is it the little miss cheerleader?" He meant Hannah, who was shaking her gold and maroon cheerleading pompoms. "She looks like fun." His eyes were glued to my face, which had lost all of its color. "If I had to bet, I'd say it's blondie." Carter grimaced. Apparently talking about Eliza was worse than talking about Hannah. "I dunno, Maguire, she looks like she could really put out—"

Every muscle in my body tensed. I couldn't help it. It was a reflex. And it was enough for Ben to realize he'd hit it right on the money.

"Well done, Maguire. With those legs, I'd bet she's a lot more flexible than little miss cheerleader. Although," he paused, "she looks like she'd say 'yes' to any—"

I didn't let him finish that sentence.

Right when my dad, the referee, the two scouts, my mom, Carter, and Eliza were all looking at me, I punched Ben squarely in the face. He doubled back, holding his jaw, and Carter jumped on him, pushing his face into the dirt.

Something—someone—held me back before I could make it two-on-one.

"Bro, he's not worth it," Austin said. "Don't." Austin had about twenty pounds on me, and there was no way I could twist out of his grip. Then, a different grip seized my arm, as Coach Dad dragged Carter and me towards the sideline.

"Sit." He pointed at a metal bench.

Ben withered in the grass, blood gushing from his face. Our trusty sideline fans stared at the scene in horror. The scouts stood by the referee, waiting for a verdict. I couldn't bear the look on Eliza's face.

My dad, L-W's mid-seventies grandpa coach, and the referee huddled on the other sideline. The ref held up his hands as if he were being arrested, and L-W's coach went berserk. His face puffed bright red, and he basically wheezed as he stammer-screamed at the referee.

"Never in m-my forty years of-of coaching—"

We missed the rest of it because my dad was heading back over. "You're in luck." He said. "The referee didn't see it."

What?! How could he not have seen it? He was looking right at us!

The referee was busy staving off legal threats from L-W's

coach, and a funny feeling struck me. Maybe, just maybe, that referee felt guilty about the time Ben had punched Carter in the face and he'd let it slide.

"He didn't see it," my dad said warned, "but the scouts sure did. I'm going to see if I can undo any of your idiot damage with them, and you'd better pray it works. If I ever see anything like that from you girls again, you will be off this team faster than you can say 'retribution.'"

The ref blew his whistle. Austin and two sophomores somehow stole the ball from Ben, only for Austin to stumble over the ball and lose possession.

The confused crowd began to cheer again, accepting that they would have no idea what happened. Nervous energy weakened my knees as I dreaded having to explain it later.

"Ben Johnson is a goddamn tool." Carter spat on the grass.

"What a loser," I said.

"Thanks, Mags. Nice to know someone else cares about my sister as much as I do."

"No worries. I've known her as long as I've known you."

Carter nodded towards the scouts. "You know they were coming today?"

"Nope. No one ever tells me anything."

Carter leaned onto his arms, trying to stay stretched for if we ever got put back in the game. "That's probably why your dad put you on defense, you know."

"What?"

"He knew he'd put you back on offense for the second half. Then the scouts would get to see you be a team player, and we'd suddenly not suck."

"We did not suck," I said. "You scored, bro."

"Still. You know I'm right."

Goosebumps sprouted on my arms as the guilt set in. The entire time I'd been on defense, I had only cared about making myself look good in front of the scouts. I hadn't been a team player at all—not like I needed to be.

Especially not to Carter.

■

Coach Dad put us back in for the nail-biting end of the game—apparently the scouts wanted to see more. I scored another goal with an assist from Carter and Austin to win the game 3–2. The scouts even shook my hand afterwards, saying they would be in touch.

"Atta boy, Nicky," my dad said as the scouts packed up. "That was a hell of a game. Best I've ever seen you play."

"Thanks, Dad."

"Proud of you." He patted my back, then went off to be congratulated by everyone's parents.

My dad.

Just talked about his feelings.

Carter and Austin hung with a group of girls near the unused bleachers. Because where else would they be?

"Nick! You were awesome!" Hannah squeezed me in a hug.

"Right cross could use some work," said Eliza. Her yellow hair brushed my cheek as she gave me a hug too. She silently laughed into my chest and I melted.

"Victory party at my house!" Jeff Karvotsky shouted. As it was a Friday night, we'd expected some kind of party, especially if we won.

"Why not?" said Carter. "We have a lot to celebrate. You ladies want to come?" He turned to Hannah and Eliza. Mostly Hannah.

"I'll have to check my schedule . . ." said Hannah. Carter all but begged her to come after that.

"You still grounded, superstar?" asked Eliza.

"After absolutely demolishing L-W? Doubt it." I'd have to double check with my mom, but I gathered that after that game my dad would throw me a bone.

On the walk back to the locker room, Austin's footsteps came up behind me. "Stop by before the party, Nick," he said. "Don't forget."

I kicked the ground in front of me like there was an imaginary soccer ball. *Like I could possibly forget about that.*

Elizabeth A. Seibert

A BRO SHALT NOT USE THE *L* WORD UNTIL HIS CHICK DOES. HE SHALT NOT EVEN THINK IT.

I'm not superstitious. At all. When people say Friday the thirteenth, I think of a crappy movie where the blond girl dies first. I think that's because my dad started showing me horror films when I was five, and he'd always point out the fake blood and clichéd plot lines. But as I got in my car to drive to Austin's house, it started to pour, when the sky had been nothing but sunny all afternoon.

It was hard not to see that as an omen.

I strutted up to Austin's front door at 8:15 p.m. As a general rule, I never get to Austin's house on time. He runs fifteen minutes later than normal human beings, meaning my 8:15 is his 8:00.

We'd discovered that Austin always runs precisely fifteen

minutes late back in eighth grade when surprise birthday parties were still a thing. It was June 10, my fourteenth birthday, and Carter and Austin had gotten our friends together to surprise me. They told everyone to be at Carter's house by 6:30 and they told me to get there at 6:45. I got there the same time as Austin, who was carrying a colorful net of balloons and a present wrapped in newspaper. I wasn't very surprised when I walked into Carter's dining room and everyone jumped out.

The doorbell dinged and Austin answered it after about forty seconds, about how long it takes to save a *COD* game. He gave me a quick "'Sup, man?" and led me to the basement, a.k.a. his man cave. Austin's house was bigger than mine, but still about half the size of Carter's. Austin's basement was a lot nicer than mine, though, seeing as he actually had one. He had a TV the size of a fluffed-up golden retriever, a foosball table, and a poker table with chairs around it. It wasn't Carter's A-lister movie theater basement, but it was a solid place to chill.

Austin tossed me a root beer from a mini fridge and we sat at his empty card table, as if we were in some secret meeting. Although his well-lit basement wasn't your typical drug dealer, mob boss hangout setting, it was not a bad place to hide a body.

"I take it Carter doesn't know?" Austin spoke first. "To get the obvious out of the way."

It hadn't occurred to me to lie to him. The secret was out.

"My nose isn't broken, so no."

"Too bad, you could've used the plastic surgery." Austin took a long sip of his root beer, with an even longer belch at the end. "How long have you two been getting cozy?"

"A month, maybe."

"Damn, Maguire. Lying to your bro's face for a month? Cold."

"Lay it on me," I said. "Don't hold back. Won't be half as bad as when Carter finds out."

"Who else knows about you guys?"

"Madison," I said reluctantly.

"Madison?" Austin clapped. "You must have some serious dirt on her, for her to not tell anyone."

You mean that she's in love with Carter?

Seriously, Nick. You're screwing over all of your friends.

I had to tell him.

"She wanted my help with trying to date Carter."

"No way. I thought I was her second choice, after you."

"Apparently half of why she was with me was to get to Carter."

Austin grinned, his eyes shining through his thick glasses. "And now it's my turn to be used. I'll definitely take it. That girl . . ."

If I hadn't known him better, I'd have thought Austin was catching feelings. He cleared his throat.

In the hour between the soccer game and my drive to Austin's house, I'd been mentally preparing myself for this meeting. I'd predicted two possible outcomes:

Worst-case scenario:
Austin starts hating me.
Austin tells Carter about my relationship with Eliza.
Carter starts hating me.

Best-case scenario:
Austin and I are still bros.
Austin tells Carter about my relationship with Eliza.
Carter and I are still bros.

It'd never crossed my mind that Austin might not tell Carter about Eliza and me. Austin was a bro to each of us, but this was too big for both of us to keep a secret, since Carter had specifically forbidden it.

"You get that I have to tell him, right?"

And there it was.

The chair squeaked as I leaned back. I tipped the front two legs at a perfect 110-degree angle, showing Austin how it was done. Like a boss.

"Can I tell him?" I asked. "I think it would be better if it came from me."

"That is an understatement," he said. "That's pretty much the only way you guys might still be able to stay friends."

"What I don't get," I said, "is why this is such a big deal to him. You dated her. Why won't he let anyone else?"

He took off his dark Yankees cap and threw it on the table, exposing his thick, black hair. Other than the cap smacking the table, the only sound in his house was the hum from the mini fridge. That wasn't unusual; his parents were probably where my dad was: watching sports at Robert Maxin's dad's house.

"He didn't, actually. Carter was really mad about it. Eliza wanted to go out with me, and there wasn't anything he could do that would change her mind, and he got used to the idea. He and I weren't really that tight when I was dating her. I think that's one of the reasons she and I eventually broke up. Well that and the fact that we both started liking other people, and I realized I'm not a relationship kind of guy. But the thing is, Nick, you're going to have to choose between Carter and Eliza. When I dated her, he didn't look at me the same. Not until we broke up, and now we're besties again—before, it was like I wasn't really there.

It's not inevitable, though there's definitely a chance that if you date Eliza, you'll lose Carter for a long time. Especially since you went behind his back."

"Carter still acts weird about your history with her, though. He won't even acknowledge that you guys dated."

Austin fidgeted with his fingers over the table. "There's a reason Carter wishes he could forget it. You don't want to hear this, bro."

The root beer cooled my lips and I pressed the can against my chin, like it could be a buffer between us. Like it could shield me from this conversation.

"Now you have to tell me."

"Yeah."

A calmness filled the room, the way sometimes people know something bad is going to happen right before it does. I still wanted to know.

"I," Austin started, "ugh, this is hard."

"Can't be as bad as when Jenny Martin dumped trash all over my car after we stuffed crickets in her locker, and you had to break the news to me."

"Worse," he said, "I went too far with Eliza. In, like, the bad way."

"Too far, like . . ." blood rushed to my ears, drowning out the humming from the fridge. I had to focus to hear him.

"No. Not all the way."

"In her pants, though?"

"Yeah."

Words clumped in my throat, unable to escape. This was starting to sound familiar.

"Remember that party they had two years ago? The one that

the cops came to and Ms. O'Connor had to call all her favors in so Carter wouldn't get in trouble?"

I nodded.

"It was during that. Jamal brought tequila. Eliza only took one shot, so I thought she was okay, but all of a sudden she wasn't. She must've drunk something before that too."

The ceiling fan seemed to pulse, as lightheadedness came over me.

I nodded.

"Right," said Austin. "Jamal told that dumb story about that one time at band camp, you know about the . . ." he made a crude gesture. "Then I joked about being a little dry down there myself, we'd never done anything like that before, and someone suggested she do something about my situation, and we went up to her room."

"That was two years ago? She was a freshman."

"I know."

"Geez."

"Carter found us up there. Eliza was in tears from doing something she didn't really want to do, and to this day I don't know why I didn't stop. Carter swears she doesn't remember it, but we couldn't come back from that."

Oh, she remembered it all right.

"And Carter didn't kill you?"

Austin shook his head. "No. That was the night of Sarah Rosen."

"So?"

"So," Austin said, "he was dealing with his own crying girl."

"Oh, damn." *Carter must have done exactly the same thing.*

Dizzy nausea threatened my every breath. My hands and feet felt hot, like an invisible fire fed off my extremities.

Elizabeth A. Seibert

"Where was I during all of this?" I asked.

"No idea."

The blood pounding in my mind grew louder, taking over my thoughts.

"Why didn't anyone ever tell me? We've made fun of Sarah so many times, neither of you ever said it wasn't—" I stopped.

What she wanted.

We both knew the answer. *Carter.* It was something Carter would never talk about. And now I knew why.

"I cannot believe Carter forgave you for that," I said.

"That's what the Bro Code is," he said. "And that night fell under it. We had to stick together on this. No matter the circumstances."

Bros before hoes.

"This is fucked-up."

"I know," he said. "Like, some guy made a sexist mandate because he was scared of ending up alone."

"Blasphemy from Austin Banks? Never thought I'd hear anyone say that about the Bro Code, especially not you."

"I literally got that from your AP psych outline."

"What?"

"Yeah, dude. When you had to take notes on whether Freud was legit or lonely. And how he didn't think being gay was normal because really he could've been struggling with being gay himself. All he actually had to do was accept himself and he would have been a lot nicer to the gays. Did you really forget that?"

Of course he had to bring freaking Freud into it.

"Look out, world," I said, "Austin Banks has learned something."

He tapped the side of his head. "All in here."

Wait. *If Austin made that connection about Freud . . . and Austin basically makes infinite gay jokes, does that mean . . . ?* Austin sipped his root beer while I digested our conversation. I gave a low whistle, shocked, my mind reeling to ask him.

I didn't. He probably wasn't gay. It was just something he'd learned. Right?

There were two kids at North Cassidy who had come out as being bisexual, and another two who'd come out as LGB . . . letters. Yeah, it's 2020 and I need to know the letters. I'll get there, okay? Here's why I've done a stupid job learning the letters and whatever so far: North Cassidy was 90 percent white, 8 percent Asian, and the last 2 percent anything else. The town liked to make up for that by having a "diversity day" at school every year, which was always awkward because, for that one day, everyone sucked up to the three black kids at our school, one of whom was Jamal. Shoot, I mean African American. I'll get there too. Diversity Day crammed an entire population's history into half-hour presentations about political correctness. And when you skip the presentations to go hook up with Madison Hayes in the student parking lot, well. Diversity Day obviously failed me. That, and I personally never needed to know the terms because I don't wake up every day having to get dressed with any other label than "white, straight, male."

Neither do my friends.

And neither do the majority of my classmates.

Until yesterday, when Eliza called me on my everyday lingo in the pool, I didn't know how legit hostile the world can seem for anyone who isn't *exactly* a straight, white, bro.

Or maybe I just didn't care.

Back to Austin.

I'd known Austin since the kindergarten playground, and it had never occurred to me that he might have been struggling with stuff. I just hoped things hadn't been too hard for him. And I hoped I hadn't made them that way.

"Dude," Austin said, "I'm not *gay*."

"I figured." Heat filled my cheeks. *Oops.* "You know you could tell me if you were, though, right?" *Yeah.* I had absolutely no idea how to navigate this conversation.

"Sheesh, Mags." His can cracked as he smoothed the metal with his fingernail. "For someone who hates putting labels on things, you sure love to put labels on things."

"Whatever," I said. The closest I'd get to *sorry*.

Austin started laughing. "You should see your face. You look like you swallowed a pregnant cow."

"How would you know what that looks like, dude?"

He gulped down the last of his soda. "Ah, wow. This is hilarious. I'm so glad you came over tonight."

"Yeah, well, I've had a lot to take in," I said. *Good job, Nick. There you go. Speak.* "Just let me know if you ever need me to talk about different stuff, or like, help you in a different way."

That had sounded better in my head.

Austin grinned and I closed my mouth. "No," he said. "Keep it up, really. This is going better than I could have thought."

My chair landed back on the carpet with a thud. "What do we do now?'

Austin's fingers cracked as he stretched them. "You stuck around when I was cut from soccer in the seventh grade. When I was at the bottom of the totem pole, you practiced with me for a month, every day after your own practice, and got the coach to give me a new tryout. When I dated Eliza, you were still around even when Carter would barely talk to me, and you didn't punch me in the face right now when I told you about the party. I'm sticking around for you. It doesn't matter to me who you date. Well, that's a lie," he laughed, "if you started things back up with Madison, I might fight you here and now."

"I think you're safe, man," I said, "and I still haven't decided about punching you." *Or Carter. What is the playbook for what to do after your best friends seriously mess up?*

"Fair. When are you going to talk to Carter?"

"I guess tomorrow. We can celebrate tonight. But, might as well get this over with, right?"

"Good luck."

"Thanks."

The table creaked, wobbling as Austin pushed it to stand up. "Who's D-D'ing this thing? Cause it's definitely not you or me, after this chat."

"Hannah," I said. "We're meeting her at the OCs' and she's driving all of us."

At least, that's the last I heard.

"Robert Maxin's Hannah?"

"Correct."

"Damn. Carter's cold too."

"No kidding," I said. "I still can't believe you guys didn't tell me about Sarah."

"I can't believe you didn't tell me about Eliza."

The basement stairs thudded as we ran up them. A slam from Austin's door and a crackly engine later, Austin sat shotgun as I pulled out of his driveway.

"Are you really surprised I didn't tell you?" I asked.

"Nah. I get it."

He texted Carter and Eliza that we were on our way. Twenty minutes later, Austin and I stood in Carter's room, watching him change shirts six million times. (Confirming everything we'd thought about him and Hannah.)

"What about this one?" he said, pulling a black long-sleeve over his head.

"Good too," said Austin.

"I liked the last one better," I said.

"Really?"

Carter had the shirt halfway over his head before I said, "Nah. Go with the black."

"Get outta here, Mags," joked Carter. The shirt settled nicely on his arms. "Great. Now we gotta do shoes."

"I'm gonna get some air," I said, slipping through the door. I had to find Eliza and fill her in on my talk with Austin. The stairs creaked as I jogged to the second floor, wondering what I could possibly say to her. I didn't want to lose either one of them.

"Nick!" Eliza answered her door and pulled me into her bright, cheery room.

"Whoa."

It looked like a hurricane had hit her room, followed by a stampede of elephants and four typhoons. Piles of clothes spilled all over the floor, like she was trying to sort through them, and her drawing paper was *everywhere*: on top of the clothes, on her desk, and scattered in miscellaneous corners of the room. All of it was very un-Eliza.

She wore jeans and a tank top, looking ready for a casual party, and had clearly been ready hours ahead of Carter. She resumed her spot, drawing, sitting cross-legged on her comforter with a clipboard and oil crayons. I climbed next to her.

"Are you redecorating?"

"I wanted to do a still life. Of my room being messy. My room's *never* messy," she said. "And that's kind of the point of the drawing."

"Very meta," I said. The headboard felt cool against my neck as I leaned against it. When I stretched out my legs, our knees almost touched.

"Mrs. Davies, my art teacher, is trying to get us all to enter this showcase thing. I'm trying to practice my still life, so it looks more like I tried, and less like I was having a seizure while I was doing it."

The page on her clipboard was mostly blank. She'd sketched her metallic drawing table, which looked exactly like it was supposed to. The shading and coloring were perfect. Better than anything I could have tried.

"You'll do great. You're probably about one drawing away from an invitation to repaint the Sistine Chapel."

"You're my friend, Nick. You're supposed to say that."

"Check and check." I brushed her ankle, with the tip of my finger.

"How's your night been?" she asked.

"You want the raw version or the sugar-coated version?"

Her crayon slipped, sending a purple streak across her page.

"What do you mean?"

Might as well give it to her straight.

"Austin saw us at the pool."

The crayon hit the only part of her floor that wasn't covered with clothes.

"What?"

"He was ready to go swimming and saw us. Before this he asked me to come over so we could talk about it."

She stood. She treaded through her scattered shirts.

Elizabeth A. Seibert

"What happened?"

"He's going to let us tell Carter."

"Oh, phew. That's not that bad."

She picked up the crayon from the floor. I took the moment when she wasn't looking at me to punt into the darkness.

"He doesn't think you remember what happened at Carter's party two years ago."

Eliza squatted on the messy floor with her face in her hands.

"Oh, thank goodness," she said.

"Why is that *thank goodness*?"

The bed bounced as I got up. Eliza shivered when I crouched beside her, pulling her into my chest.

"It's just so awkward."

My legs ached as we squatted, but Eliza buried into me. Her cinnamon scent burned into my skin.

"The story at the pool—"

"That actually did happen to one of my friends," she said. "And it happened to me too, yeah."

I stroked her hair, the back of her head soft against my hand. She pressed against me. "Are you okay?"

"Uh huh," said Eliza. "The part that really unsettles me is Austin and Carter sweeping the whole thing under the rug so I could never bring it up. And I have no idea what happened with Sarah. Those are the parts I was never okay with."

"I'm sorry, Eliza. I had no idea."

She locked her arms behind my back. "Carter's been trying to make it up to me ever since. Won't talk to me about it. Or talk to Austin. But I can tell he's trying, and I do forgive Austin. He's not there yet, but he's learning. And so am I."

Wow. She was so amazingly strong. I could only hope Carter

could forgive as much as his sister could. That I could forgive that much too. "Thanks for talking to me about it," I said. "I'm going to try and help them not suck, so none of this ever happens again. You've really helped me, um, start to get it."

"You're turning out to not be that bad. A year away from their bullshit helped a lot," she laughed. "Thanks. I'm tougher than I look."

She flexed her biceps.

I wasn't sure if I believed her, but I sure as heck wouldn't pass up an opportunity to tease.

"Oh yeah?" I said. "We doing a gun show?" I pulled my arm out of my sleeve and flexed, lining up my arm next to hers. "If you keep eating your green beans, you might get halfway there."

She brushed my shoulder, her hand finding mine, like our wrists were magnetized. "Remind me why I let you come over?"

"Because deep down inside, Eliza, you find me utterly irresistible."

Her breath tickled my ear. "You're one comment away from having your visiting privileges revoked."

"I guess we should stop talking, then," I said.

She lightly punched my chest, coming in for another hug.

The rain puttered on the roof. As her warmth melted into me, I lay my face in her hair, feeling lucky. Having this much trust for each other, so fast, was both exhilarating and terrifying. The best part was, she didn't want to hang out with me because my name was Nick Maguire, or because I played soccer, like Madison or anyone else had. For whatever reason, she genuinely liked me.

"Tell Carter in the morning?" she proposed. "That way if he murders you, I'll still have gone to a party with you with you at least once."

"Deal."

She kissed my cheek. "Think he's done picking out his clothes?" I nodded. "Time to rock 'n' roll."

■

Squeezed between Austin and Eliza, I tried not to say anything dumb as Hannah drove us to Jeff's party. Carter had taken shotgun, even though Austin had called it. Instead, Austin, Eliza, and I took turns tapping Carter's shoulder and having him guess who did it.

Jeff's Karvotsky's house made the night better. I didn't know where his parents were, but wherever they were, it wasn't there. Which made us start to respect Jeff. Getting your parents to leave your house when they know you're having a party is no easy feat. Jeff had finally stepped into bro-zone.

"Wazzup?" Austin shouted into the living room. After one step inside, I already recognized a sea of faces: the entire soccer team had showed, plus a decent number of the juniors and seniors. Jeff greeted us.

"We got drinks in the kitchen, games in the basement, and the chill room *est ici*," he told us. Jeff was the kind of nerd who took French in middle school instead of Spanish. Since he was providing this rager, we let it slide.

Jeff pointed to Hannah and Eliza. "Ladies, hats *sont là-bas . . .*" he pointed to a bin next to the couch filled with paper pointed party hats.

"Oooooh." I hip-checked Eliza as she reluctantly went over to it.

All small towns have traditions, and the tradition for the Cassidy High School house parties was this: everyone who wasn't explicitly invited had to wear a party hat. And then if you were caught as a crasher and you weren't wearing your hat . . . you had to drink a mixture of whatever the host wanted.

"What are the games?" I asked.

"T or D, something with pong."

I searched for Carter, my built-in beer/water-pong partner—the beverage didn't matter, we were in it to win it—but he was already beelining for the kitchen.

"Yo, Carter!" I shouted. "You in?"

He looked between me and Hannah, who was securing her pink party hat, and shrugged. *Forget it.* I turned to the girl next to me, who had her hands in her pockets, fidgeting.

"Want to come downstairs?" I asked.

Eliza's sparkly gold hat nicely complemented her blond hair. "These hats look stupid," she said. "Also, I don't drink anymore. Not since Carter's party."

"Understood, and you look amazing." My heart surged. For some reason, Eliza straight-up telling me she was not about the peer-pressure, partying life made her that much more attractive. Probably because I was the exact opposite of being a role model.

Hey, maybe opposites do attract.

The basement's lights were off. Instead, there was a green strobe that flashed to Jeff's rap music. Huddled together were even more of my teammates, fellow students, and Austin's new favorite topic: Madison Hayes.

"Hey, handsome." She smiled, wearing a leopard-print party hat. I wondered if she'd brought it herself. She nodded to Eliza, then leaned in to whisper in my ear, "Happy to see things are working out. Too bad I'm working on our deal by *myself*."

"You're kidding, right?" Austin was damn near crazy about her. She stalked off anyway.

"She's the worst," said Eliza. "Sorry, I know you're friends. She gets under my skin."

"Never said we were friends," I replied.

"Gross."

I stretched, able to lay my palms flat against the bumpy ceiling. "How do you think I felt about you hanging out with Daley?"

"Touché."

On the periphery of the room, freshmen finished their game of pong. They weren't doing too well, and the crowd gathered around us was probably somewhat relieved when I stood up to the plate.

"Who's next?" I asked. "Anyone who thinks they can match this squad?" I patted Eliza's party hat.

"You bet," came Austin's voice. He had his arm wound around Madison and pulled her over. She pouted, clacking her nails against the ping-pong table. I wondered if she was truly angry that I hadn't helped her with Carter more. Though to be fair, she'd barely helped me with Eliza. She'd basically sabotaged it.

"Oof. We could not have asked for a better team to play for your first time. Austin and Madison are totally hopeless at this game."

"Daaaaamn," Austin called out. "Shots fired. Too bad you're going be hammered by the end of this game, y'all."

"Nah." I searched for some new, germ-free cups. "We are playing with H_2O. If you want a drink, hold one in your hand. Don't want anyone getting arrested like last time."

"I always did love a man who took charge," Austin called back.

"Aaaaand Austin owes us pizza," I said.

Some freshman handed us drinks to hold while playing with the water. Eliza handed hers to me, unopened.

"What's this?" said Madison. "Little Miss Perfect isn't going to play the game?"

"It's fine, Madison," said Austin. "We're here for fun."

"No. I want to know why she won't play the way you're supposed to."

Austin and I lined up the cups to start the game, the goal of which was to throw the ping-pong balls into the cups, each team taking turns, until the first team to hit all the cups won. Before I could shoot my ball to start, Eliza pulled it from my hand.

"Nope. Ladies first. Let's go, Madison. Me and you."

My lips hung apart. Austin jumped with excitement. Madison took the white ball from Austin. Neither girl said anything as they took their shots. Eliza sunk hers easily in a red cup in front of Austin. Madison's bounced off a rim from our stack, and Eliza jumped to catch it before Madison could take it back.

Madison drank from the can in her hand. Eliza, since she'd recovered Madison's ball, got another shot. She lined it up and it splashed in.

"What?!" I shouted. "I thought you said you'd never played this before!"

"I said I didn't want to drink."

It took every ounce of my self-restraint to not kiss her.

Eliza and I missed a few shots through the game, though not nearly as many as Austin or Madison. I hadn't been kidding when I said they were a good team to play against, because they were terrible.

When Eliza and I had beat them by several cups, Austin let out a low whistle. "Good game. Don't think I've been creamed

Elizabeth A. Seibert

that bad in this game . . . ever. Those O'Connor genes, dude." He shook his head.

"You might want to eat some food, drink some water, or sit down somewhere," I teased them.

"That rocked," said Eliza.

"You, uh, get a little competitive there?" I grinned. "Austin and Madison never saw that coming."

Eliza wrinkled her nose.

We stepped to the wall to let the next group play. Eliza grabbed a soda can, and I slowly drank from my, um, not soda.

"There something going on between you and Madison I don't know about?" I asked. We leaned against the basement wall, half watching the next game at the ping-pong table.

"Not really."

"That's fine," I said, "Madison has trouble getting along with other girls."

"Can't imagine why," said Eliza.

I didn't take the bait. True, Madison could be awfully overbearing, dramatic, and rude. She was hot, though, and a lot of guys liked her. But Eliza was so much more. In every department.

The thing people didn't really get about Madison was that she was exactly like Austin and I were, or at least I was before Eliza, kind of. She didn't want *a* boyfriend, just boy*friends*. Lots of them. North Cassidy could forgive bros for that lifestyle, but not Madison. Especially when she rubbed her will to do whatever she wanted in the world's face like she was starring in a soap opera.

"She's hard to compete with," said Eliza.

"She's not competition," I murmured. Our shoulders brushed and God, did I want to pull her close to me.

We were still surrounded in a crowd, with some people trying to get closer to the game table and some people trying to join a different game. A large circle on the other side of the room formed where Carter and Hannah were sitting. I took a step towards that, but Eliza grabbed my finger.

"I'm sorry," she said, "you probably think that's crazy clingy. The Nick Maguire I know hates clinginess. I do too," she spoke quickly, like she couldn't get the words out fast enough, like she was afraid I would interrupt her. It was more babbling that I'd ever heard from her before. And I loved it.

"The thing about Madison is I can't stand thinking about her being with you. I can't stand thinking about me not being with you. I care about you and this way too much, and I don't want her to ruin it." She looked everywhere except for me, and I heard it in her voice. *It.*

"None of that seems crazy. I feel like that too," I said.

I'm falling in love with you.

Those words shocked me as I thought them.

What, Nick? Every voice in my head swarmed, confused, trying to figure out what that meant. It was too soon. Too fast. Too much.

You're not in love, Nick, my brain protested, *You're just happy.*

But this wasn't about me. It was about her, and how I always hoped to make her feel special. And safe. Especially safe.

"I couldn't stand not being with you either," I said. *I love you.*
"I—"

I almost told her how I felt. I probably would have, if Carter and Hannah hadn't called us over.

Eliza headed towards her friends, who were apparently all waiting for us.

I would have told Eliza if I hadn't let her walk away from me and into the circle with Carter, Hannah, Robert (obviously), Austin, Madison, Jeff, and a few juniors.

The words unsaid left a strange taste in my mouth. Like soy sauce mixed with Diet Coke.

"Lezzgo, Nick," Jeff called. "We're playing spin the bottle."

Eliza took a little stutter step, but Hannah already tugged her hand, making space (by inching closer to Carter) for Eliza to sit next to her. Carter sighed when he saw that Eliza would be playing the game and looked at Austin and me as if to communicate that as far as she was concerned, we weren't there.

If I'd ever asked for proof that the universe hates me . . . well, there it was.

"Come on, Nick," said Jeff, "We're waiting."

"This isn't really my game," I answered. *Let's go*, I tried to signal to Eliza.

"That's a lie," said Carter.

I debated leaving Eliza there. She was a big girl, and I had other people to talk to. We didn't have to be everywhere together.

"Mags, you know we can't play without you," said Austin, "Everyone wants to kiss Nick Maguire."

"Aaaaand Austin owes us pizza," said Carter.

Austin just laughed.

"Two pizzas," I corrected. "One from earlier." I took the space between Jeff and one of the girls I'd seen around but didn't really know. Though I should have, since she might have been at our soccer game? I forget.

There was no way this would end well.

First, the group itself had some really weird mojo, where Carter was with Hannah, even though he swore it wasn't going to happen. Madison kept staring at them, looking like she was going to have a panic attack. Austin kept staring at *her* and look-ing like he might panic himself.

Also, spin the bottle is a stupid game for sixth graders. It's basically a recipe for mono. Like, freaking go ask the girl out that you want to kiss. It's not that hard.

Jeff clapped so loudly and enthusiastically, it was clear that having us here meant a lot to him. *This better not ruin my life, Karvotsky.*

A guy can dream, right?

We started out with just the cheek. Jeff went first, it being his party and all, and landed on some junior girl I didn't really know. I think. I wasn't really paying attention.

Then Austin's bottle landed towards some other girl and Madison didn't even flinch. A second, sinking feeling added to my mix of wary emotions. The voodoo in the room was palpable.

Pretty soon, Madison gave a dramatic yawn. "Boring. Let's kick it up a notch *PLEASE*. Lips, three seconds."

I actually scooched back, trying to sneak away, when Robert Maxin grabbed onto my ankle. "If I have to be here, you have to be here," he said.

"Boooo," I said.

Jeff went first again. He spun the glass bottle, and everyone did this whole drum roll to play it up and make it even more suspenseful. It landed on me.

Laughter erupted from the group and spectators, and I got that sneaky feeling that takes over my every impulse whenever a big group gives me its undivided attention. I looked at Jeff and puckered my lips. "Ready when you are."

Austin got on his knees. "Nick has to buy pizza now!"

"Why you gotta assume I was joking, Austin? I think that's back to *you* buying pizza."

Austin started to protest, but the group shut him down. Through the commotion, I almost forgot to feel nervous, and Jeff backed away, grinning. Then it was Hannah's turn, and she definitely rigged it. Because it landed on Carter, and he was sitting next to her, and it's really hard to get the bottle to land on someone next to you.

Crap, I thought, why hadn't I sat next to Eliza? The one person I didn't want my spin to land on.

Carter leaned to meet Hannah halfway. Robert watched them in total suspense, as if he were frozen in time. I looked over at Madison and saw that she did too.

Damn it. Poor Austin.

Carter and Hannah legit had the steamiest three seconds ever. I had to join in when everyone was calling out and hollering about the kiss. *Get it, Carter,* I thought, kind of glad for him. Especially when they sat back, and he had this stupid smile like the luckiest guy in the Milky Way (no, not the candy bar).

Madison and Robert were the only two who didn't join in the hype.

The next few rounds were less exciting, except when a few girls got each other and decided to go for it. When it was my turn to spin, everyone did the same thing with the drum rolls and the cheering. A bunch of the girls in the circle perked up, and I honestly couldn't think of a best-case scenario. Maybe it would have been landing on Madison, since people would get over that pretty quickly. I had a 1/16 chance of landing on the worst possible person.

The bottle slowed down, inching its way towards Eliza, and as it was about to go to the next person, it swung back to her. Like a magnet—which hadn't happened to anyone else, and I had to wonder if someone sabotaged it that way. Or maybe it was fate.

Eliza went white. Carter shrugged, like it was a nonissue. Like he knew, of course, I wasn't going to kiss his sister. But I had to act "normal" around her. The way Carter was expecting.

"It's your lucky day, sweetheart," I grinned.

"What? *Oh.* Ha, you wish." She backed away.

Carter pushed me the bottle. "Spin again."

"No no," Madison called. "That's not how the game works." Madison had remained mostly silent after the Carter/Hannah thing, but now she had something juicy to live for again.

I pointed to Jeff, who could clearly see Carter's reaction. "House rules," I said, "What's the move here, Karvotsky?"

Carter relaxed, as if he knew that obviously Jeff would take his side.

Madison ruffled her hair, in total control of the situation. It seemed like she wasn't vindictive enough to out my secret by shouting it. Not yet. She was waiting for something. And I had no doubt in my mind that she would make me pay for Carter being with Hannah and not her, even though that wasn't my fault.

"I'll sub in," she said.

Austin took a long swig of his drink.

"Sure," said Jeff, relieved that he was no longer in charge of this game that he obviously rarely played. Bless his heart. "That's a good rule. First person to call in for a sub gets to do it. Perfect."

Madison went on her knees. Eliza picked at the carpet, determined not to watch this. We had a deal that we would tell Carter tomorrow.

Which, apparently, right now, meant this.

Madison shuffled closer to me, brushing into Carter on her way.

She looked over her shoulder at Eliza. "Last chance."

Eliza shrugged like the entire thing was ridiculous. Which it was until Madison sat in my lap and put her arms around my neck.

Our circle, and the excited high schoolers watching behind us, erupted.

Madison shoved her body in my face.

"Wait," said Eliza.

Madison froze, but since her lips were a few inches from mine, only I could see the big, annoying, smile on her face. She had wanted this all along.

The group stared at Eliza, especially Carter, and she glanced purposefully between Austin and Madison. She was trying to pretend she was doing it for Austin, who did genuinely seem upset at Madison's behavior.

Madison moved aside and Eliza crawled over. I tried to Jedi mind read her that she really didn't have to do this, but whatever I did wouldn't have mattered. This was a game between the girls.

"It's fine," Eliza whispered as she leaned in. All she did was press her lips against mine, as awkwardly as she could. No opening, no starting to make out. Three seconds and done. That's what she was going for. Easy. We could do that.

When the three, totally unpassionate seconds were up, Eliza started to pull away, and I—

Yup.

It was all me.

I take full responsibility for it.

It was a stupid reflex.

It.

I *had* to reach for her chin, as if to keep her there. The second my fingers brushed her skin, I realized what I was doing, and brought my hand quickly down.

Eliza pulled away, trying to look shocked. It didn't matter. Because Carter wasn't looking at her. He was looking at me.

All I could feel for her, even though it was the least interesting kiss ever, was total awe, and wanting to protect her, and all the l-o-v-e crap. And I couldn't keep my feelings off my face.

"Aww," Madison cooed. I braced. She turned towards Austin, who lounged like everything was totally normal, and said in a loud whisper, "That was cute. Do you think it was the first time they've done that? I think they look adorable together."

At which point the more excited players of our game started hollering and whooping at me.

"Shut up, Madison," said Eliza.

But I was the one who'd seen Carter's first reaction, before he sat back, expressionless. No matter how we tried to play it, how Madison tried to play it, how Eliza tried to play it, the game was over.

I never thought it would be because of me.

Elizabeth A. Seibert

A BRO SHALT NOT PUNCH ANOTHER BRO IN HIS FACE. ANYWHERE ELSE IS OKAY. JUST NOT THE MONEYMAKER.

The glare on Carter's face could cut a person down to nothing.

For a second, I almost believed he'd let it go and all my anxiety had been a waste. Except that he stood up and stomped over, pushing my shoulder so hard I fell back against the scratchy carpet.

"Outside," he said.

Jeff gasped. Our teammates closed their mouths, and I tensed.

"Carter," said Eliza.

He thudded up the stairs.

"Nick," said Eliza. I was already bouncing after him.

He waited on the Karvotskys' deck. Rain splattered on his face.

The chilly night gave me quick goosebumps, exacerbated by the rain. We were lucky it wasn't snowing, a real possibility this time of year. I slowly slid the screen door closed.

Carter was on the edge of the deck, facing me. "How long has this been going on?"

"Carter—"

"You got a lot of nerve," he said.

This was it, the moment I'd been deliberately avoiding for weeks.

Carter wasn't born yesterday, and intelligence definitely runs in the O'Connor family. He knew what I was doing with his sister. He saw it. He'd caught us right in the middle of everything, of maybe, possibly, falling hard for each other, and there wasn't much else I could say.

"You lied to me."

Only by omission.

"Didn't."

"How long?!" he shouted. "You selfish prick."

My hands began to tremble. "About a month."

Carter didn't reply. I continued, "I didn't follow your directions, Carter. That's not. A. Lie." I stepped to the side, creating some more distance between us.

It didn't work.

He lunged at me. I dodged his right hook in time for it to miss my eye, and instead it sent a searing pain into my jaw. The momentum threw me against the deck's railing and knocked out my breath.

"Carter, *stop!*" Eliza ran behind us, while Austin held Carter back.

Carter shook him off. "Did you know about this?"

When Austin didn't say anything, Carter scoffed. "Don't know why I asked."

Carter stepped back from the three of us, catching his balance on one of the stairs leading to Jeff's backyard.

Elizabeth A. Seibert

"This isn't worth it." Eliza's voice cracked. "Carter, you're being a dick."

"Oh, *I'm* being a dick?" He looked at me, folded against Jeff's house. "That is rich."

My jaw throbbed, the pain building as Carter kept going. "Why couldn't you tell me?" He asked. "Why'd you lie to my *fucking face*?"

Crickets coughed, waiting for me to answer. *Because of this.* "I'm sorry."

The porch lights made Carter's glare even more powerful. "The real irony, Nick? You're the one who always brings up the Bro Code. A real bro wouldn't pick a girl, *my sister*, or otherwise, over eighteen *years* of friendship."

"No, Carter," I said. "A real bro wouldn't make me choose."

Tears rolled off Eliza's chin. "Please stop," she said. "I can't do this, you guys."

"Have fun failing bio. I'm done," said Carter. He turned to walk off the deck. Then out into the driveway. Then off to who knows where.

"Carter." Eliza jumped after him.

He held out his arm. "I said I'm done."

"Why can't you be happy for me?" she cried, and I realized that while I'd seen the O'Connor siblings shout at each other before, I'd never seen either of them cry. "This is a good thing. We can all be happy together."

I still crouched, trying to catch my balance. I wanted to stop him as much as she did. But I couldn't move.

All I could do was play my final card, getting real skin in the game. If Carter could go there, then I could too.

"Sarah Rosen," I called after him.

Austin, Eliza, and Carter each froze. "Don't," warned Austin.

"What?" asked Carter.

"You don't get to lecture me about keeping secrets," I said. "When you weren't *ever* going to tell me what really happened. You can't build a friendship on *lies*."

"Good," said Carter. "You're starting to get it." He stepped back into the shadows. "I'm going to miss hanging out with you, Maguire." Finally, he relaxed his fists. "Always made me look so good."

The entire school watched us from Jeff's kitchen. None of them mattered. The key actors in this little drama were outside. One sobbed, one (me) was sprawled into the railing, one kicked the grass, swearing, and the other had run away. A long shadow stalking off into the night.

Done.

Elizabeth A. Seibert

RULE NUMBER 20

A BRO SHALT NOT COMPLAIN ABOUT WORKING OUT.

I spent the next day in bed. My phone was annoying me with texts and DMs, and I'd thrown it to the other side of the room onto my dirty laundry. Apparently, this was the most interesting gossip to have hit Cassidy High since a few years before when this girl had tried to marry her stuffed animal. Apparently, her parents had officiated the wedding.

Carter had taken it exactly as we'd expected him to, which was why this unfortunate reality was so disappointing. Even though I hated putting this whole situation on Carter, it was his scene that he'd caused and his misery that we were now all living in.

But I was the one who'd pushed him there.

And I was the one who should've known better.

It felt worse than any breakup I'd had. This fight with Carter, it left my heart like a dark bubble camping in the middle of my chest. It hurt to move. It hurt to think. This was truly heartbreak.

Though it could have been the tequila.

"Hey." My dad came into my room. "Let's get up, kiddo."

I put my pillow over my face. Protecting myself from the world with its plushy softness.

"Nick." He fought me for it, trying to pry the pillow out of my cold, dead hands. "Get up."

"No."

"It's three in the afternoon. If you don't eat something soon, you can kiss those six-pack abs good-bye."

I lifted up my cheek. "I don't think that's how it works."

"But do you want to find out?"

He had me there.

I sat up and he tossed me a sweatshirt. He handed me my running shoes and a pair of socks. I groaned.

"Moving's going to be good for you," said my dad. "Endorphins and all that."

I stared at the sneakers he put on my bed.

"Chop, chop. While it's still light out, please."

■

Fifteen minutes later, I ran next to my dad on one of our old routes, a stony path through the woods behind our house. The two of us hadn't gone on a run together for a few years, since his knee had started acting up again. I had to wonder if he'd be able to do this with me, but as I panted like I was about to have a stroke, my dad hadn't broken a sweat.

Elizabeth A. Seibert

After Carter ditched us the night before, Austin and I coped by taking tequila shots and eating mini donuts. I didn't even remember making it home, which meant there was a 100 percent chance my dad knew what I'd been up to. I'd never been good at going that hard and hiding it from my parents.

"I'm going to throw up," I announced, after about three more minutes. My dad didn't stop running. I trailed behind him for as long as I could, until I finally dropped to my knees and hurled my guts out.

"Feel better?" My dad jogged back to me.

"Nope."

"Come here." He extended his arm to pull me up.

"Thanks." I wiped my mouth on my sleeve. "How much trouble am I in?

"Not sure yet," said my dad. He stepped over a rock jutting out of the path and I plodded along beside him. "Your mom was going to ground you, if you were ever actually ungrounded. We're not great at enforcing that, huh?"

Blurry pebbles scattered as we walked.

"Mr. Maxin told us what happened," he said. "Robert tells that guy everything. Not sure grounding you would matter, since you don't have anywhere to go now anyway."

"Gee, thanks."

He hit my shoulder. "Mostly kidding."

We reached a fork in the trail. One side went to this secluded cranberry bog that Austin swore was where ghosts went to swap murder stories, and the other side went to the back of a cul-de-sac. Instead of choosing, my dad turned around, heading back.

"Carter'll change his mind."

"You didn't see him last night," I said.

Except for our slow footsteps, the nature around us was eerily quiet. It was too far into the fall for bugs, and still too early for birds and squirrels to prepare for winter. My dad's uneven walking thumped against the path. His knee was starting to get to him.

"He will," said my dad. "Might take years, though you guys are too close to never see each other again."

"No offense, but you're wrong."

He chuckled. "I want to tell you something."

Awesome. That meant I could focus on trying not to throw up again.

"I've never shared this," he said. "I was waiting for, I don't know. I guess a good moment."

"Okay . . ."

"This guy," my dad patted his knee, his bad one, "wasn't some overuse injury."

He was right that this was a big deal. My dad had spoken about his injury only one time—when I was six and I asked why he never played goalie for me. He'd answered that he didn't want to risk twisting his knee again. *Again?* I had asked. And he told me that a long time ago, he'd twisted his knee and couldn't play soccer anymore. That's why he'd had to quit, even though he'd been really good. Later, from my mom, I found out he was USA National Team–level good, but he'd had to halt his career before he could make it there.

"What happened?"

"'Bout twenty-five years ago. It was a Tuesday. Few weeks after junior year of college. Just started dating your mom."

"Gross."

"Right. Anyways, that day I was supposed to try out for the USA National Team."

What? I had no idea my dad had actually tried out for the team. Everyone had said he got hurt before he actually could. "You did try out for them?"

"I was *supposed* to," he said. "Had my Wheaties that day and everything. Wore my lucky socks. I was too nervous to drive, and your mom volunteered. Got to take the Green Machine." Ah yes, my dad's favorite car: the 1980s Volkswagen. I'd heard countless stories about that car and the trouble my dad had gotten into while driving it.

"What happened to that car anyway?"

"Hang on, I'm getting there," he said. "That day, your mom drove me. Route she'd taken a million times. Thirty minutes out, right on the freeway, easy. About ten minutes in, we got in this huge fight."

"Uh-oh."

"I think it was about something I said. Probably about women drivers. Your mom hates when I complain about women drivers."

"Mom hates when you make sexist comments, period."

"Whatever," said my dad. "We're on the way to the tryout, she's crying—you know how women cry—when this eighteen-wheeler comes out of nowhere. Smashes right in the back of us."

Oh my God.

"The trunk was pushed right into the front. Couldn't tell what was metal and what was us. Next thing I remember was the hospital. Your mom came out pretty okay, crying a lot, though, driver usually gets it much better. My knee'd gotten caught under the dash and didn't untwist for a few days."

His unsteady breathing grew louder. The beginnings of an emotion.

"I'm lucky to still have my leg."

"This is wild," I said. "I had no idea."

This was why my mom had been so freaked out about my car accident.

"Didn't want to scare you," my dad's voice cracked. "It's partly why I was never too concerned with you getting an overuse injury before maxing out your career."

"Shit, Dad."

"The point of my story," he said, "is that even when we were in the hospital room, when a few hours before, your mom had hated me for whatever I'd said about women drivers, in the long run it hadn't mattered. Nothing we could fight about was as big as that crash, which we made it through together. Made everything else a piece of cake. You and Carter have been through too much to not make it."

"Dad," I said, "why are you still saying 'women drivers' like that's a great joke?"

"Well, you know. You get it."

"No. Not really. I know you treat mom well. But the way you talk about women, like calling our team girls when we aren't performing the way you want . . . you can get in trouble for that now."

"No more trouble than a car accident," he said.

I groaned.

That was the truth behind my dad. He blamed how his life turned out on the car accident, and he blamed the car accident on everyone else.

The woods opened to the end of our street, and we reached our house to find my mom on the front porch with a book, watching the cars go by. She waved.

"Nick," said my mom, as I opened the front door. "Clarkebridge called."

I spun on a dime.

She was smiling.

"Full ride," she said, reaching for a hug. "You did it."

I stumbled. "That's . . . wow."

"Congrats, buddy." My mom smelled like fruity shampoo and freshly washed clothes. She held me tightly, the first time she'd hugged me in maybe all of high school.

I wasn't really thinking about what she said.

I was thinking about the one person I'd need to share this news with.

I had to know if he got in too.

RULE NUMBER 21

A BRO SHALT NOT MAKE HIS GIRL CRY.

The first place I went after my mom stopped fussing over me was good ol' Straight Cheese 'n' Pizza. The one thing Mr. Hoover ever managed to teach me was that when you don't sleep enough, or are really stressed out, you start craving fatty and sugary foods—your brain is basically screaming for energy, and fatty and sugary foods are the quickest way to get there. If you get enough sleep and manage stress, it helps with those situations.

I was aware of this, and to Mr. Hoover I say: I really needed the pizza with the mozzarella stick crust. He would know not to mess with me.

The second place I went was the O'Connors' house. I doubted Carter would be there, since when he was stressed, he went to some kind of ninja-training exercise class to get totally swole. Though I wasn't there to see him. Not yet.

I sent Eliza a text as I pulled into her driveway. She sat in their backyard against the oak tree. The perfect hiding place from the outside world, and the perfect place to be alone.

The end of the afternoon loomed overhead, beginning to fade into orange as I came up behind her. Somehow, she seemed comfortable in the mid-November air with a baggy sweater and jeans. Or maybe she simply wanted to feel the cold.

"Hey," she said, focusing on something that was not me. She had her back against the tree, hunched over a spiral notebook.

Her loose hair dangled over her writing, hiding it even as I crouched down. What was the protocol for what to say after you ruin a sibling relationship? Should I try to hold her hand? Is it even right for me to talk first? She wasn't crying, but a sad energy sat on her soundless lips.

I couldn't decide which would have been better: For her to be happy to see me, or sad like she was. Either would make what I was about to do ten times harder. Maybe I would regret this, and I was having a kneejerk reaction, like the other instances when girls and I started to get serious.

I stuffed my clammy hands into the pockets of my jacket.

"There's a rumor going around that we slept together," she said. "Carter believes it. He texted me about whether he should pick up protection. I cannot stand him right now."

"Oh no," I said. "I'm really sorry. Anything I can do?"

"It'd help if you spread that it isn't true."

"On it." Denying rumors wasn't really my M.O. All press is good press, you know? For her, I would make an exception. For Carter too.

"Probably won't change Carter's mind, though."

"Doesn't hurt to try."

The notebook in her lap stuck out like a giraffe in New York

City. I didn't want to pry, but the scribbles at the top of her page screamed at me. "Dear Nick, What keeps sticking out is the first thing you said to me: *Tell me I'm wrong.*" Her arms covered the rest.

"Wrong about what?" I asked.

It was a cold evening, with autumn starting to turn into winter. My fall jacket was on the verge of not being enough to block the cruel temperature.

"Only everything," she said.

"Are you writing me a love letter?" I asked.

"You can't handle a love letter."

"Ha." I stroked the top of her head, dragging my fingers through her hair. It took more willpower than fighting through my dad's sprinting drills to stop touching her and remember why I'd come.

"Um," I started.

Eliza closed her notebook. "It's okay. I know why you're here."

"You do?"

She nodded. "For Carter."

Her full brown eyes met mine, neither of us blinking. "I figured you might react like this, and I get it. But before you end things," she whispered, "and you want to break up or whatever, can you read this?"

I couldn't look away. Not even when she crumpled up a scratchy piece of paper and placed it in my fist. "That's what you're scared of?" I asked. "That after all this, I'd choose Carter?"

She didn't reply.

She didn't need to.

She was right.

"Please read it, okay?" The tree bark cracked as she stood. "I'm going to get another jacket. I'll be right back, and we can talk about it."

I nodded as she stalked off. *I don't know if I can do this . . .* I started to think.

"Get it together, Nick," I whispered. Then I opened up her letter.

■

Eliza took her sweet time inside, because I'd had long enough to read her letter eight or nine times. The sun had disappeared below the thinning canopy of her oak tree when she finally approached. Her letter shook in my hands, from both the cooling temperature and its contents.

"Hi," she said.

"Hi." I stood. Her eyes vacillated between mine, awaiting my verdict. Thinking she already knew what I was going to say.

The note weighed in my palm. I folded it in half, like closing a book.

"You wrote that you think you know what I'm going to do," I said.

Her loose hair floated in the breeze. She studied my sneakers.

"There's a lot you don't know." I stepped towards her. "You don't know how much I think about you. Which has been basically nonstop since forever, and especially since you came back from Australia. You don't know you're the only girl I think about." I took another small step towards her. "You don't know how nervous you make me. How that makes hanging out with you even more fun. You don't know how much I look forward to seeing you, or how I feel like I can tell you anything."

Eliza frowned. "Before you read that, you were going to break up with me."

"Yeah. I was going to take the easy way out," I admitted. "I thought if I were friends with Carter, I could still be friends with you. But I don't wanna be friends. I want to do this thing for real."

She opened her mouth. I kept going. "That grin you mentioned . . . you're the only one I ever want to give it to."

My voice cracked and so did Eliza. She threw her arms around my neck, stuffing her face into my shoulder. Her beautiful smell and warmth enveloped me.

"I—" she started.

"I know you said that wasn't a love letter . . ." I choked.

Her shoulders shook against my chest, and soon her tears dampened my jacket. I squeezed and held her closer.

"Sorry," she said, "I really thought this was it."

Wetness ran down her cheeks and I grinned. "I love you." *I said it.* Excitement shot from my elbows to my knees. "I did it, I finally told you." I fist-pumped into the air. "Hell yeah!"

"I love you too, Nick." Her laugh seeped under my skin. "Ugh, that feels so good to finally say."

Joy twisted our fingers together as she collected her thoughts. "What about Carter, though? I don't want to lose him either."

"Maybe we apologize," I said. "I tell the world I didn't sleep with you. We make it clear that we love him too. And we wait."

"I just . . ." she trailed off. "I want both of you."

"Me too." I pushed my hand through my hair. "I want this. And you. And I hope that's good enough for him."

"I think he just needs time. He'll do the right thing, I know it." Eliza kissed my cheek. "So did I tell you that I love you yet?"

Really stinking cute.

The tree's bark caught my jacket as I backed into it, with Eliza's chapped lips against mine. Breathing my air, Eliza slipped the letter out of my hand, allowing it to flutter to the grass. I didn't need to read it again anyway; its contents had burned into my memory, as the taste of her had, and the subtle sound of her knotting her fingers in my hair.

She pushed her passion into me. We kissed until the sky turned purple, savoring each other until the last ray of sun had set our hearts on fire.

RULE NUMBER 22

A BRO SHALT CHEAT ONLY ON HIS HOME-WORK. NEVER ON AN EXAM, A GIRL-FRIEND, OR HIMSELF.

Things were not the same in the weeks, then months, that followed. Carter had meant it when he said he was done. He began to treat me even worse than we treated the freshmen when we hazed them, like when they would talk to us, and we'd talk over them like we couldn't hear them. When we walked past the froshies in the hall, we would bump into them and pretend they smelled like women's deodorant. It had recently occurred to me that we should stop doing that.

When Carter walked by me in the hall, he didn't react in the slightest. When I started talking at our lunch table, he waited for me to finish, and changed the subject. I would have preferred for him to be blatantly rude.

But *I* was the one who'd broken the stupid code.

Elizabeth A. Seibert

Carter had really put his money where his mouth was too. He'd completely ghosted Hannah and stopped inviting people who weren't Austin, Robert, or Jamal to do anything with him. According to Austin, Carter was more focused than ever on college and had even driven down to Clarkebridge for a pre-med acceptance meeting. I was still studying for the AP bio test, miles away from the program I wanted to attend.

There was that, and then the fact that I now had to do all of my own homework. Austin and Carter still shared their answers with each other, but Austin couldn't give me as many of his. It wasn't that he didn't want to; he didn't have time.

I was starting to get why people say high school is hard.

At least I had Eliza. After the soccer season ended, we'd established her room as our after-school study spot. We were "allowed" to do that because Olivia felt bad for me. (Though her pity cupcakes were almost enough to make me feel normal.) While I poured over my biology textbook, Eliza worked at her drawing table, building her portfolio for art school.

The afternoons always got worse, however, when the back door slammed and heavy feet climbed up the stairs. Carter wouldn't say anything as he passed Eliza's room, where we waited, hoping this would be the day he'd come talk to us. He'd stomp all the way down the hall and slam his door, through which the opening melody of *Fortnite* sang down to us. Eliza always called out a hello and waited for him to say it back. And I always wondered if I should go up there to say something.

Carter never said hello back.

I never went up there to say something.

Sooner than I wanted, the critical day in February was upon us, and my fate was in the hands of the AP bio test. The exam room was a few towns over, and I had to wake up at 5:00 a.m. to not miss it. On a *Saturday*.

I shuffled into the exam room ten minutes before it began, as instructed. It was a stuffy, moldy-smelling classroom, and my head immediately began to throb. The shiny floors made walking in feel like boarding a spaceship, but I managed to show the exam proctor my ID. He was a twenty-something skinny dude that must have been a grad student. His square glasses and ultimate frisbee jersey made him an ultra-nerd. Before, I would have written him off in my book, though after starting to appreciate nerds for their intellect and ability to help me study, I actually began wondering what this guy's deal was. Who was his baseball team? Which *Smash* character did he play?

The proctor pushed me a thick exam packet and a number two pencil. "Fill out your name on the front and don't open it until I start the exam."

Sir, yes sir! I turned to take the one empty seat left in the room (apparently nerds show up on time to things) and stopped cold. There, sitting three rows away, and next to the exact seat that I had to take, was Carter O'Connor.

There were two possible days to take this exam, today and the week after. Of course we'd picked the same day. Why hadn't Eliza warned me that he'd be there? *She probably didn't know*, I thought.

"Hey, man." I plopped the packet on my heavily graffitied desk. "Guess all the studying with me paid off," I tried to joke.

He paused, considering actually speaking to me. Finally, he nodded back. "Good luck."

I bubbled in my name on the exam sheet. I yearned to turn to Carter and start making fun of the exam proctor. I didn't.

"Good morning, everyone," the proctor finally said. "The exam will have four sections, each forty-five minutes. Do not skip ahead to the next section . . ." he rattled off the terms for every standardized test in existence. "Turn off your cell phones. No talking. Your time starts now."

Packets shuffled as everyone raced to begin the first section. I sighed and went to Question #1. My heart pounded in my throat—I had no idea what I was reading. *It's okay.* Deep breaths.

My testmates scribbled in their exam books, well underway with their answers. Carter glanced over. Seeing how nervous I was, he nodded. Either to say I could do it, or to say I was wasting time. No matter, it helped me pull myself back together and begin the freaking test.

■

That. Was. Exhausting. By the end of the three hours, my stomach growled like I was officially starving out of my life, while it was barely lunchtime. I packed up my stuff and turned on my phone to see a few emails and a voicemail from Eliza. While the rest of the test-takers filed out, her message played.

"Hey, superstar." Her voice was loud on the receiver, especially in the mostly empty classroom. "Wanted to say good luck today! So good luck! Love you."

I smiled. That was cute.

Carter stood at the front of the classroom, right by the door, waiting for me.

"You hitting the road now?" he asked.

"Probs. Traffic's gonna suck on the way back."

Carter nodded, like he was in the same boat. "Hey, real quick, want to grab lunch?"

What?

"Yeah," I said, "of course. Where were you thinking?"

Carter led me to a pizza joint next to the school. Because where else could we have our first discussion together in months?

Pizza was the great equalizer.

We each ordered a slice and a Coke. Carter picked out a booth by the window, and I have to say, it felt very *Godfather*-y. This was the part where I was either about to be warned about impending death, or he was about to demand wads of cash.

"I'm going to get right to it," said Carter, looking down at his pizza. He was uncomfortable because he was being direct, but not meeting my eyes. Carter was the OB person who had told me that directness is all about looking someone in the eye.

"I . . ." he searched for the right words, another sign that grabbing me for a quick bite was a total impulse move, ". . . I didn't realize she loved you."

The pizza melted in my mouth. That was not what I expected him to say. "I was shocked by that as well. Given what she knows about me, and all."

Carter nodded. "Do you—"

At the same time I said, "I try—"

We stopped, each gesturing for the other to finish their sentence.

I went first. "I try to give her everything she deserves. So yeah, um. I . . . I love her too."

A few other test-takers scattered into the restaurant, creating enough noise that we wouldn't be easily overheard. Our exam proctor dug into a calzone the size of his head a few booths over. Mad respect.

"I'm sorry I didn't tell you why she and Austin ended, or what really happened with Sarah."

"Super shady," I said.

"Yeah. I don't like the guy who did those things, or the guy who hid it. I'm trying this new thing where I'm not that guy."

"I was always planning to tell you about Eliza," I said. "It was going to be right after Jeff's party. Which, yeah, was a month after it started."

"No kidding. I guess all that happened in the worst way it could have happened. Jeff's party was . . . Seriously though, how does Madison actually end up in the middle of every tiny piece of drama?"

My pepperoni smacked in my mouth. "Honestly, it's impressive."

Carter took a big bite of his pizza, now starting to actually look at me. "That night Austin told you about—with Austin and Eliza, and me and Sarah—I didn't really understand it. Felt guilty, mostly. And a lot of guilt went into protecting Eliza."

He looked away. "I should have trusted you to be with her, but I didn't trust my judgment. And then when I found out you were seeing her behind my back . . ."

"That was the worst way it could have happened," I repeated.

"I talked to Sarah a couple weeks ago."

"Really?"

Grease rolled down Carter's wrist. He ignored it.

"I didn't think I had it in me. Turns out, I was only a blip on her radar. She thought how I treated her was normal."

"Geez," I said.

"I gave her my whole apology anyway. Broke down during it. Maybe now she and I are even. I told her she deserves better. I hope she finds it."

I swallowed. I had always thought that Carter was the best of us. The last few months, not so much, but he'd proven that he was human, and even he makes mistakes. This, however, was next-level Carter. Owning up to his mistakes, respecting people beyond how anyone expected him to, this was Carter all along. He'd just gotten lost for a while.

"Anyways," he continued, "Eliza told me you'd be here today, and that I should be nice to you because she loves you. Today's the first time she's told me that." He paused, "I don't know. Maybe you guys are actually perfect for each other. Eliza deserves the chance to find out."

"Thanks," I started. He wasn't finished.

"It took me longer to come around to whether or not you deserve it. Of course you do, though. I'd made it about me. Since I didn't feel like I deserve another chance with a girl, ever."

"You sound very self-aware about this," I joked.

Carter smiled, somewhat sheepishly. "I've started seeing someone."

"What? Who, Hannah?" As far as I knew, that was long over.

"Nah. Like, a shrink. You know, to unpack all those mommy and daddy issues." He coughed and listened to the bustle of people eating pizza. I stayed quiet, unsure if he wanted to tell me more.

He did.

"Finally aired all the B.S. I've been thinking about my dad," said Carter, "how he actually played into what happened with Sarah, where he abandoned his own family and had no concern for our emotions and treated us and my mom like garbage. I couldn't deal with that. I gave myself so much responsibility to do the right thing, after what he did. Especially when it came to Eliza. I'm starting to be able to weed through it all, though. It's helping a lot."

"Wow." It took a lot of courage to admit to seeing a therapist, and the rest of what he'd said. Especially from a bro. "Good for you."

"Yeah. I'm trying to get Eliza to go too. Anyway, the doc suggested a while ago that the first step in forgiving myself would be to forgive you. So . . ." He held up his soda. "Cheers?"

Grinning, I lifted up my can. "Maybe I should go see this miracle worker."

Carter looked out the window at the high school campus. It was much bigger than ours was, and a lot of students loitered about for a Saturday. "I should've told you I was going to be here today. Would've saved some gas, maybe."

I rested my elbows on the table. "I should've told you a bunch of things," I said. "Now we know."

"Now we freaking know." He crumpled up his greasy napkin and tossed it onto his paper plate. "Anyways, we gotta talk senior pranks," he said, a familiar glint appearing in his eye.

"Ah. The real reason you wanna be BFFs again. I always was the better pranker."

"Dick," said Carter.

"You didn't deny it."

"I'd say we're about even. Which means with our ideas combined, this year could go down in history."

"Fair enough. What are you thinking?"

"Chef Pizzeria," he said.

"Obviously."

"We build a giant pillow fort inside the school and put him at the end. Like a king."

"We dress him in pajamas and give him one of those eye masks," I said.

"Exactly."

"Not bad." I scratched my chin. "I'll raise you one. The pillows are filled with Jell-O."

"Bro," said Carter.

"Bro." I reached for a fist bump.

Our fellow test-takers had begun to file out of the restaurant, and our proctor waved to us as he tossed away his plate. With the noise dying down, Carter's voice lowered.

"You still want to do Clarkebridge's PT program?"

I nodded. "Helping people with their injuries. Giving them hope again. I want to help people, on that level."

Carter leaned back against his seat cushion. "That's what I want to do with pre-med," he said, "I want to be a goddamn superhero. I don't know if she told you, I'm going to Clarkebridge too." He laughed. "They're going to have no idea what hit them."

"If I get into that PT program. That exam was a doozy from hell."

Carter shook his head. "You'll get in. You crushed that exam."

"You know something I don't?"

"I may have sneaked a few peeks, to check on you."

"Do you mean to tell me," I said in a rushed whisper, so no one from the exam would overhear, "That Carter O'Connor cheated?"

"It's not like I copied you. Wanted to check—"

"Sure," I said. "Surrre you didn't."

Carter chuckled; he'd never give himself away. "How sick is it going to be to play soccer there, though? You're on the team, right? PT program or not?"

"Hell yeah."

"Same." He lit up, and I finally, fully recognized the kids from Eliza's letter. The old Carter, and the old me.

"And now we're here," I said. "New team, same digs."

The table clanged as Carter drummed it with his fingers. "Damn, we're gonna be good."

EPILOGUE

"*Cannonball!*"

"*No!!*"

"Stop it!" The girls on the side of Carter's pool shrieked as the splash crashed into them.

Carter surfaced from his jump and doggy paddled through the crowded waters to where Austin and I baked on the pool's edge.

Austin held up nine fingers. "That was solid, dude. But I bet you can beat it."

"Four," I said. "I've seen better."

Carter pushed water at me, splashing my swim trunks. "Whatever."

"Nice try." I adjusted my sunglasses. It was a hot May afternoon, perfect for us and a hundred of our classmates to celebrate our very last day of school together.

"I was going to give it a three," my favorite voice called behind us.

A soft kiss landed on my cheek and Carter stuck out his tongue. "Can you guys stop being adorable, please? It's nauseating."

Eliza slid her arm around my bare shoulders, making my world feel complete again. "Don't hate us 'cause you ain't us."

"The good thing about you being wifed up," said Carter, "is you'll be extra able to wingman for me with the college girls."

"I am the best wingman." Though we all knew Carter wouldn't need one.

"Mags, I can't believe you're giving up college girls before you've even met them," Austin sighed. "No offense," he added as Eliza feigned complete shock.

"Not my fault you blew it in high school." I fist-bumped Eliza. She leaned against my shoulder, relaxing under the sun. A year ago, I'd have agreed with Austin. I'd have said there was no girl who'd be worth basically unlimited girls at college. Now, I knew college girls would be the same as high school girls. Only more of them. And none of them would be as perfect for me as she was. So it didn't matter.

"You're going to bring cupcakes when you come visit though, right?" I asked. "Otherwise we might not have a deal."

"Will you help me?" Eliza said to Carter.

He grabbed my legs and she pushed from behind, launching me into the water. Which, after sitting in the heat for a few hours, felt amazing.

When I came up, Robert and Hannah strode over to us, hand in hand. I elbowed Carter and he sighed. After Carter had decided he didn't really want to try things out with Hannah, she finally gave Robert a shot. My boy must've done all right, because she pretty much never left him alone. Not that he wanted her to.

Behind them, Jamal and Josh Daley waded in the shallow end, taking turns spiking an inflatable beach ball at Madison, who sunbathed on the pool's steps. After the bottle spinning disaster, Austin realized he wanted something from Madison that she'd never be able to give him. Madison had stayed hung up on Carter for a few weeks, until one night she and Josh Daley hooked up and never really stopped. They were good for each other too; both of them had lightened up and become consistent faces in our friend group. Last I heard, Madison and Josh were planning a gap year to bike across Africa.

"Karvotsky's looking for you guys," Robert announced.

"Ooh, yeah." Austin stood. Carter and I pushed ourselves out of the pool.

"We've got to do a thing," I said to Eliza, as Carter scooped up the top-secret notebook from underneath his bright beach towel. For real, the thing even said *Top Secret*.

"Can you tell Olivia to turn up the music?" she asked as we headed away from the pool and into the O'Connors' backyard.

Every year, Eliza and Carter held this huge end-of-school party, which was an even bigger deal this year, because of graduation and everything. Ms. O'Connor had it pretty much down to a science. Snacks by the pool, snacks by the badminton net in the yard, snacks inside—mostly it was a party full of snacks.

She and my mom were in the kitchen at that moment, in fact, making sure the snack situation was under control. My dad was as far away from this party as he could be, since most of the soccer team was there. And his presence would've been weird.

Coach Dad had stopped pushing me as hard after I got my Clarkebridge scholarship. Turned out that when he wasn't spending as much time with me, he could spend more time with my mom. I didn't know whether he'd cleaned up his act with her, but they seemed happy. They hadn't grounded me since Jeff's party either.

They'd been close, however: When Chef Pizzeria showed up covered in Jell-O and pillows in the school hallway, no one knew who the culprits were. My mom even suspected Jamal until pictures made the town newspaper, featuring striped pillowcases that looked suspiciously like mine. She'd yelled at me for half an hour. But with the image of me at college and unable to cause trouble at her house looming in the near future, she ended up just letting it go.

She was the only one. Chef's pillow fort de Jell-O would obviously go down in Cassidy High School's history. The owners of Straight Cheese 'n' Pizza even proudly displayed Chef's newspaper picture on their wall, next to a picture of their three extremely handsome and quite stylish best customers. They never said anything to us, but they knew.

Shrieks from the pool faded as we reached our former soccer teammates by my favorite tree in the O'Connors' yard—the most sacred place Carter and I could think of to do this. Jeff Karvotsky, the new captain, and the youngest ever at Cassidy High, had the troops rallied for us. The guys diligently waited as Carter, Austin, and I pulled them away from the party.

"We got you guys a good-bye gift," said Carter, "because we're the best."

"And because we're going to be way too far away to bail you guys out of trouble," said Austin.

"Not that we would anyway," I added. Even though Carter and I were going to Clarkebridge together, Austin was going to college in Canada. He wanted to try living in another country, though that barely counted. Something about foreign girls.

Carter held out the *Top Secret* notebook like ancient priests held out their scriptures. The underclassmen rolled their eyes at us, like they no longer had time for us anymore. I knew they were anxious to be the big dawgs, but no matter what they said, the three of us would always "have it."

Jeff reached for the notebook, but Carter took it away at the last second. "Uh uh," he said, "First, you guys gotta promise that this will *never* fall into the wrong hands."

"Is it pictures of your mom?" said a kid in the back.

"Hey," shouted Austin. "That's someone's mom you're talking about. Show some respect."

The guys calmed down. I grinned. *Yup. Still got it.*

"Do you promise?" Carter asked. "You won't show this to anyone outside of your broskis. No adults. Definitely no teachers."

"Obviously, we promise," said Jeff.

"You have to swear it," said Austin.

"We swear, okay?"

Carter handed Jeff the notebook. Our former soccer teammates gathered around Jeff to see what all of our overhyped nonsense was about. Jeff's jaw dropped. "No way . . ."

"The Bro Code?" said Kevin Light, one of the guys on defense. "I didn't think this was real."

"Seriously, dude?" Jeff shook his head.

"Get it together." Another defender, Paul Jones, clapped Kevin on the back.

"It's real all right," said Austin, "Just, um . . ." he looked at me.

"Updated," said Carter. "We're leaving you guys with everything we know about it."

"Learn from us," I said. "And don't screw up."

Jeff flipped through the notebook. "Rule number 15," he read aloud, "A bro shalt not ghost."

Carter nodded. "That's right. You send a text."

"No taking the easy way out with her," I added. "You'll be glad you didn't."

"Or him," said Austin. "Per rule 18."

Jeff balanced the fat notebook on his arm. Kevin and Paul helped him, flipping the pages back as fast as they could.

"A bro shalt not make fun of," said Paul, "the sexual or gender orientation of other bros. The consequence of such an assumption results in that bro buying the other bros the dinner of their choice."

"It can get very expensive," said Austin.

"Thanks, guys," said Jeff. "We won't let you down."

"You'd better freaking not, Karvotsky," said Carter, "or we'll come for you."

I caught Austin's eye and he smirked. Both of us suppressing the urge to say *that's what she said*. Which, as we'd discussed, violated rule 18.

The guys immersed themselves in the treasure we'd bestowed upon them.

"Bye, high school," said Austin.

Carter laughed. "Good."

Austin shuffled his feet as the bittersweetness started to settle in. "We're still gonna . . ." he said.

"'Course," said Carter.

"Carter already bought an extra sleeping bag for our room," I said. "We're expecting you to come visit like every weekend, man."

"Nice." Austin looked at me. Then Carter. "Those cannonballs aren't gonna explode themselves."

"Lezzgo," said Carter. They ran back to the out-of-control pool. I chased after them, but also tried to slow everything down and soak in the last memories I'd have of high school.

"Hey, Maguire!" someone called as I made it back to the edge of the pool.

Eliza held one of Carter's massive Super Soakers. "Any last words?"

I tapped my chin, pretending to think about it. "I think you know already, O'Connor. Something about remembering me being eighty—"

She cut me off by pulling the trigger and jetting water, video-game style, like I'd taught her.

It stung as it hit my stomach. "Oof," I said.

"Are you okay?"

"Why don't you come here and see?"

"Are you going to push me in the pool?"

"Nah," I grinned. "That doesn't sound like me."

Eliza dropped the gun and tiptoed across the pool deck. It took her a few seconds as she had to weave around guys punching a volleyball and girls lounging on the deck. "You look fine," she said.

"Don't you forget it."

"Shut—" she began to say, until I leaped off the edge of the pool and pulled her in with me.

THE BRO CODE

By Austin Banks, Nick Maguire, and Carter O'Connor—the OBs

Rule Number 1: Bros* before hoes**

*A bro is any dude, chick, they, or robot in a bro's circle of friends.

**A hoe is any dude, chick, they, or robot who is toxic, disingenuous, or only wants to be around you for attention.

Rule Number 2: A bro shalt love barbecues.

Rule Number 3: A bro shalt always honor a high five, low five, fist bump, chest bump, knuckle knock, and so on.

Rule Number 4: A bro shalt not gloat about winning, their team winning, or their bro winning . . . after the weekend is over.

Rule Number 5: A bro shalt accept the outcome of rock-paper-scissors.

Rule Number 6: A bro shalt chew with their mouth closed.

Rule Number 7: A bro shalt treat their mother like a queen.

Rule Number 8: In a game of truth or dare, a bro shalt choose "dare."

Rule Number 9: A bro shalt not let other bros be alone on holidays.

Rule Number 10: A bro shalt not skip ab workouts.

Rule Number 11: A bro shalt text a love interest whenever a bro wants.

Rule Number 12: A bro shalt only gossip face-to-face. Never over text, social media, or otherwise.

Rule Number 13: A bro shalt not let bros do stupid things . . . without taking a video.

Rule Number 14: A bro shalt not mock a bro's love interest.

Rule Number 15: A bro shalt not ghost.

Rule Number 16: A bro shalt always be willing to pick up the tab. Or split it.

Rule Number 17: A bro shalt not be ashamed of what makes them happy. Unless it's Californian sports teams.

Rule Number 18: A bro shalt not assume the gender or sexual orientation of other bros. The consequence of such an assumption results in that bro buying the other bros the dinner of their choice.

Rule Number 19: A bro shalt only make bros and love interests cry happy tears.

Rule Number 20: A bro shalt always finish telling a joke. They will never, under any circumstances, let it go without a punchline.

Rule Number 21: A bro shalt shower at least once a week, whether they need to or not.

Rule Number 22: A bro shalt not cheat.

Rule Number 23: A bro shalt never make their bros choose between other bros.

Rule Number 24: A bro shalt not lose on purpose . . . to anyone over the age of ten.

Rule Number 25: A bro shalt decide for themselves which rules are worth following.

ACKNOWLEDGMENTS

First, I thank you, cool reader, for spending hours of your life you'll never get back on reading this. And thank you for reading the acknowledgments, since almost no one does. I hope you laughed at least once. What I wrote on these pages means one thing to me, but when you come to it with your own experiences and perspectives, it becomes something new entirely. Thank you for making *The Bro Code* come to life.

To my Wattpad readers and friends, thank you for supporting my writing and helping me grow. Special thanks to Wattpad readers who read this story when I originally wrote it in 2012 and have come back for this tale eight years later. We would not be here without you.

Thank you to my superhero editor, Jane Warren, for your incredible help taking a book I wrote in high school and pushing me to turn it into this. Your belief in this story and characters helped me see myself as a "real" writer.

Thank you, Deanna, Caitlin, Jen, and the wizards on the Wattpad Books team who selected this book for publication and worked so hard to get it into the world. Your dedication and time spent on producing this into an actual book blows my mind, and I'm so excited and humbled to have had this experience with you.

To Gabby, Maggie, Emily, and Maisie, thank you for unloading the dishwasher when it was my turn, but I was on a word count roll, and never complaining when I made noise in the kitchen at 1:00 a.m. while I was writing. You truly lived with the blood, sweat, and tears that went into this project.

Thank you, Mom and Dad, for having me, making me waffles, and not reading this until I told you it was ready. Oh—and thank you for pushing me to take writing classes and never telling me that being an author was a bad idea, even if you wanted to.

Thank you, Apple and Maddie, for reading this a million times and letting me know if something was stupid. Thank you for the dog gifs, the giraffe memes, and being my biggest fans. Or, at least, pretending to be.

To Kevin, thank you for teaching me about sports and video games. And thank you for always bringing me a snack or tea, especially when I didn't ask for it. Without you, this book would have taken twice as long,

To my friends and teammates, thank you for the anecdotes, slang tips, and ideas about being a bro. Thanks for being there to keep me sane and understanding when I had a deadline. You guys are the true O.Bs.

Thank you to the #MeToo movement for bringing important stories into our culture, championing women artists, and for making my ex-boyfriends wonder if this book is about them. It's not.

To everyone else, thank you. You know who you are, and you know why.

ABOUT THE AUTHOR

Elizabeth A. Seibert has been an author, sunscreen-obsessed lifeguard, barbecue-loving waitress, finance reporter, nine-to-five marketer, and aspiring superhero. Her stories on Wattpad have amassed over thirty million reads, and she's been featured in *Imagines: Celebrity Encounters Starring You* (Simon & Schuster). Elizabeth currently lives in Massachusetts, USA, where she loves to cook and play board games and ultimate frisbee. *The Bro Code* is her debut novel. Visit at www.elizabethseibert.com.

wattpad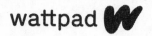

Where stories live.

Discover millions of stories created by diverse writers from around the globe.

Download the app or visit www.wattpad.com today.

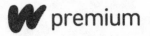

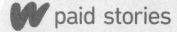
Best Friend's Revenge

by Losalini Kaloucava

When Liz Charleston's ex-best friend suddenly returns with a plan to take revenge on her, drama seems inevitable - but who knew revenge could be so... handsome?

Read the Free Preview on Wattpad.

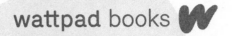